MY DATE
WITH A WENDIGO

Visit us at www.boldstrokesbooks.com

MY DATE
WITH A WENDIGO

by

Genevieve Sara McCluer

2020

MY DATE WITH A WENDIGO

ISBN 13: 978-1-63555-679-7

This Trade Paperback Original Is Published By
Bold Strokes Books, Inc.
P.O. Box 249
Valley Falls, NY 12185

First Edition: March 2020

Credits
Editor: Barbara Ann Wright
Production Design: Stacia Seaman
Cover Design by Tammy Seidick

Acknowledgments

Thank you, Jessica, Danny, Alexandra, Kassandra, and Ryuu, for all of your support and help with my getting this out there. And a special thanks to my editor, Barbara. This definitely wouldn't have happened without you.

MY DATE WITH A WENDIGO

CHAPTER ONE

Elizabeth

I throw on my jeans and tank top and fumble my way to the door, ignoring the snoring woman in the bed behind me. My phone battery is still at thirty percent by some miracle. I've missed three calls from Carol, which I will continue to ignore for the rest of my life, and ten calls and a dozen texts from Sandra. That is a bit more pressing. As I call her back from the girl's porch, I wish I'd thought to grab my jacket before I went into tonight's bar. Christ, it's cold.

"You're alive!" a voice from the other end announces.

"Thanks for the update. I wasn't sure." That was corny, but if it can keep us from discussing anything serious, I will be cornier than early James Bond.

"Liz, I've been worried sick. Are you okay?"

"I have a few painful scratches on my back. What is with girls only keeping two of their nails short?"

"Great. You should've let her cut you up some more."

I sigh, grinding my foot in the gravel of snoring girl's driveway. "Would you come pick me up? My car is still at the bar." Besides, I'm probably not sober enough to drive.

I only have to wait in the cold for fifteen minutes before her SUV pulls in, crunching the gravel as it idles beside me. I could've waited inside, but that would have increased the chances of spending more time with snoring girl. I climb in and rest my aching head against the leather headrest. "Thanks, Sandy."

She turns down the greatest hits of Lynyrd Skynyrd and glares until I meet her eyes. "You promised you'd stop doing this," she says, the car staying annoyingly still.

"I didn't promise you anything. Let me sleep. You can yell at me when we get back to my apartment."

"No, you promised yourself. Remember? I think it was, 'I'm tired of doing this to myself. I'm going back to school, I'm going to find a nice girl, and I'm going to stop drinking myself into a stupor and having one-night stands every night.' That sound familiar?"

I open one eye enough to glare back. "What part of that did I not do? I went back to school, then grad school, and even got myself a nice job as a therapist. It was my day off; I can have some damn fun."

"I know you're still hurting from Carol, but this isn't the right way to handle it."

I close my eye again. "I dumped her. I'm fine. I just needed to get laid."

"You dumped her because she said she loved you. Yesterday. You are clearly not fine."

"It's almost three thirty a.m. It was two days ago."

"Well, it wasn't when you did this stupid stunt."

"I can't believe you'd call this girl a stunt? For all you know, she could be my one true love." I feign offense, my hand almost resting on my heart, but I can't quite be bothered with that much movement right now.

"What's her name?"

"Do I have to know that to love her?"

She shakes her head, staring up at the roof. "Elizabeth, this is getting ridiculous. You and Carol were happy together. I promise, you can be close to another human being without exploding."

"Well, I don't want to take the risk." If I fall asleep now, I won't have to listen to any more of this.

"Liz." She places a hand on my shoulder, and I can feel her stupid empathetic eyes attempting to bore into my soul.

I refuse to open mine. "Sandra, drive. I don't want to talk about it."

"I'll drive after we have this conversation."

"I should've called an Uber."

Her hand drops. Is she actually going to drive? Thank God. "Liz, I'm sick and tired of watching you crash and burn."

I open my eyes and turn to fully face her. I'm sick of this; she's been giving me this lecture for six years. "I'm not doing it anymore. I'm a therapist; I have my shit together. I'm successful; I have a good life. You don't need to worry about me. I just wanted to go have one night of fun to help me forget about whatshername."

"Carol."

"Was that it?" I lean back, lacing my hands behind my head.

"You were together for a year; you know damn well that you haven't forgotten her name."

I shrug. "I thought it was Cassandra."

She groans and shifts the car into reverse, backing out of the driveway. I win. "We're still talking." Damn it.

"How about you talk, and I take a nap?"

"Call Carol. When you're sober, and it's not a ridiculous time. Call her in the morning, okay? I'm not saying you have to get back together, just handle things like a mature adult."

"She said she never wanted to speak to me again." She also called me three times, but Sandy doesn't have to know that.

"Well, maybe you should suck it up and call Abigail?"

If there was a brake on my side, I'd have slammed it. I stare, my mouth hanging open. I haven't thought of Abby in years. Why on Earth would I talk to her now? "Fuck you." It is clearly *not* a sore spot.

She rolls her eyes and focuses on driving rather than returning my look of astonishment and anger. "Right, because bottling all of that up is healthy. What a great therapist you must be."

"I'm the best therapist," I say, holding my head up high and doing my best to shake what she'd said. I'm fine. Not like Abby would respond, anyway.

"It's been long enough, Liz. You need to either forget about her or ask her what happened. How bad could it really be?"

I glare out the window, choking back whatever I want to say. I can barely think. A tear runs down my cheek, and I hate myself for it. It's been six fucking years. I'm fine. "I'm fine." Totally, completely fine.

"All right. I went too far. I'm sorry; we can drop it. You're too tired for this tonight."

This is just residual emotions from my breakup, or maybe I'm sad that I didn't find out what snoring girl's name is. It has nothing to do with her bringing up my best friend of eighteen years who vanished off the face of the Earth without so much as a good-bye after I told her how I felt about her. I handled that fine. "Can we stop for food? I could really go for some Timmies right now."

"Doughnuts aren't food."

"Then they don't have any calories."

She paused to consider, stopping at a red light and hitting her blinker. "I can't argue with that logic. We can eat all we want."

I admire her restraint for not adding, "Besides, it's healthier than drunken one-night stands." Though I suppose that point would be somewhat nullified following a drunken one-night stand.

❖

With a dozen doughnuts, a large box of Tim Bits, and two coffees on my table, I can finally ignore Sandra. She can't call out my decisions while shoving her second Boston cream in her face. I bury my own feelings under a pile of fried carbs. With the coffee to wash it down, it's not that hard. Doughnuts will never abandon me. The thought that I've been the one abandoning people is enough to show that I am far too sober. "Want some wine?"

"Wine to go with our coffee and doughnuts?" That damn judgmental stare.

"It's been a rough week, okay?"

"How much have you had to drink this week?" Her raised eyebrows and warm brown eyes manage to radiate both their traditional judgment and compassion. As a therapist, I should learn to do that. Though maybe judgmental isn't a great look for me.

With a sigh, I add, "This is the only night I've had anything to drink. I promise I'm not an alcoholic. Somehow, addiction doesn't seem to be one of my self-destructive tendencies."

She sighs, glancing toward the cabinet above the stove where I keep the wine. "Help yourself if you need it. I'm not in the mood."

Well, that certainly sucks all the fun out. I drain my coffee, hoping that it will make me less self-aware. I think the double chocolate doughnut actually manages. "Thank you. For picking me up, I mean, not the lecture."

"You're welcome for both." She runs her fingers through her long black weave. "I'll do it anytime, you know that. Please don't make me keep having to."

I groan and stuff another bite in my mouth. "Fine. I'll try that whole healthy thing. I suppose I should at least take another look at it, if for no other reason than so I know what I'm talking about when I tell my clients to do it."

"One-night stands can be healthy; you just don't do them in a healthy way."

"Is this 'cause I don't know her name? I bet it's Laura. She looked like a Laura."

Sandra shakes her head. "You're exhausting."

"It's just late. I'm a delight."

She checks the time and lets out a long groan. "I'm tired. I've been up since six yesterday morning. I couldn't sleep because I was too worried about you."

"Want to crash here? I'll need you to help me get my car in the morning."

"I'm too tired to stay up, but after all that coffee, I don't think I could sleep either."

I consider for a moment, my eyes falling on the TV in the living room. "Want to binge shitty movies until we pass out on the couch?"

"Fine, but I get to pick the movies."

I narrow my eyes and take a sip of coffee. "Can I at least pick the genre?"

"Nope. You owe me." She grins, her almost perfect teeth showing as she meets my gaze. "We're watching romcoms."

"Damn you and your straight shit."

"You love it."

"I do not." I throw a doughnut hole at her. I'm very mature.

She catches it and pops it in her mouth. "Thanks. You're so considerate. How about *The Proposal*?"

"I said I'd watch movies with you, not marry you."

Rolling her eyes, she stands from the chair and prances to the living room. "Come on. It's good, I promise."

It isn't. I hate it. Halfway through whatever second movie she picks, I am mercifully granted sleep by whatever deity or being controls insomnia. They are, however, a fickle bastard, as I dream of Abigail. She's walking away, and I can't quite reach her. Then I'm late for class because why have one nightmare when you can have two?

The couch is soaked with sweat when I wake up, and the sun is only starting to shine through the western window. The credits to some movie are scrolling on the screen, but Sandra is sleeping peacefully, her head propped up on the armrest of the couch and my favorite blanket wrapped tightly around her.

I shower and throw on some clean clothes before heading back downstairs. I want to wake her since I need a car, but she stayed up twenty-two hours straight because of how much she cares about me, and even I'm not heartless enough to wake her after that. I grab a book and fall back on the couch. Somewhere around chapter three, I fall asleep, but this time, my dreams are far less contentious, and I make it through a few more hours.

❖

My client is convinced he's dead. I'm a little jealous, but I'm also trying very hard to contain my excitement. Cotard delusion is rare, and I didn't think I would ever have a patient with it. I try my best to recall how to treat it. I wish he'd bothered to tell me about it before scheduling the appointment.

I give in and look it up, doing my best to look as if I'm taking notes. I didn't expect to ever deal with it. The class that mentioned it must've been four years ago, and I didn't have any reason to retain that information. Unfortunately, treatment is primarily pharmacological, and I am not a psychiatrist. It is usually part of another disorder, so maybe we can work toward that.

"I'm dead, doctor. It's not a delusion, I swear. The whole world keeps going by, but I'm not part of it anymore. I'm just a walking corpse."

He doesn't show any signs of decay, but contrary to his claim, I am not a doctor, so I'm far from qualified to pronounce him. "I know a good psychiatrist I could recommend. I'm happy to keep seeing you, but she'd be a lot more helpful."

He shakes his head vigorously. "No, I don't want to see anyone else. No one else notices me. I looked you up, and you're the best; there's no one else I can talk to."

My reviews are good, but the best? I'm pretty sure my therapist is better. I should give her a call; it's been a few years. "Dennis, I'm happy to keep talking to you for as long as you need. I think it would be helpful if you also saw Dr. Marovsky."

"No, I can't. He'd look right through me." He does look

a little dead as his eyes stare at nothing. He's still breathing. I wonder if pointing that out would help? From what I recall, confronting a delusion only tends to make them double down on it.

"Why is it that you want therapy?" Let's toss him a low ball; maybe then I can figure out how to proceed.

"I need someone to really see me." His gray eyes just keep staring into me. I shudder. "I was going to try a medium, but they'd have to summon me, and I wasn't sure how long it would take to get them to notice me. Your name popped up at some point, and I knew you were the answer. I knew you'd be able to help, that you could hear me, that you could talk to me. I need to feel whole, to feel alive again. Please, Ms. Rousseau, I can't talk with anyone else; it has to be you."

Am I stealing his money? There's not a lot I can do for him. Maybe, if I earn his trust, I can convince him to see a psychiatrist? I'm sure there's some therapy I could pursue, especially if I can find out what's causing his delusion. Other than that, I can have him talk to someone else and help him realize that others can see him too, and maybe that would convince him to talk to a doctor? It's worth a shot. "Of course, Mr. Bernard, I'm happy to help."

We make it through the rest of the session without any real progress, but the first session is really to meet the patient, do an excessive amount of paperwork, and figure out what path the treatment should take, and I've done the two parts that I'm not dreading. That just leaves paperwork. I feel so much better than I did this weekend. It's a nice reminder that I know what I'm doing with my life, and it's hard to feel alone when I have people paying to talk to me.

After my sixth patient of the day, I'm out of appointments and ready to pack up. Helping other people work through their stuff does wonders for me. I check my phone as I head to the car and find another call from Carol. Maybe she left something important at my place and wants it back. If that's the case, it would be cruel to ignore her. I take a deep breath, trying my best to pretend this isn't one of the things I want to do least in the entire world. Even working on Dennis's file was more appealing. I start the car and call her back, letting it play through my speakers.

She answers on the second ring. "Lizzy?"

I never did like that name. "I'm here."

"Oh thank God." She lets out a shuddering breath. She's been crying. This was a terrible idea. I resist hanging up only through the knowledge that she would call back a dozen more times. "I've missed you."

I haven't. Maybe I'm the one who's dead inside. I don't miss her at all. No matter what my behavior Friday would suggest, she's been the last thing on my mind. "I'm sorry." It's all I can give her.

"Can you please tell me why?"

I blow out a breath as I stop at a red light. There's a Mexican place on my left that sounds delicious, and it would give me an excuse to get off the phone, but she deserves better than my brushing her off, no matter how little I want to deal with her. "It needed to happen. I'm sorry I hurt you, but I didn't want to keep stringing you along. I don't love you. I don't know if I'm even capable of love. When I realized how serious you were, I had to end things. It was for your own good. I should have done it months ago before you grew attached." I'm so healthy. I'm an expert on healthy. Literally.

She sobs and coughs before meekly replying, "You really don't love me?"

I try to search within myself. I'm fond of her. I hate that I hurt her. I wouldn't mind having her in my life once she's had some time to move on. But I don't love her. "I don't."

She hangs up. The light changes. I try not to enjoy my Mexican food too much. It seems in bad taste to be stuffing my face with a burrito when the girl I was considering moving in with is crying on the other side of town, but it is an incredible burrito.

At least I can have one healthy relationship.

CHAPTER TWO

Abigail

I wash the blood from my hands in the bathroom sink. There's no mirror, but I don't need to see my reflection to know I must look terrifying. The smell of the well water fills the room as I splash my face, and I'm pleased to see that no blood comes off. It had been a clean hunt and a quick kill; the only blood is on what can charitably be called my hands.

It's a little past eleven, and I need to get to my diet support group. It's only a fifty-five-kilometer run away. I stuff the deer carcasses in a heavy-duty burlap sack and make it in about forty minutes. My stomach growls, but I do my best to ignore it. There aren't any people around, which helps a little. Nothing else would do.

The Community Center is as packed as ever. The run-down mall, whose only notable feature is the impressive number of broken windows, keeps away all but the most curious explorers. It doesn't look as if there is anything left in it to destroy or loot.

Though if anyone did make it in, they'd be eaten or sold within minutes. Rows upon rows of stalls fill the hallway, with each large room hosting numerous events throughout the night. There's a long line at the fake ID stall, as always. I have a few more years before I'll have to look into that.

I find my favorite venison dealer and hand him the heavy bag. He glances inside, peeling fabric away from the wound, and in a thick Russian accent announces, "Two good-size bucks. There must be almost two hundred pounds of meat here."

My skeletal fingers unfurl as I hold my hand out. "Cash, please. Canadian."

"If you'd like to trade, I could get you a much better rate." He scratches at his horn; it always seems to itch when he's trying to rip me off. I would love to play poker with him.

"Boris, I can't eat any of the stuff you sell. Give me the money."

He sighs and shakes his head. "I have a good deal on silver. You never know when you could use it."

"Why do you even have silver?"

"I ask myself that question every day now." He rubs at his thick beard as he stares at the carcasses. "Very well. Five hundred dollars."

My mouth drops, and he takes a step back. I close it in what I hope looks like a smirk. "I could get someone to sell it to humans for two thousand easy; that'd still leave me with at least fifteen hundred."

"Then go do so. That is the best I can offer you, Abigail. Venison doesn't move as quickly here as it does in other markets."

"One thousand."

"Because I like you, I will give you eight hundred. You know this kill was not difficult for you. I think you will take deal."

He's right. I will take deal. "Fine, but only if you throw in that silver necklace."

He holds up the one I'm looking at, a small but ornate cross. "Eight hundred and fifteen grams of silver? May I ask why you want it?"

I shake my head and stare down at him. "I can trade it to someone else later." He doesn't need to know that it's because having something shiny to wear might make me feel pretty for half a second. He'd laugh. "Do we have a deal?"

"Very well, Abigail, very well." He places the bills and the necklace in my outstretched hand. I stuff it into the pockets of my torn-up XXXXL hoodie. I weave through the rest of the stalls toward the third converted room on the left. The door is still open; my haggling must not have taken as long as usual. I should've tried for more. I walk in and plug my phone in the corner. There are rows of charging stations around the building, and no one would dare steal here, but I'd rather keep an eye on it. It's the only thing I have left from my old life.

I look around at the large circle of beings. Most sit on chairs, and those that can't have found a spot on the floor, save for the one hovering. I sit between Ashley and James. They've been coming here even longer than I have and are the closest friends I've made since I started. The remaining members file in and find their seats, and Ben closes the doors. There's no time to chat, but I'll talk to them after since they always stick around for a while. Neither of them has any place worth heading back to either.

"I see we have a new face joining us today," Benjamin says, gesturing to a hooded figure I don't recognize. Ben rises, his five-foot frame making the change hardly noticeable. "Would you like to introduce yourself?"

The figure shakes its head.

He nods. "That's okay. Take all the time you need. We don't judge. Is there anyone who does want to share?"

Robert stands. From what he told me when I started out with him as my sponsor, he was one of the founding members, but plenty of others have said that isn't true. All I know is that he's been coming here longer than I have. "I messed up last night. I know this is why we avoid having relationships with humans: it's not safe. I haven't talked about her before since I really didn't want to get that lecture, but I guess I needed it. You all were right. I really screwed up. I ate her. I couldn't stop. I've been so hungry."

The man next to him—I think his name's Frank, but he's pretty new—puts his hand on Robert's shoulder. "It's okay, man. We all make mistakes."

I nod, as does Ben. "The important thing is not to give up,"

Ben adds. "I know you fell off your diet, and it's okay to be disappointed in yourself, but you can't take that as an excuse to eat more."

Rob nods. "I know. I know. I've heard it all. I can't believe I did it. I thought she was the one. Twenty years clean, five years with her, and I messed up." He licks his lips, and my stomach growls again. How did he hide her when I was at his place? I should've smelled her. "I told myself that I could just have a nibble, that it'd be fine, but I kept going."

"It's how we live," another voice says. I'm not sure who.

Rob shakes his head. "I can eat animals, and I have been. I'm not starving. I don't have an excuse. She looked so delicious, and I messed up."

"It happens," I say. "Just because you can eat other things doesn't change how hard it is to stay clean. You're not made for it. The fact that your body can handle eating other things better than mine doesn't mean that it's what's natural. Instincts take over; it's why we keep our distance from them, but you were brave to try otherwise. I'm sorry it didn't work out." Every fiber of my being wants to do the same. To find someone and devour them. I can't. I won't. Not again.

"Abigail's right," Ben says. "You're an ogre. It's in your nature."

"She's all the evidence I need that I failed." He gestures toward me. "She can only digest humans, and here I am, able to live just fine off other foods, and yet I ate my girlfriend. I'm a monster." He holds his massive head in his hands, weeping. "I really loved her!"

My claws dig into the reinforced metal chair. I miss being around people; I miss my old life, even after all these years, but I won't go down Robert's road. It's too dangerous. I can barely smell a human without wanting to eat it, and I'm starving.

"Can I speak?" I hope I'm not interrupting, since Rob definitely needs to be comforted, but his story is making it hard for me to think about anything else. "If Robert's done, I mean." It's taking so much work to keep my voice; it almost falters into a bestial growl. The hunger is too distracting, but it always is.

Robert raises his head and nods, baring his tusks in a pained smile.

"Thank you." My nails rake on the metal as I try to gather my thoughts. "It's been two years since I've last eaten. I know I should find a place to live that doesn't smell like my last victim, but it's hard to find a place out in the country." Several people nod, and a few voices echo my thoughts. "I've been a wendigo for six years. I know most of you already know my story, but I figured I should be fair to the new guy."

The figure inclines its head.

"The hunger has been getting worse. I'm scared that I won't be able to go on. My stomach growls constantly, even more than it did when I first changed. I don't know if I'm immortal; I don't think anyone like me has ever gone this long without eating. Maybe I'll keel over tomorrow." A few gasps and polite chuckles answer me. "I don't know what to do. All I can think about is food. I need to eat. I tried eating a deer the other day, even though every fiber of my being told me not to. I threw it up right away."

Robert stares. I'm sure I'm making him feel guiltier, but I need to get this off my chest.

"Is there anyone else here who can only eat humans?" There aren't many of us.

The hooded figure raises its hand. That's something, but it doesn't help me figure out how to keep going. He's too new. He has no experience.

James the incubus taps my shoulder. I turn and meet his eyes. "I'm sorry," I say. "I know you're in a similar situation."

"I know I could probably feed without killing. I have it easier than you do."

I grumble. He's right. I have it the worst of anyone in this room. There was one other wendigo in the group when I joined, despite how much more common we've become, but he left a week after I'd started. I look around for anyone else.

"Maybe it isn't so wrong to give in sometimes?" James offers. A hushed murmur runs through the group. It's always a taboo subject. We don't require abstinence; it isn't as if you're kicked out of the group if you eat someone, but it is frowned upon. Actually suggesting moderation is seen as enabling.

I meet his eyes, tears forming in mine. "The hunger is insatiable. If I give in again, I don't know if I can ever stop."

He frowns, chewing on his lip in what even I have to admit is a sexy manner. Lucky bastard. Nothing I do is sexy anymore, but then again, I'm not a sex demon. "Save pieces for later and eat them sparingly?" he offers.

It's tempting, but I shake my head. "I can't. I just can't."

Ben clears his throat. The hooded figure is still holding its hand up. We all quiet as we wait to see what might come out of its mouth. If it has one. "Thank you," it offers in a soft, heavily accented, masculine voice. I can't quite place it. It pulls down its hood to reveal no head at all. I'm not sure how it supported the hood in the first place. "My species is defined by our cannibalism, much as yours is." The words clearly take some effort, and they still sound muffled without the hood. "I was scared that I wouldn't be able to do this. I wasn't sure if I would be welcome here. I'm glad to see I am not alone."

I finally realize that the words are coming from his torso. So he's an anthropophage. He is a long way from home. "Me too," I admit. Maybe we can make it through this together.

A few more people share, but it's just the usual catch-up like, "I've been five years without eating a human because I can live off animals." One other person has fallen off their diet, but it's been almost an entire week, and they say they are managing to stay off the human again.

The hooded man bows to me once the group ends, but someone grabs his attention before I can talk to him. Ashley and

James stay by me, Ashley pulling me into a hug. She smiles up at me, her desiccated cheeks doing their best to dimple. "I'm really proud of you, Abby."

I sigh and lean back in the chair, my head several feet above the headrest. "There's not much to be proud of."

"There's lots. You're still managing. I didn't say it in group because I didn't want to make a big deal out of it, but I fell off the wagon a month ago. It's why I wasn't in group then. I was tempted to go back. I mean, I can just eat dead people; it's not like it hurts anyone."

I wondered why she hadn't raised her hand when I asked if anyone else could only eat people. She really wanted to avoid having to say anything. I knew it was a stupid question anyway. "But you managed to stop?"

She nods, yellow fangs showing through her slight smile. "It wasn't easy. I ate three people that week." Her eyes widen, and she waves a gray hand before her. "They were all dead beforehand. I wasn't hunting."

"I've wondered if it would be worth it for me to try the same. If they weren't too rotten, it would probably work, but I don't know." I sigh, and it comes out as a whistle as the air pushes past my fangs. "It's the curse of my kind; the hunger keeps growing and growing. If I ate, what would stop me?"

She holds me tightly, and I rub her back, careful not to scratch her with my claws. It's nice to be touched. It has been a long while. If only she wasn't straight.

"We should get going," James says. "The slave market is getting started up next door, and I know how the smell gets to you."

He's right. Fresh meat calls to me, and my stomach lets out a roar I'm sure everyone hears. I wipe a speck of drool from my chin. "Yeah, let's get out of here, please."

We hang out for another hour before parting ways. They both have some shopping to finish before the stalls start closing, and I'm not up for being in the building. I hug them and let them finish their errands. I take a casual walk back to my cabin, sticking to the woods and sparsely populated areas as best I can.

❖

After I lock the door, I climb the stairs and throw myself into the too-small double bed, my legs dangling over the edge. I pull my phone out. It's at ninety percent. I should be able to use it until tomorrow night.

I've grown adept at using the screen with my new hands. I barely have to touch it. I learned this the hard way and had to find someone at the market who could replace the screen twice within my first year. I rest it against an open palm and let the thumb of my other hand glide across the screen. I have a missed call.

From Elizabeth.

I stare, swallowing, trying not to think of my hunger. Maybe it was a butt dial? There's a text message too.

Hey, is this still Abigail's phone? I know it's been a long time. It probably isn't your number by now, right? Sorry, random person who isn't my old friend, just ignore my rant.

I miss you. I know I messed things up between us, but you were my best friend for so long. I have other friends, I'm a functioning adult, I'm managing, but even after all these years, I still catch myself wishing I had you to talk to about my day. You meant so much to me, and I'm sorry I threw it all away. If you've come close to forgiving me, do you think maybe you could call me sometime? We could catch up.

I stare, blinded by tears as I reread it again and again. I miss her too. More than she could possibly know. My stomach growls, and I exit out of the message. I can't. It's too dangerous. I could hurt her.

The phone vibrates, and I risk a look. It's her. She's calling again. At two in the morning.

I don't know what possesses me to answer the phone. It

might be the bit of me that still wants to feel human, the bit that bought the necklace I'm wearing, the bit that wants to see how my old friend is doing and pretend that everything is normal. I fear that it's the part of me that wants to eat her instead. I should fake a voice. I can sound like anyone in the world; I can tell her this isn't her friend's number anymore, and she should stop calling.

But it's two a.m., and my friend needs me. I'll let myself believe that's the reason. "Hello?" My voice is my own or at least the voice that was once mine. It's the only voice I ever use. The other wendigos I've met all talk in the horrifying bass growl I make when I'm not paying attention. I guess I'm just pretentious.

"Holy shit." That's Elizabeth all right. "It's really you. Which is good because I just realized how late it is and how crazy I sound."

Hang up. Abby, just hang up. "It's me."

"Wow." She sniffles, and I can see her like she was the last time, young and stubborn and ready to take on the world. And head-over-heels in love with me. This is a terrible idea. "I've really missed you."

I choke back a sob, the sound coming out so utterly inhuman, I'm amazed she doesn't ask what it is. I wipe away tears. "I've missed you too. I'm sorry I haven't been in touch."

She lets out a dry chuckle. "That's a hell of an under-statement. It was my fault, though. I know it was. I shouldn't have tried to change things; we were perfect as best friends, and I was just being an idiot asking for more."

Oh, you stupid fool. You really think that was why? I loved you too. I told you I did. "It's okay."

She sighs. "Where are you living now?"

Lie. Come up with something. Maybe she's moved? "I'm just outside Toronto." It has to be the hunger taking over. That's why my body isn't doing what I want, isn't it? I'm luring her into a trap. I'm not just desperate to see my best friend. I'm going to kill her.

"Oh really? Find a nice place in Mississauga?"

I glance outside the window to the still woods surrounding my cabin. "Not quite."

"Well, I'm still here. I have a practice in town, actually. I'm a real live therapist."

I could use one of those. I'd chew on my lip if there was enough left of it. I should tell her to never call me again. It's the only sane course of action. "That's amazing. I'm so proud of you."

I can hear her grinning over the phone. "What about you? Did you end up as a sociology professor like you wanted? You weirdo."

I could certainly write an interesting thesis on the culture I'm in these days. "I didn't."

"Oh." She falters, clearly not sure how to reply. She's spent this whole time thinking that I'd run off on her and ended up with the perfect life with everything I ever wanted. It's a little hilarious. "What do you do?"

"You'll laugh," I reply, trying to buy time. What the hell should I say?

"I won't, I promise."

"I'm a hunter." At least it's the truth.

She laughs. The lying bitch. "I'm sorry. I just can't imagine that. My Abigail as a mighty huntress." If only I was still her Abigail. "The pay any good?"

I put the eight hundred from earlier in my wallet. "It's not bad."

"That's good at least. Do you like it?"

I honestly have no idea. It's just quick and easy and lets me order things online. That is, after I use the ATM at the Community Center, which I forgot to do. Oh well, I still have enough from last time, and I don't have anything too pressing to buy. "It's a living."

"Are you happy?"

Tears continue streaming down my cheeks, getting caught

in my fur as I lean back in bed. "I'm happy hearing from you," I offer lamely. No, that was stupid; it's just going to make her think she can see me. I need to tell her to leave me alone. Even if I have to say I hate her, at least it'll keep her safe.

"Wanna grab coffee sometime?"

I blink. I don't think I even need to blink anymore. I stare at the ceiling, trying to think of any plausible excuse. I need to buy time. "I'm out of town right now, but maybe when I get back?"

"That sounds great. When will that be?" She sounds so happy.

I don't want to take this from her. I want to see her. I hadn't even realized how much I've missed her. "A few weeks?"

"All right. Let me know when you're back, and we'll make plans."

"Can't wait. I should probably get some sleep. You have a good night." I hang up without waiting for her response. What the hell did I just agree to? I have to cancel or not show or change my phone number and let her think I ran away again. Anything is better than this. I can't let her see me like this. Let her keep the memory of the woman she loved, not the monster I've become. My phone slides from my hand to the floor, and I bury my face in my pillow. I'm pretty sure I end up biting a chunk out of it as I try to muffle my sobs. This is such an awful idea, and the next diet group isn't for another week. I need someone to beat some sense into me.

The beating can wait for tomorrow, though. If I go out in this state, I might eat someone. I let myself fall asleep. It's the closest thing to sustenance I allow myself. My dreams are of food. They're of Elizabeth.

CHAPTER THREE

Elizabeth

I'm really trying to listen to this client, I swear I am. I've just heard her say it all so many times before. It feels like I'm stealing from her at this point. I walk her to a solution, she decides to take it, and then the next week, she's right back in the same spot. It's amazing her insurance is still covering it.

That's not the only reason I'm barely listening. I still can't believe that call last night. I'm gonna talk to Sandy about it in another hour. She should be proud; she wanted me to talk to Abigail. I just didn't think it would really happen. Or that I'd be calling her at two in the morning after tossing and turning. I can't even blame it on the booze. I was stone cold sober.

"I can't betray my vows," she says for what must be the hundredth time since she became my client. "I won't do it. It's wrong. We made vows before God. If she can't love me as I really am, I'll just stay with her and suppress it." One of the two solutions she comes to before walking away every single week.

"I can't tell you what to do," I tell her as I always do. "If you think that's what's best for you, you should do it. I just want you to think about what you're sacrificing, and if it's really something you can live with."

"But I love her."

"Does she love you?" I actually don't specialize in this stuff, but a friend of hers found out that I am gay because I am not always great at keeping up that wall between therapist and client and recommended that she see me since I might understand. I don't, but she seems to like venting to me anyway.

"Of course she does. She doesn't treat me as badly as you seem to think. She does love me." She grabs a tissue from the box on the plush couch's armrest and wipes her eyes before blowing her nose and tossing the tissue in the general direction of the wastebasket. "She really does."

Every week. "I can't judge that for you. I only want to make sure you've thought everything through before you do it."

She kicks at the carpet, stirring up the chip crumbs from my last client. "There's no other option. It's the only way."

"If you're sure." I let her continue ranting for a while. This is one of the more religious days, and it's never fun listening to her insist that God doesn't approve of homosexuality in addition to the divorce, transitioning, and all kinds of other things she's convinced He doesn't want her to do. It gets old. I've never had much patience for that sort of stuff myself. Religion is exhausting all on its own.

"What do you think?"

I suck on my teeth as if I've been listening and am trying to sort out my feelings. "I think you should pick whatever is easiest for you to live with. If that's staying with her and burying who you are again, then while I worry about you and think we should discuss it more, I can't make you choose otherwise."

Chewing on her lip, she turns her gaze to the shag carpet. It came with the place. "It's what God wants."

Well, God also wants this session to be over. It's 4:50. "If that's what you believe. It looks like we're out of time. I'll see you next week?"

Standing up, she straightens her skirt and brushes off a crumb I'd missed from the couch. "It's scheduled for noon, right? I need to do it during lunch."

A couple clicks on my laptop bring up my schedule. "Yep, Twelve o'clock next Wednesday. I'll see you then."

She pulls me into a hug, and I pat her back. "Thank you so much. I don't know what I'd do without you to talk to."

"It's my job. I'm happy to help." I walk her out and grab a handheld vacuum to clean up the crumbs. I have a maid that comes in on Thursdays, but I'd rather not have every client stepping on chips in the meantime. When I'm confident I've vacuumed all the mess, I lock up and climb into my black Subaru sedan, tossing a few files in the back.

I'm supposed to be meeting Sandra at her favorite sandwich place in half an hour. It's only fifteen minutes away, but I have an audiobook to listen to.

❖

"What did you want to talk about?" she asks, popping a pickle into her mouth. "I assume you didn't ask me to meet you here just because you knew how badly I was craving a good sandwich."

"No, that's the reason. I'm psychically attuned with your stomach, and I knew you needed this." I smirk, sipping my Orangina.

"I really did." She takes a bite that has to be too big for her and melts into the chair, a smile spreading across her face. "It's perfect."

"Good. It should be." I blow on mine. I'm not burning my mouth again.

"Work was so long. I swear, I can still see numbers dancing in front of my eyes. It's the worst. I had to fix someone else's work that was off by almost a million dollars. It took me the entire afternoon to figure out where they'd made the mistake."

I should own up to it. Why am I so scared? Do I think it was all a dream, or am I just dreading the "I told you so" lecture? Whatever. "I did it."

She raises an eyebrow and sets her sandwich on the plate, quirking her head. A speck of lettuce is stuck to her cheek, and it makes it very difficult to take her seriously. Maybe it'll make the lecture easier to stomach. "You did what? I'm pretty sure I'd know if you were the one that fucked up the books for that client."

"What you suggested over the weekend." God, I'm coy today.

She wipes her face and leans forward, staring intently. Damn it, now she's intimidating again. Her black eyebrows furrow as she studies me. "You called Carol?"

"I talked to her on Monday, but that's not what I meant. She didn't take it well, but I did it. Did I not tell you?"

"No, you most certainly did not." She continues eyeing me but pulls back and picks her sandwich up. "All right, so other than hurting that poor girl even more, what did you do?"

I sigh, my gaze falling to my own lunch. Maybe this would be easier if Abby had told me more. I still don't know what happened. "I called Abby."

She drops her sandwich. Fortunately, it lands on the plate, but a few pieces of lettuce and a pickle fall out. "You what? Holy shit, Liz. Are you serious? How long has it been? I mean, you were calling her almost every day without an answer until, what, five years ago?"

"Yes. Thank you for that. I definitely needed to be reminded of how awful that year was." Taking a swig of my drink, I turn away. It was not an easy time. Even the year I took off from school hardly made it worth it.

"Well, what'd she say?"

I grumble. "She didn't say much. Just that she really missed me too, and that we could meet up when she's back in town. I just wish I knew what had happened between us. Maybe I really did scare her off when I confessed."

She wraps her arms around me, resting her chin on the top of my head. "I know how badly she hurt you before, but isn't getting this chance for closure a good thing? You can see her and confront her. You won't need to spend the rest of your life feeling like there's something wrong with you."

"Who says there's something wrong with me?" I spit back, holding back tears in the crowded restaurant. I know I'm overreacting. She just kind of hit the nail on the head. Abby running off definitely made me feel as if I was broken, as if I wasn't worthy of love. I'm over that, though. As a therapist, I give myself a clean bill of health and add that I am absolutely perfect and amazingly functional.

"You did, all the time. Hell, Friday you were insisting you weren't capable of love."

"That's not necessarily something wrong with me," I point out. Capable of love is not the same thing as worthy of love. I'm fine. "Can we leave? We can eat in the car. I'm sick of making a scene." Trying not to cry is way less fun than crying in a friend's car. I'm obviously only crying as part of my being fine, not because of how much Abby hurt me or anything.

She nods, chin pressing into my head. "All right." She grabs our sandwiches and heads for the door. Taking a moment to collect myself, I wipe my eyes before I follow, carrying our drinks.

We sit in her SUV, classic rock playing quietly in the background as she watches me and delicately eats her sandwich as if in fear of a drop landing in her car. It's not my car, so I dig in. Maybe the veal can fight back the complicated array of emotions I'm going through. In my defense, she told me to call Abby, so any mess in her car as a result of that is really her fault. It's sad how bad I am at emotions considering that I'm a therapist. I can handle other people's fine, but I'd rather just get rid of mine. They're annoying.

She lets me finish before asking, "Do you know when she'll be in town?"

I shake my head. "I wish I did. She said a few weeks, so hopefully less than a month."

She contemplates that as she chews. "Keep talking to her, then. Maybe you can get answers before she gets back? You don't need to wait that whole month for closure."

I shrug. "I don't think she wants to talk. She seemed pretty desperate to get off the phone."

"Did she say that? She answered the call and said she missed you. You're probably overthinking things."

I'm supposed to be the therapist here. "I was blowing up her phone. I'd sent her a really long message and called earlier in the day. Then I couldn't sleep, and I tried calling again, not thinking about how late it was. She probably wasn't paying attention to who it was. I mean, who calls at two in the morning without something important to say?"

"It *was* important, Liz." She finishes her sandwich and washes it down with the rest of her water. "Try texting her. Just one message, and give her a day to reply."

"Maybe."

"If you think you harassed her into talking to you, take a step back, let her know that you still want to talk more, and leave the rest to her."

"If I'm doing that, shouldn't I wait for her to message me?"

With a shrug, she puts her hands on my shoulders and stares into my eyes as if to make sure I don't miss a syllable. Way to be overly dramatic. "She wants to talk to you. She may be worried you were drunk or that you're still mad at her. Just one message, then wait for her move. I promise, she's gonna talk to you more. She already made plans to see you. Clearly, she wants to."

The tears come again, and I do my best to fight them. "Then why'd she leave?"

A quick squeeze to my shoulders and she calmly says, "Ask her."

I guess I can't argue with that. "Fine." I pull out my phone before I can chicken out. "I'll message her right now."

I type out a quick message. *It was really great talking to you last night. I can't believe how long it's been.* There, that's harmless, right? Hopefully, she doesn't read it as passive aggressive. I just didn't want to ask her anything and sound presumptuous, as if I'm trying to force her to talk to me. "I messaged her."

"Good." She rolls her neck and tosses the garbage into a grocery store bag sitting at my feet. "Is it all right if I head home? I'm meeting a cute guy for drinks tonight, and I was hoping to clean up and look presentable first."

"Yeah. Go knock him dead. I'll be all right."

"I love you, Liz." She hugs me for the umpteenth time, and I swear I feel a tear on my shoulder.

"I love you too."

"See, you *are* capable of love." She crushes my spine and sits up. "Now get out of my car."

"I can see when I'm not wanted." I wink as I let myself out and head back to my sedan. I guess I'll head home too. I don't have a hot date since *someone* decided to chew me out whenever I have a one-night stand. Not that that's what I really want right now. I hope she'll message me soon, and those two things are completely unrelated. It's not like I'm any good at relationships.

❖

When I'm getting ready for bed, my phone chimes. It's probably an email from a client or a potential client. That's what it was the last time I checked. The time before, it was just Sandra making sure I made it home safe. She really is a good friend. There's no way it's Abby. I give in and set my toothbrush back down and dash to the phone. Dental hygiene can wait.

It's her. *It was nice talking to you too. I know what you mean; it kinda feels like it's both been so much longer and so much shorter than six years. So much has changed.*

I'm not tired anymore anyway. *You free to call?*

My phone rings. I didn't even know custom ringtones could carry over from phone to phone. God, that's embarrassing. "Hey," I say, holding my breath as I wait for an answer. I can scarcely believe it's real. No, I'm not still in love with her—I'm definitely not—it's just nice hearing from my best friend.

"Hey." She doesn't sound at all nervous. Maybe slightly distorted. I could swear her voice was a little higher before, but it's probably just the phones. Maybe it's the connection since she's out of town.

"How's your day going?"

She doesn't answer for a few seconds, and I glance at the screen to make sure she hasn't hung up. "I actually just woke up."

"Oh." Do hunters have a night shift? Maybe it's her day off?

"It was nice having that message to wake up to."

I lie back in bed, any thoughts of my nightly routine far from my head. I've missed this. "I'm glad I could make your morning special. Your night?"

"Morning is fine." A low sound, something like a sigh, crackles across the phone. "How was your day?"

"Just boring work stuff. Nothing I can talk about." I definitely didn't cry over you both in a restaurant and in my best friend's car. Christ, what is wrong with me?

"Right, confidentiality and everything. Wow, that has to be tough to get used to."

I stare at the unmoving fan above, the light shining in my eyes. "It's not that bad."

I hear movement on her end. "I guess it was your dream job. Plus, you had a while to adjust to it. I'm sorry I wasn't there for it."

Don't say it. Just enjoy catching up. Put a pin in the insanity for once in your life. "Why weren't you?"

There's only silence for a long moment. I'm about to check the phone again when a barely audible sound comes through the speaker. Something almost like a growl. "I don't want to talk about it. I promise it wasn't you, okay?"

There, I got something. It wasn't my fault. There goes six

years of anxiety, only to be replaced with a million new fears. Just take it and change the subject. "Then why? Abby, you disappeared. I called you every day for an entire year. I dropped out of school. I was a wreck. I'm trying so hard to move past this and be friends again, but I need to know what happened." Like I said, I'm the picture of mental health.

I wait for her to hang up. It's about the only sane response to what I unloaded on her. "But you're a therapist now. I thought everything worked out perfectly." Her voice still seems oddly perfect, as if she's not blubbering like a little baby. Maybe that's just me.

"I've mostly turned things around, but it took me a long time, and I'm still dealing with a lot of baggage. You were the most important person in my world, and then you vanished without a word for six years."

I can't come close to placing whatever that sound is. A dog howling, maybe? Does she have a pet? "I'm sorry," she finally says, her voice still crisp. Still unaffected.

"No, it's fine, don't worry about it. I'm being crazy. I should go to bed."

"Wait."

Like I was really going to hang up. "What?" I whisper, terrified of what she might be about to say.

"I need some time. Give me a few days, then maybe I can explain. It's really complicated. I promise, I'll give you some sort of answer. I never meant to hurt you so badly. Or at all. Just give me the weekend, maybe a week? You can text some. I'd still love to hear from you, but I need some time. A lot has happened; my life definitely didn't go as planned."

That's not unreasonable. I waited six years. "One week?"

"Probably less. I just need to sort a few things out. I don't know what I can tell you or what I can do." She pauses, and I hear the creak of floorboards as clear as day. Loud house. "I'll call you soon, I promise, and then I'll tell you. Just, in the meantime, know that it had nothing to do with you. I…" She stops. She loves me? Is that what she was going to say? No, I'm being crazy, I don't even want her to say that. I'm not capable of love, remember? "I have to go. I'll talk to you soon."

Right, that's what she meant.

Maybe I'm still a little hung up on her.

CHAPTER FOUR

Abigail

I knock on the door to the mausoleum. Ashley is a bit of a drama queen and such a classicist. She found the Platonic form of a mausoleum; it's a large marble structure with tall hedges near the back of an ancient and ill-kept cemetery. It's the most dramatic place possible, so it is absolutely where she would live. When she doesn't answer, I bang louder, waking up a restless spirit who promptly tells me off. "Sorry," I mutter.

Right when I'm about to leave, the door opens, and a very sleepy ghoul peers out. "Abby?" Is it that she's surprised to see me, or she can't tell if it's me or another wendigo in a massive hoodie and sweats? They're more common than you'd expect.

"Yeah, it's me."

She takes a step back, yawning as I follow her inside. "What are you doing here? It's like ten p.m. I was sleeping in. I had a long day."

I pace around the stone chamber. There's a casket in the back, but she sleeps on the pink four-poster bed behind it. I've only been here once before. The unicorn poster really livens up the place. "I forgot how much of a girl you are."

"Thanks for the reminder. I forget sometimes."

I glance at my skeletal body hidden beneath shapeless clothing. "I know the feeling."

"Is there a reason you're pacing around my tomb? You're

leaving claw marks in the rock." She walks through the narrow entryway past what I guess could be called the foyer and sits on the stone casket.

I continue pacing. "Yes." I toss my arms out to the side. Where do I even begin?

Her foot taps on the stone as she crosses her legs. I can hear every little twitch. "Well, tell me before I go crazy."

"Is it too hard to resist eating when you live surrounded by all these bodies?" I ask. I guess I'm still a coward.

She rolls her milky eyes. "Embalming fluid makes me retch. It can definitely be tempting, but I just remember that taste."

"You could stay at my cabin if it'd help. I know how tough it's been for you lately. You know you can call me anytime you're having trouble."

"And you can call to see if I'm awake before you come over."

"I did." I just decided to come anyway despite her not answering. In my defense, this was rather urgent. I've been losing my mind.

She leans on the casket, arms splayed dramatically. "I would've called you back in like an hour. I'm sleepy! Did you wake me up to ask if my home is tough for me, or did you want something?"

I manage to stop pacing and try to casually lean against the wall. "Yes."

"Yes to which?" She raises her head, staring hard.

"Yes, there's a reason. It's just scary. I know we're not supposed to do this kind of stuff."

"Just tell me!" She jumps to her feet, taking the two steps to meet me. She glares up, barely managing to meet my eyes. "What happened?"

"This girl called; she was my best friend, maybe more, back when I was still human. I ignored her for so long. I don't know what possessed me last night, but I answered, and I really hurt her when I disappeared, and she wants me to tell her everything, and

I don't know what to do. Should I just tell her? Can I? Would she understand? What if she hates me? Or worse, what if I go see her like she wants, and I end up eating her?"

She takes a step back, eyes widening. A gnarled finger scratches her scalp. "Fuck, Abby. That's a tough one. I actually forgot you were gay."

"Thanks."

"Am I your type?"

Straight girls, I swear. "Ashley, please, this isn't about you."

"Fine." She blows out a breath, although I don't think she needs to breathe. "I cut contact with my boyfriend when this happened to me, but it was a lot easier back then."

That's enough to distract me from my problems. I tilt my head, staring. She's never talked about when she was turned. I thought ghouls were born that way. How old is she anyway? "You were worried you'd eat him?"

Shaking her head, she replies, "No, I just knew he wouldn't think I was beautiful anymore, and there was no way I was willing to face that look in his eyes."

That makes me think of how Liz may react when she sees what I've become. I can see the terror on her face already. I don't think I could take it. What if her freaking out makes me mad, and I lose it and eat her? Or what if she runs away and never wants to talk to me again? "So you don't think I should tell her?"

Her milky eyes look almost sad. "The girl is still hung up on you six years after you up and abandoned her. You may be underestimating her. Besides, girls are a lot less shallow than guys, so maybe she'll still be into you."

With a shrug, I reply, "Maybe. I just want to see my friend again."

"And not eat her?"

I nod.

"Well, if she's that important to you, maybe you should tell her."

"You're not gonna talk me out of it? Isn't telling a human

about us a terrible idea? Don't we explicitly say that dating humans is a recipe for disaster and is an easy way to fall off your diet?"

"Those rules are just guidelines."

"Ashley—"

"Abby! You're looking for excuses. If you want me to talk you out of it, I guess I can, but I don't think that's what's really best for you. Clearly, there's some serious unsettled business between you two. Even if you can't see each other in person, it's worth it to address it. Maybe you can both move on then, or maybe you'll see that she can be pretty cool about everything. Hell, maybe she's a sexy vampire or something now. It's been six years; she could've changed too."

Picturing Liz as a wendigo, I can't help but laugh. Her long blond hair gone, replaced with dark fur, that cute little nose replaced by this proto-snout, and her slim figure corrupted as the bones stretched and widened. At least she'd be taller than me again. "I'm pretty sure she's human."

"Well, even then, I'm sure she's decent for a human." Her wry smile looks cute, even on the patchy gray skin. "Talk to her, okay? I promise it's worth it."

"Will you help me figure out what to say?"

"Of course I will. I can't believe you're even asking." She wraps her hand around my index finger and leads me out of the foyer, letting me take the coffin while she sits on her bed and pulls out a laptop.

"Do you have electricity here?"

"Yeah, I bought that generator you showed me online." She gestures toward the small box in the corner.

"Oh. I don't tend to use mine much. I mostly go to the Community Center for that kind of stuff."

"I don't know how you live without internet."

"I have my phone."

With a shrug, she says, "I guess that's enough. It just sucks for Netflix." She opens an empty document. "We can plan out a whole script. What do you want to say to her?"

We work until the sun rises, ironing out exactly how I should talk to her, what might be a bad idea to mention, how to phrase everything, and how to handle it if she freaks out. We end up with a pretty decent plan, considering what I'm about to confess. Not wanting to risk dealing with morning traffic, I spend the night in her tomb, leaning up against the wall as I sleep on the floor.

❖

Back home, I call Robert. I haven't called him in ages, but I need to speak with him. How long has it been since I came close to needing my sponsor? Maybe he'll talk me out of this crazy plan. "Hello?" His basso voice booms through my phone's speaker.

"Hey, it's Abigail."

"Oh, hey, Abby. It's been a while. How can I help you?"

"I'm sure it's not an easy topic for you right now, so I'll understand if you're not up for talking about it, but I wanted to ask about what it's like dating a human." Why am I asking about dating? I'm just trying to be her friend again. Obviously, we wouldn't get together. She wouldn't want that now. I meant to ask what talking to a human about being like us is like.

He rumbles out a laugh that causes my speaker to crackle. "Has the fair wendigo got herself a crush?"

I feel my cheeks turning red. I wasn't entirely sure if they can do that anymore. I've never checked. "It's not like that. I don't think. Maybe. I started talking to a friend of mine from when I was a human, and she doesn't know anything, and I'm not sure how to handle it." Other than the massive script I printed off at the Community Center an hour ago.

"A girl? I had no idea."

"Yeah, gay wendigo, it's really amusing," I grumble, my

natural voice slipping in for a second. "Please, just tell me. How did she react?"

"Before I ate her?"

"Yeah." Great role model you've got yourself, Abby.

"Well, it wasn't like I could hide it. She thought my place was abandoned and was sleeping off a bad high there. At first, she was convinced I was a hallucination. We talked for a while, and I ended up finding that I enjoyed her company. I wasn't even thinking about her as food at the time, and that's rare for me." I wish I could say the same. "We kept everything pretty separate. She had her human world, and I had our world. I sometimes wonder, if I had just let her into my life a little more, I wouldn't have ended up doing what I did."

"So I should tell her everything?"

"I can't tell you what to do. I don't know what it's like to be a wendigo, and I don't know what your girl is like. I will say that it's probably a lot better to know for sure that she can't accept you than it is to spend the rest of your life wondering. Especially with how long our lives can be. Besides, if she freaks out, you're totally justified in eating her; you don't need that kind of negativity in your life."

I roll my eyes. "I'm pretty sure that's still against our diet."

"It's a cheat day when they're mean to you."

I growl and so does my stomach. "I'd really rather not think about eating her. I'm already scared enough that I will."

"How long has it been since you ate anyone?"

"Two years. You know that." What is he trying to get at? Anyone can fall off at any time. He hadn't had a morsel in twenty years.

"And how often are you tempted?"

"Always," I admit in a growling whisper.

"I don't have that appetite. I wasn't used to resisting that much. You're a lot stronger than I am. I don't think you'll eat anyone you don't want to. You're sort of awesome like that. I've never seen another wendigo last over two weeks, and you've made it two years. Don't doubt your self-control. You won't eat her. You might eat her out, though."

"Thanks." I forgot how gross straight men are. "All right, I'm gonna call her."

"Good luck. Let me know how it goes."

"I will."

We say our good-byes and hang up. I barely pay any attention. That's two different people who both told me to call her. I'm really doing this.

Maybe I'll end up bringing her to group. That would be funny. Actually, I think we have a strict no humans allowed rule; it's like bringing doughnuts to a Weight Watchers meeting. Man, I miss doughnuts.

I stare at my phone, my heart thundering at what must be a rapid ten beats per minute. I have the script sitting next to me on the bed. Through squinting eyes, I find her last call and hit the button to call her back. On the third ring, I'm about ready to hang up. It's three a.m. She's obviously asleep.

"Abby?" she asks, her voice sounding tired but completely alert.

"Sorry, did I wake you?"

"Don't worry about it. Holy shit, I wasn't sure I'd ever hear your voice again."

That hurts way more than it should. I deserve it. I did abandon her for six years. "I told you I'd call."

"You did. I shouldn't have doubted." I can hear her sitting up, the springs lightly squeaking. "I'm so glad to hear from you."

"You might not be. I have a long story to tell."

"All right, let me start a pot of coffee. I don't want to miss a word."

❖

A talon lodges in my blanket as I fidget, too terrified to start. I have the whole thing planned out, but it seems woefully insufficient. I pull the nail free, sending a puff of fluff into the air, and tap a rapid beat on my thigh. She's going to think I'm crazy. Or worse, she'll never want to talk to me again. I've missed her so much. I can't lose her all over again.

"Abby?" she asks, sounding worried. "Are you there?"

"Yeah, sorry." I let out a breath, producing a whistle as it blows across my fangs. I'm not sure I really need to breathe, but I've never felt up to testing it. Well, not since that one time, but that wasn't the main goal. "Are you sure you're up for this? It's pretty unbelievable. You're going to think I'm crazy."

"You're not crazy. I'm sure there's a perfectly reasonable explanation for why you vanished for six years. Maybe you were abducted by aliens. I won't judge. Please, just tell me. I promise, I hear crazier things at work every day."

I really doubt that. "I guess I should start with the last time we saw each other."

"You mean when I confessed my undying love for you?" She only sounds a little bitter.

I sniffle, the memory bringing with it a swell of emotion and nostalgia. A tear starts to run down my cheek but gets caught in a clump of fur. "I told you the same."

"Well, yeah. I know you did. I just thought you were trying to spare my feelings."

"I wouldn't lie to you, Liz." My foot scratches a long line in the hardwood. "I didn't want to tell you because I knew you'd worry and want to go with me. Not about my feelings, sorry, I'm skipping ahead. I went to see my parents over winter break to finally come out to them." We had such dramatic timing, telling each other just before we went home for break, not that home was exactly far.

"Oh." I can already hear her mind racing, saying, maybe she was sent to a Pray the Gay Away Camp, maybe her parents sold her off to some rich man, or maybe her parents decided they had to have her studied in a lab to see if they could find the source of her gayness. She always had fanciful ideas like that.

"We were going to go mountain climbing like we used to all the time before I left for college and always did every winter break. I decided to wait to tell them until we got to the campsite. I told myself it made more sense, but if I'm being honest, I wanted any excuse to delay it."

"So you've been stuck in the Swiss Alps or something for the last six years?"

"Let me finish the story, Liz."

She sighs, creating static in my shitty old phone. "You're right. I'm sorry."

"It was a lot of fun. I always loved it growing up."

"Is that why you had those sexy abs and legs?"

"Among other reasons." Wow, it's so weird to think of myself as sexy. That's not a thing I've been for such a long time. Now I can never let her see me. I need someone to remember who I used to be. "Well, we made pretty good time. I guess those legs weren't just for show." I smirk. "We made it about halfway up the mountain and set up camp for the night. We were still tired from the canoe trip.

"Manitou Mountain isn't that tough a climb. It should've been an easy hike. We just wanted to go someplace different." Stick to the script, Abby; you're freaking out. I breathe in and out slowly, laying my hands across my lap. In and out. I haven't even gotten to the tough part yet. I can freak out then. "Sorry. Apparently, the forecast had changed in the two days we'd spent canoeing. A blizzard started up." If my voice was real, it would crack. Instead, I stifle a sob, my voice its normal cheerful self. "When we woke up, we couldn't even start a fire outside. We had a little heater inside the tent, and we gathered around it and ate energy bars. I figured, hey, they can't be mad at me when we're marooned on a mountain in a blizzard, so I might as well tell them now. My mother wasn't surprised. You know her; she'd seen how we always were. She'd expected this to happen someday. My father…" Without willing it, my voice is his. "He didn't handle it well. He went outside." I catch myself, switching back to my own voice. This is my story, damn it, not his. "He was pacing in the snow. It was almost to his knees. I think he screamed. I didn't think it was loud enough to set off an avalanche."

"Oh God." I hear her gasp. Her coffee cup clinks on the table.

"It knocked the whole tent off the mountain. I don't know how far we fell, but the snow hadn't been as liberal there. It barely padded the fall, and there were so many rocks. I broke my legs and hit my head hard enough that I must have been unconscious for a little while because the sun was setting when I woke up My mother had a huge gash in her head, and stuff that I didn't want to think about was leaking out." The thought is enough to make me salivate. Breathe in, breathe out. Another whistle on the exhale. Crying and hungry, what a fun combination. "She wasn't moving. Unfortunately, my father wasn't quite dead. He had a bad black eye and was covered in blood." It looked almost like a snow cone, but I leave that detail out. "I just remember him glaring, the one eye almost swollen shut. I knew he blamed me. If I hadn't told him, we would've all lived."

"It's not your fault."

"Isn't it?" I had no idea I still felt so guilty. I don't feel guilty about eating them, so why do I feel guilty about killing them?

"You only wanted to be yourself, for them to accept you. There's nothing wrong with that, Abby. I'm so sorry that happened. Did you end up in a hospital? How long were you there?"

She's still trying to figure out why I hadn't contacted her. She would've been there for me, nursing me the whole while if it had been that simple. "I didn't. I was buried up to my shoulders under what must've been a hundred pounds of snow. Maybe more. I couldn't walk. I couldn't drag myself free. I could reach my mother, barely, and that was it. I held her hand, her cold, lifeless hand, as I watched my father deteriorate. His injuries must've been worse than they looked—internal bleeding, probably—but he refused to talk to me. He died before nightfall. I made it two more days."

"Before rescue came?" That hope in her voice, that optimism…I should just lie to her, let her think I was just too traumatized to talk to her, that her friend is still out here, even if I can never see her. I should let her believe that Abigail Larson is still alive.

"No. The blizzard kept going. There weren't any more hikers coming, the river was frozen over, and I hadn't had a thing to eat in three days." I hold back a laugh. Three days? That's child's play. "I was still holding my mother's hand, and I was so hungry."

"Oh." She sobs, sounding as if she's trying to hold it back. She doesn't want to let me know how much this is upsetting her. I'm going to upset her either way, so it might as well be sooner rather than later.

"I ate it. With a newfound strength, I dragged her toward me. I wanted to wait, to not give in to that hunger, to just believe that rescue would come, but I was starving. I didn't know where the food we'd brought was, but I couldn't move, and I had all the food I needed. I ate my mother. I ate every last bit of her. Then, when I had the strength, I pulled myself through the snow to my father. My legs were still broken, but I had other options. I didn't have to eat him. Our supplies must have been somewhere. I could've looked. I finally had the strength. I didn't want to; something inside me had broken, and I gave into it. I ate the miserable bastard. He tasted amazing."

Liz has the decency to gag. Maybe she threw up in her mouth. Now she knows what kind of monster I've become, but I haven't gotten to the real horror yet. "Abby—"

I don't let her continue. I need to finish my story. "Something changed within me. I don't mean my mind; that had already happened at that point. My body felt wrong. The bones seemed to be not only mending themselves but growing. I could walk again, but my legs seemed longer than before, my feet were bursting from my hiking boots, and my shoulders were ripping my coat. I didn't need them anymore. The clothing was restraining me, and I ripped it off."

She makes an odd sound. I suppose she must've always pictured me naked when we were younger, but there's horror in it too, as if her dream and nightmare have been mixed into one. She's not scared of me yet, I don't think, but the story is definitely getting to her.

"It hurt so much. I thought I was going to die. I think I did. My body tore itself apart; my skin ripped and cracked. My lips were so dry and cold, I couldn't feel them. I think I'd eaten part of them with my father. My head, my chest, my hips, every inch of me was stretched and contorted until I didn't even resemble myself. I ran, trying to escape from the pain, but it kept tearing me apart from the inside, remaking me as something new. I collapsed as my body writhed and reforged. I tried to find help, though I don't know what I would've done if I'd found anyone. Maybe I'd have eaten them too. It must've been hours, maybe even days, but when the pain stopped, or at least subsided enough that I could think again, I wasn't myself anymore."

"Abby? What do you mean? None of that makes any sense."

This is what the script is for. "I wasn't human anymore. I tried to eat some berries that were buried under the snow, but I threw them up. The rabbit I caught was the same, but I caught it without even thinking. I saw it running, and I snatched it out of the air. It must've been yards in front of me, and then I was right there. I was larger, fiercer, faster. I was a monster." I hate that word. "I could barely think. It wasn't like I was any dumber or like I had brain damage. I just had so many instincts fighting for control. I let them control me, Elizabeth. For four years, I hunted and killed what was once my own species. It's why I couldn't let myself be around you. I knew that if I saw you again, you'd just be food. I couldn't do that to you. I don't know at what point I finally gained control of myself. I want to say it was four years, but I don't think it was even a month. I remember everything I did, and I remember loving it. That's why I can't be around you. I'm in town right now, but if I see you, you won't be safe, and I will never let myself hurt you, even if it means I can never see you again." The tears start up again, trickling around the matted clumps of my fur, falling onto the floor beneath me with a light patter that's almost deafening.

I can hear her breathing, sobbing, her grip tightening on the phone, but she doesn't say anything. After a few minutes, I think maybe she's going to hang up. I wait for her to do so. I won't say another word, I've already hurt her enough. "I'm so sorry," she finally says, her voice cracking as she heaves out a sob, collapsing back into tears.

I freeze and stare at the phone. "What? Why are you sorry?"

"You had to go through all of that alone. Your father's rejection, the avalanche, everything that happened after. I'm so sorry, Abby. You're my best friend, I love you, and I wasn't there for any of it." Love? That must've been a slip of the tongue. It's been six years. I'm sure she's moved on by now. She can't still love me, not after everything I've done, after what I've become.

"I'm glad you weren't there."

Whimpering, she gasps, "Why?"

"I already told you. I don't want to hurt you, and I would have."

"No, you wouldn't. Even when you were doing all of that, you kept away from me. That's proof you can control yourself. You would never hurt me. I know you wouldn't." That makes one of us. "You're home, right? Where? Let me come see you. We can figure this out together." She takes in another breath as if collecting herself, her hand brushing against flesh as she wipes away tears. "You're not a monster."

The tears stop, my mouth runs dry, and I can barely say a word. She wants to see me? After all that? "No. I can't. It's not safe."

"Let me be the judge of that."

If I keep talking, I'll tell her where I am, and she'll be here. It's too risky. I can't. I hang up.

She calls me at least a dozen times, but I resist. I won't answer. I won't hurt her.

CHAPTER FIVE

Elizabeth

I have to get her help. She's lost her mind. My poor Abigail, let me look after you. I should get her to a hospital. No, if I do that, she'll tell them that story, and they'll think she's a murderer. There's no way she really did all that, is there? Having to eat her parents to survive certainly could have messed her up. She said she died. Does she have Cotard delusion too? Well, I was reviewing that anyway. Maybe I can help.

I call again, and it goes straight to voice mail. I leave yet another message. "Abby, please call me back. I promise, I can handle everything. I just want to be able to help you. You mean the world to me, and I hate that you had to go through all of this alone. Call me, okay?" I hang up and check the time. It's a little past seven, and I have my first appointment at eight. Normally, I don't open until nine, but it was an emergency. *Abby, just fucking call me! I need to know that you're okay before I leave. I need to know you're not running away again.*

I finally found her, and now this happens. I don't know how much of what she said is true, but she seems to believe it, and I have to help her. Wiping away tears, I try to focus on anything but this. My client needs to be my focus. I've been self-involved enough. Maybe I should just cancel.

I splash some water on my face. I can't cancel; my client is having an emergency. It's my job to put away my own shit and help them with theirs. This can wait. At five o'clock, I will do whatever I have to do to find Abby, but until then, work calls.

I check my phone again, hoping that I somehow missed a call amid the few dozen times I called her. Nothing. I throw on a blouse and pants, finish getting ready, and send her another quick message before I leave for work. *Please, Abby, call me tonight? I have to head to work, but I'm worried about you. Don't run away from me again.*

With only five minutes to spare when I arrive, I throw the lights on in the office, make sure the room is clean, and set my bag in the corner. The second I'm done, the front door opens, and my eight o'clock steps in. "I'm sorry to make you come in early, Ms. Rousseau."

"It's fine." I take the short redhead's hand and lead her into my office, letting her take her normal seat on the couch. "Would you like to tell me what's bothering you?"

She chews her lip, looking everywhere but at me as she scratches her wrist, her leg tapping a steady beat. "You can't have me committed without my consent, right?"

"I don't think that would be best for you either way. Please, tell me what happened."

She'd barely said anything on the phone last night, just that it was an emergency, and she asked how soon I could see her. I told her I could talk on the phone, but she didn't seem to want that, so I agreed to open early. "I was going to kill myself last night. Maybe I would have if you hadn't answered. I needed to hear a friendly voice, so thank you for that." She sighs, clutching her wrist and holding it to her leg. It continues to tap occasionally. It's a little more distracting than when it wouldn't stop.

I keep my expression placid. She's clearly fragile, and I don't want to risk upsetting her. "What led to that, Cindy? Was there a reason?"

Her foot beats rapidly again, and the scratching starts back up. "It wasn't even anything that important. I was overreacting." She stares as if expecting a response. I don't oblige her. "I just felt so alone. My husband hasn't been around much, and work has really sucked. I could've tried calling a friend, but I felt like I would be a burden. Why would anyone want to deal with me? It started weighing on me. I started thinking how no one would miss me, they don't want me around anyway, and I'm just this useless bitch they put up with because I never leave them alone."

"You're not useless." I should have insisted on talking her through this last night. She'd been doing so much better. I had no idea she was having this bad an episode.

"No, I am. I really am. I gave it a week. Just after our last session. I know you said that people really do care about me, and you almost had me believing it, but I thought I'd test it first. I didn't contact anyone, I didn't talk to my husband without him starting it, I didn't approach any coworkers, and I didn't call anyone. I let the whole world wait. Guess what? Not a single person tried to talk to me. I gave them time, and none of them cared."

There was so much more I could have done. Damn it, I really thought she was doing better. "I'm sorry, but just because they didn't contact you doesn't mean they don't care. I guarantee, you could call any of them right now, tell them how you're feeling, and they'd drop everything to be with you." Don't offer a guarantee like that. I'm acting as desperate as she is, and it's not helping.

She shakes her head, staring at her open palms, her eyes wide. "Then why didn't they call me?"

"Cindy, people can be busy. Maybe they don't always take as much time for their friends as they should, but it doesn't mean they don't care. Take a minute to talk to your husband or friends, and they'll make the time for you too. I know that sometimes it feels like you have to start every conversation, but they might be worried they're being a burden to you if they contact you. Some people have trouble starting conversations or showing that they care, but none of that means they don't."

She takes a tissue from the box but doesn't cry. Instead, she holds it a few inches from her face as if she's forgotten what it was for. "If they cared, they would go out of their way to show it. I wouldn't always be the one to start everything. My husband wouldn't spend all his time at work or playing golf, and my friends wouldn't be too busy working and going to parties without me."

"Do they ever invite you?" I know the answer, but I want to lead her to the conclusion herself.

"No!"

I take a deep breath, and she does the same. "Why did they stop inviting you?"

Her foot taps a single time. "I don't like parties, and I kept telling them I didn't want to go. They'd still invite me some, but I'd rather be at home. I told them I had a book to read, and they said they understood. It didn't mean I didn't want to spend time with them."

"Do you think that might be why they stopped inviting you? Maybe it wasn't that they didn't want to see you, but they knew you didn't enjoy going out. Does that seem possible?"

She hesitates, the crumpled tissue falling to the floor. "Maybe."

"Then maybe you should find something you could do together and invite one of your friends to do it with you, or maybe you could invite your husband on a date. Do either of those sound doable?"

"They'd say no." She bites her lip hard. I'm a bit worried it might start bleeding. It's the first time my mind has started to wander back to Abby's story since I got to work. She might have eaten part of her lip with her father? How would that even happen? "Ms. Rosseau?"

Shaking my head, I reply, "Sorry. How about this? You agree to try inviting a few friends and your husband out on different nights. If they all say no, I'll admit you're right."

"I am right."

"You don't want to prove me wrong, then?" I meet her gaze, allowing the slightest cocky smile. I know she can't resist that.

Her eyes narrow as she stands. "I know what I'm talking about. No one cares about me, and they'd be better off if I was gone."

"I care about you."

She pauses, sinking back onto the couch. "Oh."

"They do too. Give them the chance to show you."

One more tap of her foot. "Fine. But you're wrong."

"We'll see."

She glances at the clock. She still has twenty minutes left. "We still have an appointment for Wednesday, right?"

"We do."

Another tap. "I didn't really have anything else I needed to talk about."

I allow myself a light chuckle. "That's a good sign."

She doesn't smile, but she nods. "I guess. I'm sorry for worrying you."

I'm still worrying about her. "You don't need to be sorry; just take care of yourself. If you feel like that again, know that you can always call me." I'm glad I gave her my cell number. It would've been awful if she'd only called the office.

"Thank you." A tear finally trickles down, clinging to her nose, and she grabs another tissue. "I don't know what I would've done if you hadn't answered."

I don't even want to think about it. I'm not sure I could handle losing a client like that. "Any time. I'm happy to open early or see you after hours if need be. Just as long as it's actually an emergency."

She nods. "I understand. It's not like we're really friends."

Shit. "It's not that I wouldn't want to be your friend, but I can't help you without keeping it as a professional relationship. I do genuinely care about you, but violating those boundaries by having a dual relationship like that makes it so that I can't be objective and could end up with me losing my license."

"Oh." She places her hand over her mouth. "I'm sorry. I didn't think—"

"It's okay. I'm just explaining why. You're still a dear person, and I'm happy to help you as much as I can." I think that saved it. I need to watch my mouth today so I can stop sticking my foot in it. Maybe it's because I didn't sleep.

Letting out a shaky breath, she glances back to me. "Okay. I understand. Thank you, Ms. Rosseau. I'm gonna go, and I'll talk to my friends like you suggested. I'll see you on Wednesday?"

"I'll see you then." I walk her to the door and wave as she drives off. I can't let myself get distracted like that. It's unprofessional, and if I hadn't caught myself as well as I did, it could have done some serious harm.

I manage to make it through the rest of the day barely thinking of Abby. That is, until my interesting new client goes out of his way to remind me.

❖

"Can you really still see me?" Dennis asks the instant he walks in.

"Yes. You're right in front of me."

He breathes out a sigh of relief and takes a seat on the couch, shrinking to the side and pressing up against the armrest. "That's good. I was worried. No one else is able to still. They look right through me."

I take a seat and stare. I've been doing so much research on this disorder, and I still don't understand. People obviously interact with him. I know it's a delusion, but why am I an exception to it? I know this isn't quite what Abby is going through, but it sounds similar. "If you're dead, what kind of being are you? Are you a ghost?"

He shrugs. "I don't know. I would have thought I was, but I'm not sure it would really make sense. I just know that I'm not alive."

"When did you die?" Abby says she died that day with her

family. He should be able to answer that, right? What are the chances of meeting two people with Cotard delusion?

He blinks. "When did I die?"

"Yes."

Hesitating, his gaze drifts around the room as he ponders. I guess he's never thought of it before. "I think it must've been about six months ago. That's when I first noticed." Damn. I was really hoping that'd be a breakthrough. Oh well, back to the only plan that seems plausible: I'll get him to trust me enough that I can talk him into seeing a doctor for psychiatric medication or ECT.

"Of course. That would make sense. Has no one interacted with you since?"

"Well, it's not unheard of. There are some people like you. People who are special."

"Oh? How many of those have you met?"

He sighs. "I'm not really sure. It can be tough to tell if people can really see me or if it's a coincidence. Sometimes I think I went through a whole interaction with someone, thinking they could see me, only to later realize that there was a far more rational explanation. Often, they're just going through the motions, but sometimes, I'm pretty sure there was just someone behind me."

I jot a few quick notes on my laptop. "Going through the motions? What do you mean?"

He leans back, staring at the yellow curtains as they filter in soft light. "Like people in shops. Someone sets something on the counter, they don't even need to see you, and they'll say the whole spiel anyway."

I lean forward, studying him. "People in shops can see you?"

Shaking his head, he continues to watch the window. "No, of course not. They don't need to. Seeing me isn't part of their job. They're practically zombies themselves. They just ring up the item and take the money that appears on the counter."

"Are you a zombie?"

He turns back, staring. "No. I don't think so. It wouldn't make sense. More of a ghost, if anything."

"Right." Give him time. It might feel like I'm getting nowhere, but I need to let him grow comfortable with me, and maybe he'll listen enough that I can do some actual good. "That makes sense." I hope I'm not enabling him. I need to make sure I challenge him enough that he keeps thinking about it, but denying his delusion won't get me anywhere. Maybe I should do the same for Abby? Just take her at face value and see what happens? Maybe eventually, we can figure things out together.

The rest of the session goes much the same. He doesn't ever drop the delusion, so I'm pretty sure he genuinely believes it, and I'm unable to make any serious progress. When we say good-bye, he drives off. The car seems to think he's real. I look over my office to make sure everything is in order, grab my bag, and head out. I check my phone before I start the car, but I haven't heard from Abby.

It seems like I'm taking up way too much of Sandra's time with my shit, but hey, what're friends for? I call her.

❖

An hour later, I've finished ordering pizza when she knocks on the door of my little town house. "The door's open, Sandy," I call, grabbing drinks from the fridge.

For a second, I'll admit, I was imagining Abby had found her way here and was going to talk to me. Still no message on my phone, not that I've been keeping an excessively close eye on it or anything.

"Hey, honey," she says, pulling me into a hug.

I reluctantly hug back, half-heartedly patting her back. I'm in no mood, and I haven't slept.

"I've been worried about you. I'm really glad you called."

Fine. I hug her back properly and pull away as soon as she releases me. It's not that I don't like hugs, but she likes them too much, and I don't want to encourage her. It does feel nice, though. Maybe I'm being weird because I don't know what to tell her about Abby. Or because I've been awake for thirty-six hours. "Why have you been worried? I'm fine."

"Fine? Liz, you basically went off the deep end as soon as you heard from Abigail. I know you've missed her, but…are you checking your phone to see if she's messaged you right now?"

I put it back in my pocket. "Sandy—"

"No, Liz, this is ridiculous. Tell me what happened. Did she tell you why she's been gone? It wasn't about you, right?"

No, I had nothing to do with it. She just killed and ate her parents, then started a murder spree. You know how it goes; it was just one of those weeks. "She told me."

Sandy falls into the couch, propping her legs up on a throw pillow, and looks at me expectantly. "Well, spill. What did she say?"

Maybe I should tell her everything. It would certainly be interesting. Then maybe she can help me figure out what to do about it. But what if she goes to the police? I don't know if Abby actually killed anybody. Maybe she's just delusional. She did say she was dead, so maybe her victims are only as dead as she is. I can't hand her over to the police, she needs my help. She said she was home, so maybe I can find her. "She left to tell her parents about me. It was winter break, and they always went mountain climbing." Sandra will absolutely tell other people. I can't. "They didn't take it well. Maybe that's why they didn't answer all those times I called their house." I looked it up, and they were never reported missing or dead, so maybe that was part of the delusion. I'm not exactly lying.

She stares and pats the couch beside her. I must have been pacing this whole time. I sit down next to her. She doesn't need to know how nervous I am. "So she's, what, been in conversion therapy?"

Should I just say that? I wish she'd been in some kind of therapy, though conversion certainly wouldn't have helped. What am I going to do? "I think she got sort of scared and ran. She felt like she was a monster due to the way they reacted. She felt like she couldn't be trusted around me, so she tried to keep her distance. That's why she was ignoring me. She was trying to protect me." Didn't even have to lie.

"That's really messed up. It sounds like her parents did a number on her." She pats my knee. "But she seems better now?"

"Maybe." I mean, she did seem like she had herself under control. She's fighting against her delusions, and she's winning. She won't hurt anyone else, even if she really did do what she said. Who could blame her if she had, anyway, after everything she went through? "She's still really scared. She hung up last night after I asked her to come see me. She still thinks she's going to hurt me." I try my best to hold back tears. I can barely see through them. "I keep telling her that she's wrong, that I trust her, that I know I'm safe with her, and that I love her, but she won't listen."

Sandy sits up, her eyes locked on mine. "You said what?"

"I asked her to see me in person."

"No, not that. You said you love her?"

Blinking away tears, I nod. "Well, maybe *loved* her. I don't know. I did say it, and I think I meant it, but it's been so long."

"Liz, I've never heard you say that about anyone else, not the way you just did. Not romantically. You're still in love with her, aren't you?"

I nod again. I feel like such an idiot. She pulls me into another hug, and I give in, letting my tears soak her shirt. "I think I am."

"Oh, honey, it's okay." She squeezes me tighter, squishing the air out of my lungs. Okay, maybe this is why I called her. I guess I really needed a hug. The doorbell rings.

"Pizza's here." I try to pull away.

"I'll get it." She leaves me on the couch trying to collect myself and stop the stupid waterworks while she pays. "The delivery driver was cute," she observes, setting the box on the coffee table.

I eye her suspiciously. "Come to think of it, you didn't tell me about your date. How did it go?"

She giggles. "Pretty badly. I just didn't want to bug you since I knew you were dealing with enough, and it was more amusing than painful. He claimed he forgot his wallet, and he was just, in general, a complete ass. It wasn't anything worth talking about."

"Oh, I'm sorry. I still wish I'd been there to help."

She waves me off. "It's fine. I really don't mind. I just have the worst luck with men."

"Well then, go see about getting that driver's number." We can hear the car start and drive off. "Or not."

"I can call the restaurant and ask."

"Yes, do that. It's definitely a good idea."

She shakes her head and quirks an eyebrow. "Come on, Liz. I'm not that desperate."

"You're desperate enough to try online dating."

Her cheeks turn red. "There's nothing wrong with online dating."

"Of course not. Nothing at all. There's no reason you'd be embarrassed about it."

She takes a slow, playful swing at my cheek, but I duck. "You're lucky you're cute because you're a total bitch. Does Abby know? Maybe I should give her a call and let her know that her girlfriend is picking on me."

My own cheeks color as well. "Shut up and eat your pizza." Maybe I need a night to relax with a friend. Hell, maybe Abby needs the same. I'll let her be for tonight. She just better call me soon, or I'm going to hire a private eye or something. I'm not losing her again.

Chapter Six

Abigail

"I made it another week," Robert announces to a round of gentle applause. "It's not even difficult. I miss her too much to eat any human. I'd be more likely to eat myself rather than her if I had another chance." His fist clenches against his thigh, ripping a hole in his leather pants that must have been custom-made to fit him, as big as he is. This is why I can't do it. I won't be like him. He meets my eyes. "I know I could've done better. I could resist it if I just had another try."

The anthropophage from the previous week pats him on the back. I find myself clearing my throat as everyone turns. Holy shit. I guess I should share. "I've been really considering breaking one of our guidelines."

"Which one?" Kara asks. Her pelt sits on the chair behind her, and half of the group has been eyeing her like meat. Maybe we should add that selkies need to wear their coats as another rule. "Is it the 'no wearing clothes made of human skin' rule? You would look amazing in a human-skin jacket." Her eyes run down my body, and I cover myself with my arms.

I open my mouth to reply and pause. Is Kara flirting with me? She should've tried a week earlier. "No. A human girl that I haven't talked to since I was turned—out of fear of hurting her—has been talking to me." Does Kara look disappointed, or am I reading too much into it? There's no way a selkie would have a crush on me. She's hot. Liz only even likes me because of what I used to be. Not that Liz likes me. I'm jumping, like, four steps ahead. "I told her Monday morning what I am, and instead of freaking out, she started trying to see me in person. I haven't talked to her since. I wanted to wait and let you guys talk me out of it. I'm beyond terrified, but I've really missed her." I glance to where I would normally be charging my phone, but it's not there. I left it at home to avoid the temptation. I even spent the day at Ashley's to be sure.

Ben's expression turns grave. His mouth puckers in. "It's a rule for a reason, Abby."

"It's a soft rule. We only have one hard rule."

"Don't eat people," we all say in the usual bored chant.

I stick my tongue out at Ben. It's a bit impressive, if I do say so myself, as it sticks out a full two feet. Kara blushes. I guess there is one thing I have going for me. Go, lesbian wendigos.

Shaking his head, Ben stares at the ceiling as if to say, Lord, give me the strength to put up with these bitches. "It is. You've been clean for two years. I believe in you, and I think you could be around that temptation without giving in, but what kind of future could you have? Look at Robert. They were together for five years, and it still happened." Okay, seriously, how did he keep it a secret for that long? "It's just not safe."

"She loves me."

He blinks, his jaw hanging open as he stares. "How the hell are you already moving that fast? I thought you hadn't decided to date yet."

I show my fangs in what I am sure is an awkward smile. "We confessed our feelings for each other right before I changed. I was sure she'd have moved on by now, but I was wrong. I'm hurting her even more by keeping my distance. She even said how painful it was with me avoiding her for the last two days. Maybe it's worth the risk. If I'm gonna hurt her either way, I'd rather be able to hold her in my arms." Not in my mouth. She's not food. Don't picture it. Fuck, I still remember that dream so clearly.

"You're starving, Abby," he continues, catching the point he'd so quickly dropped. "Even more than most wendigoag." I know it's the proper plural, but I think wendigos comes out more naturally. "Maybe you could manage to be around her, but we've all heard your stomach growling." Great. My hands fall to my belly. I didn't know it was that loud. "If you're going to be around her, you might need something to dull the cravings, and that would be going off your diet. I know you don't want to do that."

"Maybe if they were already dead," I offer meekly.

"See? You're already thinking about it. She's a bad influence."

"I'm always thinking about it! I'm so fucking hungry I can't take my eyes off Kara, just like the rest of you, but I'm still not doing it, and I wouldn't for Liz either. I know how to handle my cravings just fine, thank you." I'm surprised to find I actually believe it. Can I really manage?

Kara blushes and looks around the room, her eyes finally leaving me to take in everyone salivating over her. She puts her pelt back on and the resulting grumpy seal glares at us. "Happy?"

"I'm fine." My eyes are locked on Ben's, predatory and hungry. I can be very intimidating. "I won't eat her."

The little goblin backs down. Maybe he's wondering if I could digest him. I start to calm down. I scared him. I'm sick of scaring people. What if Liz makes that same face when she sees me? Who am I kidding? I know she will. She's going to run away. So that's all the danger there is. I don't need to worry about a relationship. I just need to have the courage to face her and get my answer, then resist all of my instincts telling me to hunt her down as she flees. I can do that. I can handle those few seconds looking at her beautiful face. What if she doesn't run, though?

"You're right," he finally says. "You're one of the strongest women I've ever met. If you really think you can do it, then do. But call me if anything starts to happen, okay? Robert probably isn't in a good place for that yet, so I'll do it. Just call me if you think you're going to eat her, and let me talk you down. Deal?"

I nod and extend my arm. Another advantage: I can shake people's hands halfway across the room without getting up. See, being a wendigo isn't literally the worst thing ever. "Deal." Wait. Did I just say I'm going to see her? Holy shit.

❖

James and Ashley pull me aside once the group ends, taking me toward a quiet corner by a few unpopular stalls. "You're really going to do it?" Ashley all but squeals. "I'm so happy for you."

James stares. "What? No." He looks back to me. "Abigail, you know how bad an idea this is. Fuck, if I found a cute human and tried to date them, even though I know that I can feed without killing, I don't know if I could do it. I would end up killing them just because, in the moment, it never sounds like a bad idea. It's what happened to Robert. Don't let it happen to you. Please."

"Well, I don't eat by having sex."

"Don't you?"

I stare at him, cocking my head as I narrow my eyes. "What?"

"How would you have sex, then? I might not be an expert on lesbians, but I'm pretty sure those claws would skewer her."

I glance at my hands. He has a point. "I do have a tongue."

"Exactly." His smirk is pissing me off. I wonder if I can eat an incubus. He smells vaguely like food. "You really think you could have a taste without eating her? I can't. I start feeding a little, and I want to go all the way. What would stop you from deciding to take a bite when you're down there? Maybe you'd just eat her thigh. 'She has two legs, what's the harm,' you'll think, and before you know it, you've eaten the woman you love. Tell me I'm wrong."

I meet his eyes but find myself faltering, looking at the floor. What if he's right? "We could just not have sex."

"Is that fair to her?"

I heave my shoulders in a massive shrug. "I don't fucking know, okay? But I need to find out. We've spent six years missing each other so much. I need to know if we could work."

"Even if it costs her life?"

A guttural growl escapes from my throat unbidden. He takes a step back. "No, but it won't. I can control myself. I'm not ripping *you* apart, am I?"

Another step back, his eyes widening as he stares. "Nice wendigo, it's okay. I'm your friend, remember?"

"Exactly my point. She's my friend too. If I can avoid eating you, I can manage just fine with her, even if I do end up having a taste." I snarl. "I'll hold myself back. I have two years of practice, and I can keep doing it. I can control myself." I can. Right?

Ashley leaps at me, throwing her arms around me. I catch her. "I'm so proud of you. You can do this. You two are going to be the cutest couple. I can't wait to meet her. I am going to get to, right? Maybe you could bring her to group."

"She's not bringing her to group," James insists, finding new ground to stand on.

"I'm not." I look between the two of them. If she can handle me, she can handle Ashley, right? Can they handle her? She gave in and ate just a month ago. She might not be safe for Liz. "Of course. You're my best friends. You can handle being around her? You won't eat her?" I linger on her eyes, willing her to reassure me. I want to be able to trust my friends.

"Of course I won't." Ashley's arms loosen, and her milky eyes manage to look hurt. "I would never hurt your girlfriend. You know that?"

"Yeah. I know."

"I'm not sleeping with your girlfriend, Abby," James adds. "She's safe with me."

Yeah, I can trust them. I know that. I nod. "Of course. I know." I offer the least threatening smile I can manage.

Ashley squeezes tighter. "I'm so excited. It's like *Romeo and Juliet*. Two lovers from different worlds, but who love each other so much they can overpower that. It's like one of my soaps." Squealing, she squeezes all the tighter. She'd be crushing me if I was a human. "You'll tell me everything? I can't wait to hear about your first date. It's so romantic!"

"You know Romeo and Juliet die?"

She waves, almost hitting me in the face. "Not important. Their love was still powerful enough to overcome their differences, and that's what we're focusing on. Besides, neither of them ate each other, so you're still in the clear."

I set her down. "I guess that's something, at least."

"That would be a very different play," James muses. "I kind of want to see it. The intensity, the fervor. Rather than succumbing to poison, they devour each other in the heat of their passion. Shakespeare would be proud."

"I don't think our group would be allowed to see it."

"You do have a point. I might be willing to break my diet if it meant I could see a spectacle that beautiful."

"I won't be providing it for you."

"Good." He smiles, his perfect teeth flashing. His curse is so much better than mine. "I believe in you. I'll second Ben's suggestion; call me if you need help resisting."

"After everything you just said, you won't be my first choice."

"Because I'm an admirer of beauty? Don't be so cruel, Abby. You know I'll talk you down."

I growl. "Unless it's beautiful."

He gives a barely perceptible nod. He was never human. He doesn't understand. I suppose I can't blame him. "If I can resist the beauty of my own acts, I can resist it in yours. I promise, I shall only give you the most helpful of advice."

"Thanks." It's probably around 1:30. I don't want to wake her up again. I should call around six. I'd be going to bed then, but that's a normal time for people. "You guys want to do anything? I have some time to kill. I'm gonna call her in a few hours."

"Want to come watch *Grey's Anatomy* with me?" Ashley asks. "The vendor over there just got all of the DVDs. I was gonna load them up on my laptop and marathon them over the next week."

"I thought it was online."

"I wanted the special features," she whines.

I chuckle and shake my head. "All right, fine. I can watch a couple episodes. James, you up for it? It may be a little triggering for you."

"I can watch sex scenes that are tame enough for syndication. What do you think I am?"

"An incubus who's given up sex?"

He raises his hand, and it immediately falls back to his side. "Well, I'm made of sturdier stuff than that. Ashley, lead the way."

❖

Fucking hell, Liz! I haven't used my phone in two days, and it was at eighty percent the last time I got off the phone with her. She's called me so many times that it's almost dead. I rush downstairs and fetch my generator. I don't tend to use it as there's not much I have that's worth powering. That may change if she starts coming around. I bite my lip, clenching the wrist of the hand holding the phone. Holy fuck, this is really happening. I stop biting. There's already not much of it left, and I'd rather not accidentally eat myself. I'm on a diet.

I plug the phone in and let it charge up to fifteen percent. It's still not six. I was a little overly excited. I can't wait any longer. Maybe she's already up.

It makes it to four rings, and I'm about to hang up. Maybe she's mad at me for avoiding her? She isn't wrong to be, but I needed some time to think. "Abigail?" she says with a pant. "Sorry, I was in the shower. Are you still there?"

Tears are already forming in my eyes. I let them fall since it's not like she can see me. "Yeah, I'm here." My voice is crisp, clean, and chipper as always.

"Holy fuck. I was so worried."

"I'm sorry. I just needed some time to think. I've never told a human about it before. Hell, I've never talked to a human without eating them since it happened."

"So you really think you're not human?" She sounds so skeptical. I can hear her tapping on a computer. She's going all therapist on me. I didn't consider that possibility. I'm a monster; how could she not believe it? Well, she will when she sees me.

"I am quite certain I'm not."

"Well, send me a picture. I'd like to know what I'm dealing with."

I hesitate. My phone has a camera, so I could just take a picture, and she'd know. I hold the phone up, see my face, and it falls to the floor. I can't. She can't see me like this. What am I thinking?

"Abby? Are you okay?"

I pick the phone back up and hold it to my ear. "I can't. I can't take a picture of this. I'm sorry."

"Abby, I know you've been through a lot, but it doesn't make you a monster."

"It really does."

She taps a few times, probably trying to find the right article. "So you said you died. You think you're dead?"

My little therapist, always trying to diagnose and fix. She can't fix what's wrong with me. "The human I once was is dead. I am very much alive and may be forever."

"You think you're immortal? It was about the right age for

schizophrenia to set in," she mutters, quiet enough that a human probably wouldn't have been able to hear it.

"I wish I was schizophrenic. It would be so much simpler."

"Well, I'm not discounting that yet." She taps a few more times. "You're not Algonquin, are you? I mean, it's a pretty cultural-based disorder, and I think I would know if you were. Wendigo syndrome definitely sounds like your story, though."

A monstrous howl echoes through the cabin as I double over in laughter. Holy fuck. She actually got there.

"What the fuck was that?"

"That was me," I say, my voice still its natural growl. I fix it. I just can't bring myself to talk to her like that. "I'm maybe an eighth Algonquin, but I'm definitely a wendigo, and it's not a delusion."

"You're what? So you do think you're a wendigo? I mean, I guess it would make sense. So that's why you feel like you have to eat people? There's not a lot of notes for treatment, but I'm sure we can figure out something. Would it be okay if I write a paper on it? No, wait, I can't treat you. I'm not having a dual relationship, but I know a really good psychiatrist in town; maybe she could treat you?"

"Liz, I told you, I'm not delusional. I'm really a monster. I'm really a wendigo."

"Right, that's your delusion. I'm sorry. I shouldn't say that." She chuckles. "I just realized you were in the Algonquin park when it happened. Maybe that's why? It awoke something inside you that snapped when you saw and did everything to survive. I promise, Abby, we can get through this together."

She's not listening. There's no way I can convince her over the phone. I'm going to have to give in and talk to her in person. I want to so badly, but every time I think I'm ready, I chicken out again. How can I face her after what I've become? I'm a murderous cannibalistic monster. She deserves so much better. "I know, Liz."

"So you'll let me help you?"

With a shrug, I lean back against the bed. What else can I do? "Sure. We'll see what you think when you see me." There, now I have to do it.

"You'll see me? Yes, that's amazing. I love you, Abigail. I'll do whatever I have to do to help you be happy again. I'll make you see yourself the way I see you. You're not a monster; you're a wonderful, amazing, beautiful woman who has been through way too much."

"Thanks." We'll see if she's still saying that when she sees me.

"Wanna grab coffee? I don't have an appointment until ten today."

My jaw drops. I figured we'd make plans for this weekend or something. "I can't," I manage after far too long a pause. "I don't go out, not around people." The coffee shop at the Community Center might be open. She's *totally* ready for that. I've never actually seen someone faint, so it might be worth it.

"Then I'll grab coffee and meet you at home." She's really not giving up. "Where do you live?"

"I'm like an hour from Toronto up a dirt road."

"Oh." I can hear her grinding her teeth. She's considering taking a sick day, isn't she? "Then I could bring dinner tonight?"

What? No, no, no, no, no. Liz, you would *be* dinner. "Eat before you come." No, that sounds worse. I'm fattening her up. "I don't eat. I'd rather just talk to you."

"You don't eat? I knew you'd given up eating people, but you have to eat food. Are you anorexic?" Still diagnosing me. Great.

"No." I am very skinny. I look like a skeleton. A light chuckle erupts from my belly. Maybe I am anorexic.

"Are you okay, Abby? Was that you again?"

"That's me laughing."

"Well, I'll be over at seven or eight. I'm not sure how long it'll take to get there. Give me your address." Not a bad recovery.

She's trying so hard to pretend that every sign of my inhumanity is completely ignorable.

"Okay. It's in Hamilton. I'll text it to you. I'm going to bed. I'll see you soon." What am I gonna do? Fuck. Why did I agree to this?

"I'll see you then. Sweet dreams, Abby. I love you."

Without thinking, I find myself saying it back. "I love you too." I still do. My lips curl up in what must be the most terrifying smile. If my cheeks could hurt from smiling, they would. I love her, and she loves me. I know it will never be real, but I'll at least have one day to dream that it is.

CHAPTER SEVEN

Elizabeth

I blow out a shaky breath. I barely had an appetite, so I grabbed a burger at a fast food place on the way. Her house is about an hour and a half away from my office. I'm still wearing the red button-up blouse and black slacks I wore for work. It's not my preferred going out clothes, but I was a lot more femme when she knew me. It doesn't go with the hair, but maybe she'll think I'm cute like this. Am I really thinking of dating this woman who might be schizophrenic? Well, yeah, it'll be fine. Dr. Labelle will get her an antipsychotic prescription, and she'll be normal in no time. She'll be my girlfriend. No, she'll be my best friend. I'm getting ahead of myself.

She claimed she was in town, but I'm not sure this actually counts. My tires catch in a divot on the abandoned dirt path. I have to gun the engine for a good thirty seconds before it manages to climb out. It doesn't look as if anyone has driven on this road for years. How does she manage? Is she really that much of an agoraphobe? Are those footprints? They're massive. An indentation from what looks like a human foot but at least twice the size sits on the side of the road with a few less-clear twins a good five feet on either side. She can't have been telling the truth. Dread starts to rise in my belly, but I swallow it down. Monsters aren't real.

They pepper the path here and there as I slowly climb the hill, unable to stop from studying the strange markings as I pass.

There are so many of them, and many seem to be smeared by an identical print on top. What the hell is going on?

I park my Subaru a few feet from the door. She doesn't seem to have a vehicle of her own. "Abigail?" I call. I doubt she can even hear me in there.

"The door's open," her voice calls from the dark woods behind me.

That's not creepy at all. I turn to stare, narrowing my eyes to catch the tiny bit of light provided by the moon. "Abby?"

"Sorry. Just give me a minute. I didn't want to have you stuck in a closed room with me."

A strange scent catches my attention. I must have been smelling it since I've gotten out of my car. It isn't entirely bad. It's sort of like meat mixed with roses. It's disconcerting but hardly enough to scare me off. "I'm not going anywhere. You can come out."

She takes a step closer but stops, standing at the edge of the trees. Her breath seems to whistle; her arms are wrapped tightly about her chest. She's wearing a baggy hoodie, but that's all I can make out. Wait, did she grow? She used to be shorter than me.

She manages another step, and there's just enough light to make out a few features. What the fuck? I stop myself from taking a step back, barely. My eyes widen as I take in what's become of my best friend. She wasn't lying. I squeeze my eyes shut. I'm not trying to wish her away, but I have to calm my nerves. I won't show her how scared I am. "Abby," I breathe, finding it hard to swallow.

"I *did* tell you," she says, her eyes locked on the ground at her feet.

Her feet! She's not wearing shoes, and they're an exact match for the prints in the road. "Is it really you?"

She doesn't say "No, it was all a trap," and lunge forward and eat my face. So I assume that's a good sign. "It is. I'm sorry, I don't know what I was thinking. You should go home. I knew this was a bad idea."

I take a step toward her, using all of the courage I have not to run away. It's still her. I can even see a few familiar features in her strange, twisted appearance. "It really is you," I whisper. "Oh, Abby. I've missed you so much."

I take another step, then another, until I'm covering the distance in a sprint. I fling my arms around her, and rather than devour me like one would expect, she hugs me back, gently, as if I'm a porcelain doll. "I've missed you too. More than you could ever imagine."

I look up and realize just how much she's grown. Her chin is a full foot above the top of my head, and I'm not short. I rest my head against her chest. It's not as soft as it once was. It's feels like bone with skin stretched taut over it and maybe some fur under her jacket. It's not warm or comfortable, but it's everything I've ever wanted. I finally found her.

We stand like that for what feels like hours. I don't dare to say a word and can scarcely bring myself to breathe. I think I hear her heart beat a few times, but it's so faint, so slow, so quiet, almost as if she really is dead. I can't believe I doubted her. She's been through so much, and I need to hold her and let her know everything is okay. I stand on my tiptoes and am still too short to kiss her cheek, so I plant a soft kiss on her collarbone, just above the chain of some necklace hidden under her sweater.

She stirs, her black eyes widening as she looks at me. I think she's smiling, but it's definitely a little concerning. If I didn't know her, I'd think she was going to eat me. I'm sure she's considered it. I smile back, doing my best not to let the fear show. We actually covered this in one of my electives in graduate school: dealing with clients with disabilities. I suppose it's not quite the same, but you can't ever show that sort of reaction to any injury or disfigurement in a patient as it can severely and sometimes irrevocably damage the trust in a client/therapist relationship. I don't want to be her therapist, but I sure as hell don't want to lose her trust when I'm finally regaining it. "I've missed you so fucking much." I know I've said it a dozen times already, but not in person, and it's still so incredibly true. I don't care how much she's changed. I just need her in my life.

"I've missed you too." Her voice doesn't match the pained expression on her face as a tear runs down her cheek, disappearing in what I assume is fur.

"Can we go inside? It's freezing out here."

She nods and takes me by the hand. I grip it as her long bony fingers wrap around me. I'm desperate to keep some form of connection as we walk lest she fade away like a dream. It's hard to believe this is real. It's all so alien. Monsters aren't supposed to exist. The love of my life isn't supposed to gain two feet in height, fangs, and a hunger for human flesh. It's all so absurd.

Inside the surprisingly spacious wooden cabin, the decoration comes as a surprise. Well, even more of a surprise on top of everything else. Outside, it looked like a hunting lodge, and I would've expected deer heads or something of that sort, especially since she's a hunter. Or was that a lie? How does she survive? Instead of grotesque displays of kills, the cabin is decorated with paintings of varying skill and size but all in the same style, at least from what my amateur eye can tell. I think there's one of me, there's one of her as a human, and there's some abstract thing that makes me feel a little queasy. "Did you paint all these?" I ask.

Her eyes widen, and suddenly she's five feet away, blocking my view of one of the paintings. So it *is* me. "I did." Her gaze falls to the floor as her fingers nervously scratch a hole in her pants. Wow, those things are sharp. Poor lesbian wendigo. I can't believe I'm seriously calling her a wendigo. They're not real! Well, they are. I guess.

"They're beautiful."

She takes a hesitant step to the side, barely enough for me to see the painting again, a shy smile on her face as she glances at me before returning her gaze to the ground. "You really think so?"

In the picture, I still have long hair, but she got the brown of my eyes perfectly. It's like looking in a mirror, although my reflection is wearing a dress. I can't even think of the last time I did that.

"You changed your hair." Her eyes travel up and down me. I'm not sure if she's checking me out or sizing me up for a meal. "You've changed a lot. I wouldn't mind painting a new one if you wanted to model."

"Holy fuck, yes. That sounds amazing. When did you start painting? I don't recall you ever doing anything like that."

"About three years ago." Her voice is as clear as ever, despite the fact that she's talking to the floor, and none of her shyness seems to have touched it. I did hear her use another voice when she was telling her story. I thought it was my imagination, but it sounded like her father. Does she have some weird power with voices? Is her old voice gone? Unless, of course, she's just a monster that can use anyone's voice and is only pretending to be her.

No, Liz, you're being dumb. She would've already eaten you then. "It was when I was starting to hate what I'd become. For so long after it happened, I reveled in it, enjoying my instincts, enjoying—" She cuts herself off, likely to save me from having to hear more. "Well, about three years ago, I started to feel sick with myself. I hated everything I'd been doing for so long. I think part of me always did—otherwise, I wouldn't have been concerned for your safety—but I never used to let it get to me. Then a little after I ate the guy who owned this place, I started to really miss being human. I missed thinking about more than my next meal. I missed having someone to share my life with. I missed being alive. I went to the Community Center, and they were having an art class. It was mostly angsty vampires and the like, and I got a few weird looks, but it really spoke to me. This is actually the first one I ever drew. It looked way worse then. I've painted back over it, but it was you. You were what made me realize that I couldn't keep living that life."

"I was?" My cheeks heat up, and I continue to stare at the

painting to avoid meeting those intense, hungry black pools she has for eyes. "Wait, community center? There's some youth outreach program for monsters?"

"Not exactly. It's more of a black market but with some programs like art classes and support groups." Her eyes widen. "Oh, if you ever do meet another or if you go with me to the Community Center, most of us don't like the term 'monster.' 'Fiend' is actually the preferred term."

"How is it any different?"

"Monster sounds silly. Fiend sounds, well, fiendish. It makes us sound evil, not like a boogie man hiding under the bed."

I shrug. "I guess that makes sense. Kind of."

She sits down on the couch, crossing her legs. Even seated, her head almost hits the ceiling. "It's a really interesting place. I think you'd like it, assuming you're there as a customer and not a product." Her mouth twitches strangely. I'm not a hundred percent sure of the human equivalent of that expression. "The point is, you were always my inspiration. I tried so hard to put you behind me, but I never could."

"I know the feeling." I sit beside her and hesitate for only a second before leaning against her bony arm. She wraps it around me, and I breathe in her strange scent. I hate to use the term, especially when it's apparently not PC, but it's monstrous, and at the same time, it's comforting. It's not her old scent, but I know it's her, and I want to bask in it forever. Wow, I really *am* still in love with her. "Losing you really messed me up. I've fixed most of it at this point. I mean, it *has* been six years, but I could never quite move on. I think if we'd broken up, or even if you'd died, maybe I would've been able to find someone else, but that lack of closure left me waiting for a relationship I was convinced would never come, but now it finally can." I sit up, looking into her eyes as I swallow the lump that just formed in my throat. "I mean, if you want to. I know you're probably still sorting things out. We haven't even talked in six years. I don't mean to jump the gun."

"You'd really want to? I don't know what I can offer you. I

could never give you a normal life, we couldn't go on dates—at least not any place with humans—I don't know if we could ever have sex, and I can't move to the city or anything. I mean, I absolutely guarantee that you're better off without me."

Standing on the couch, I stare into her eyes and run my fingers through the soft fur on the back of her head. "I don't need normal. I need *you*." My eyes catch on her fangs for just a second, but I close them and lean in. She doesn't lean in, but she doesn't pull away either as my lips slowly meet hers. They're not soft or warm like I'd imagined. There's barely any lip at all, but her hands rest lightly on my back, almost completely enfolding me as she falls into the kiss.

Her tongue presses against my lips, and they part to allow her in. I think it reaches my uvula. What was that about no sex? She actually tastes kind of good. I was worried it would be like kissing rotten meat, but instead, it's more like a Popsicle. Her tongue is weirdly cold, and teasing it with mine sends a chill down my spine, but I can't think of anything I'd rather be doing. I lean into her, letting my own tongue into her mouth, lightly grazing a fang.

She pulls back, her eyes wide as she wipes her mouth. She looks away and starts breathing in and out slowly. Her eyes shut, and she sits there without saying a word.

"Am I moving too fast?" I ask.

"No. Not at all. That was amazing." It's not her voice. It's more of this weird growl. It would terrify me if it came from anyone else.

I take a step forward, still standing on the couch, and rest my hand on her shoulder.

She pulls away, suddenly standing at the stairs. "Just give me a minute. I'm not going anywhere, I promise. I just need a minute."

"What happened?" I step off the couch but don't move any farther.

"You cut your tongue on my tooth," she says.

It takes me a moment, but I think I understand. "It made you want to eat me."

She nods, her eyes squeezed shut. "Just a little. I mean, it was all really romantic, and I want to be with you, and if you're sure, then yes, I one hundred percent want to go out with you, but I just tasted human blood for the first time in two years, and I'm fucking starving. If I waited another second, I'm scared that I wouldn't have been able to settle for only *tasting* your tongue."

Oh. Ow. "So leave my tongue in my mouth?"

Another nod. "Yeah. It's not worth the risk. I don't want to end up eating it."

"Yeah, me neither." Shaking, I sit back down. I didn't think dating a wendigo would be so complicated. "You mean it, though? You want to be my girlfriend?" Focus on the positives.

"I do. I really do."

I'm sure some blood shows on my teeth as I beam up at her. "I've been waiting six years to hear those words. Abigail Lester, my girlfriend."

She lets out a slow breath, and her fangs show in a pale imitation of a smile. Her breathing has returned to normal, and she takes a step toward me. "I have too. This is everything I've ever wanted. Although I never pictured me like this when I imagined it." She gestures at her body, hidden as it is beneath the shapeless clothes.

"You're still beautiful," I say, and she is. It's not what I'd wanted either, but she'll always be beautiful to me.

❖

My eyes flutter open, and I see Abigail towering over me. If this is how I die, I guess I can live with it. After a massive yawn, I blink away sleep. "I'm sorry. I just passed out. Did you finish the painting?"

Her teeth show in what I am learning is her smile. "I did. It's fine. I'd already finished your face before you fell asleep. You looked beautiful, even sleeping. I think you were having a nice dream. You looked so happy."

"I know it sounds corny, so give me a break since I just woke up, but I was dreaming about being with you."

She takes a nervous swallow, her smile vanishing. "As a human?"

I shake my head. "No. Just as you are now." It's true. I felt so safe in her arms in my dream. I'm still a little scared of her, but it's vanishing quickly. It's Abigail; it's really her. "You're perfect."

She lets out a shaking breath. "Would you like to see it?"

She's spent what must be the last eight hours on this, since the sun's up now. She was too scared to touch me after that incident last night, so she decided to paint me. I had to lie on her couch and model, and I guess that was a bit much for me. I rise, stretching, my arms almost hitting the ceiling. How does she walk in here? "Oh, wow." In the painting, I'm lazing on a very old-fashioned couch, propped up on my arm, with sunlight filtering onto my face, and every part that's untouched by it is drawn in more detail than the parts in the light. A red, toga-esque dress covers my body, slipped up to expose one of my legs from the thigh down. I look like a Greek goddess waiting for her servant to bring her grapes. "It's beautiful. You're an amazing artist, Abby." I take a step forward to kiss her.

She leaps back, appearing by the window. I guess the sun doesn't hurt her. "I'm sorry. I'm just scared. I need to know I can control myself."

"You can." She doesn't run away as I take her hand and pull it to my lips, pressing them against the knuckle of her middle finger. Her hand is so large and yet so slender. Unfortunately, it's also so sharp. Avoiding the talon, I look into her eyes. "But we can take all the time you need. I'm not going anywhere." Shit, what time is it? "Except possibly work. How long did I sleep?"

"It's just past seven. I'm sorry. I know I should've woken you up, but you looked so peaceful."

"It's okay. I have time. Do you have a shower?"

With a quick nod, she replies, "I do. It doesn't have hot water, though."

"It's fine. Where is it?"

"Upstairs. Do you want me to show you?"

"Of course." I never got the tour last night.

She leads the way, stooping to make her way up the stairs. She points me to a small bathroom off her bedroom, which has a bed too small for her to fit in. I may have to see about changing that. "Take your time."

I shrug out of my shirt and let it fall to the ground. Her eyes drift over me before she turns around, hiding her face. It's nothing she hasn't seen before; we've known each other for a long time. Though I'll admit, I'm mostly teasing her. I refrain from asking her to unhook my bra, as that could lead to things that neither of us is ready for and that I definitely don't have the time for, and quickly shed the rest of my clothes in the bathroom so I can take a brief shower in the freezing water. I could probably use a cold shower, anyway.

She walks me to the door when I leave, and she looks terrified that I'll never come back. "See you tonight?" I ask.

Her face lights up. It really is a smile. I can sort of see it now. "Yes. Of course. If you want." It's a good thing she can completely control her voice; otherwise, she might've sounded a little overeager.

"I can't wait. What time?"

"As soon as possible. I'll be reasonable, though. How about ten?"

I smile back at her. I'll save the kiss for tonight. Maybe she'll be feeling a bit more up for it by then. "Until tonight."

Back in my car, I navigate the dirt road, the footprints now a source of comfort instead of alarm. I just need to avoid gushing about this to any of my clients.

❖

After work, I give Sandra a call. I'm not heading back to Abby's until ten. It's Friday, so I can spend the entire weekend with her. I just need to be patient for a few more hours.

My phone rings through my car's speakers as I wait for her to pick up. Sandra needs to know what's going on in my life. She's been worried about me, and she was the one who was there for me these whole six years of my being a total fuckup because I couldn't get over Abigail. I won't tell her that she's a wendigo, but I will tell her that we're dating. I'll just come up with an excuse for why she can't meet her.

"Liz, you're alive."

She'd have way more reason to be surprised if she knew what I knew. "I am, not for lack of trying." Wow, that sounds so much dumber than any time I've said it before. Had I been depressed? "I had the most amazing night last night."

"Oh really? You doing anything? I'd love to hear about it."

"Well, I have to leave for a date by about 8:30, but until then, I'm not. I could swing by?"

"A date?"

"I thought we were gonna talk about it in person. You'll just have to wait."

"You're terrible." A light chuckle drifts through the speakers. "I'll see you soon."

Twenty-five minutes later, I pull into the parking lot in front of Sandra's place and take the stairs up to her apartment on the third floor. The lack of an elevator would bother me so much more any other day. I knock on the door and hear her voice from behind me.

"Hey, sorry, I was grabbing us food. A chicken sandwich okay?"

"From where?"

"Where do I get sandwiches?" Giving me the stink eye, she unlocks the door, and I open it for her.

We take our usual seats in the living room, and she gestures pointedly toward the TV tray I'm meant to eat over. I deserve that. I probably made a mess in her car with that veal sandwich last week. I take a bite, leaning over the tray as dramatically as I can manage. Damn, their veal really is better. Normally, I love their chicken sandwiches, and today of all days, everything is perfect, but I would enjoy their veal so much more. Though of course, I'd have to get a human sandwich for Abby. I wonder how much that would be.

"Are you going to tell me or not? It's been half an hour, and the suspense is killing me! I'm not a young woman anymore."

"You're twenty-eight."

"Like I said. I have, like, three gray hairs, and I'm a year older than you. Respect your elders, and tell me the damn story."

Leaning back, I receive a prompt glare that sends me back over the table. I chew angrily. "Abby called me back yesterday morning."

A Cheshire grin spreads across her face. "Go on." She is, unfortunately, not steepling her fingers as she learns that her diabolical scheme has finally been realized.

"I went over to her place, and we started talking, and she painted me, and we made out, and we're dating!" I squeal. "We're really dating. I've waited, like, ten years for this. I can't believe it's finally happening. She's so amazing, and she makes me feel beautiful, and she's so beautiful, and she's gotten so strong and absolutely incredible at art. That picture was a fucking masterpiece. I want to plaster every wall in my house with it and see the very representation of her love for me every time I open my eyes." I'm such a girl. I haven't been this love-crazed since… well, since I figured out I had feelings for Abby.

She lets out a long whistle. "That is the most romantic thing I've ever heard. I mean, you're clearly completely besotted and mad at this point, but I can hardly blame you. I've been waiting for you two to get together since I've known you. I can't believe it finally happened. I thought for sure it was a lost cause after she…well, you know. I'm so happy for you!" She takes a bite of her sandwich and grins with a bit of eggplant stuck in her teeth.

"I'm seeing her again tonight. I'm gonna ask if I can spend the whole weekend with her."

"That's wonderful. Oh my God, I'm going to die from sheer joy. This is the greatest news I've ever heard in my life."

My smile turns sympathetic. "You'll have the same before too long, I'm sure. Any guy would be crazy to resist you."

"Yet they all seem to. Or even worse, they want me and are just terrible."

"See, this is why you need to go gay. Ladies are great."

She glares. "I would if I could. Believe me."

"Oh, you think about it for me?" I wink.

"You have a girlfriend now, missy, so you'd best put a stop to that flirting nonsense."

She has a point. I've been such a slut for so long that I'm not sure how to handle being in love. "You're right. I love her so much."

Her smile regains its full force. "Have you told her?"

"I have." A quick nod and I turn back to my sandwich. I wish I could share it with Abby, but even if I can never share a meal with her, it's worth it. After this long a wait, I'd give up anything for her.

"And did she say it back?"

I laugh, a bit of sandwich falling on the floor, but she doesn't seem to care at this point. "She did. She really did. Holy fuck, Abigail Lester loves me. It's finally happening. My life is finally working out."

"Enjoy it. With any luck, you'll have all the time in the world, but don't let a day go by without savoring every second of it. It's just fantastic to see you happy again."

"I couldn't be happier." Well, I'll be even happier in a few hours when I'm back in her arms.

We make it through dinner, and I manage to stick around

until 7:30, checking the time every few seconds. After the end of some show I was barely paying attention to, I give Sandy a quick good-bye kiss on the cheek and run to my car so I can get ready in time to see Abby.

CHAPTER EIGHT

Abigail

The sound of tires tearing along the dirt path drags me from bed. I throw on a nightgown and make it to the front door before Liz's car pulls up. I haven't worn this thing in a year. I felt horrid in it, like a monster playing at being a woman, but after how she looked at me, even though I could smell her fear, I feel like maybe I'm not so disgusting. She makes me feel pretty again. The cross hangs from its chain around my neck. I was never particularly religious, but I haven't taken it off since I bought it last week. Maybe I could get a new necklace, something that suits me more now that I'm feeling comfortable enough to consider it. It's weird thinking about clothes as anything more than a disguise.

As soon as the car is parked, she leaps out and runs up to me. I fight back any instinct to attack. She's so slow that it's not like she'd be a threat anyway. I sweep her into my arms, holding her close, and am surprised to find her lips on mine again. Maybe this time I can manage it without wanting to eat her, at least any more than I always do. She smells amazing and not only because it's appetizing. It's like the scent of home that I've long since forgotten, only to find it again and feel like I was never gone. My nose wasn't so sensitive back then as to pick up every detail the way I can now, but it's still so familiar, and I can't believe I ever allowed it to slip from my mind. I give in to the kiss as gently as I can, trying to be careful not to let my teeth so much as brush her lips.

I don't let my tongue into her mouth this time. Her taste was too enchanting on its own, even before the blood, for me to risk it right now. I just hold her and let our lips press together as best they can as we share each other's feel, scent, breath, and, I suppose, taste. I wish I had better to offer of any of those. Why does she even want me?

"I love the nightgown," she announces, beaming at me when we finally pull away. A finger traces over the soft fabric. "It suits you."

"Wasn't that long ago it would have suited you too."

"Yeah, but now I'm a total badass."

I bare my teeth at her. I hope she reads it playfully and not threateningly. "Oh, you think you're more badass than me?"

"I could take you."

I breathe in her scent again, savoring the closeness before I set her down. "That reminds me, I have a present for you."

Giggling happily, she follows me inside. "Really? What'd you get me? Is it pretty?"

"I think it is. Though I'm sure it's not what you were hoping for." I present her with a delicately wrapped gift. I had Ashley help with the wrapping. My hands are great for slicing, stabbing, rending, and surprisingly painting and piano—not that I've much experience with the latter—but not so much for wrapping. I did slice the paper, though, just to feel useful.

Seated on my couch, she rests the box on her lap and slowly unwraps it. She used to tear presents apart. She might just want to save everything to do with me for fear that I'll disappear again. I promise, I'll prove otherwise. "Oh. It's…huh." She stares at the silver dagger slid a few inches from its sheath.

"It's not much, but it'll keep you safe." I hope. "It might not be able to kill me—I've heard mixed things—but it can hurt me, and it can kill a lot of other things."

"I would never hurt you."

"But I might hurt you." I sit on the far side of the couch. I'm starting to feel more comfortable with my ability to be around her, but the second I actually let myself believe that she's safe is the very instant I'll devour her. "Besides, I need to know that no one else will hurt you, either."

With a sigh, she slips the dagger into a jacket pocket, leaving it protruding halfway out. "All right, I guess, but I really don't think you'll hurt me."

"We need to find a better way for you to carry it. There's a harness for it, but I wasn't sure how you'd want it." I pull the leather strap from the box, thumbing it idly as we talk, and I try to figure out how best for her to carry it.

"You don't need to worry. I know I'm safe with you."

"Well, I was hoping, maybe you wouldn't be with only me all weekend."

"You want me to go? Or are you suggesting a threesome? If so, I gotta warn you, I don't think I'm too up for sharing what's finally mine."

I feel my cheeks heat up, among other parts. I didn't know those still worked. "I don't want to share you either. However, I do want to let you see what my world is like, what my life is like, and who my friends are. I know I can't be part of your life, and it's not fair to either of us, but you can at least be part of mine. If you'd like to, I mean."

She takes the strap and holds my hand in her lap, running her thumb along the dark fur. "Then I'll happily wear it. I'd love to meet your friends. They won't be offended by my being armed?"

"We all have built-in weapons, and you don't, so it just seems fair."

"You also have superpowers."

"I don't have a way to give you those."

Resting her head on my arm, she pulls herself closer. "I'll have you at least. Can we go tomorrow? I really just want to spend tonight with you."

Her hand brushes my thigh, and I take a shaky breath. "Liz, I can't, please…I'm not ready. I'm too scared I'll hurt you."

She pulls her hand back and looks up at me, guilt clear in her eyes. "I'm sorry. I wasn't thinking. I know. I wasn't even trying to. I just want to be close to you, and I've used sex for that for so long at this point that I think I forgot how to be intimate without it."

What happened to her? She used to be one of the slowest-moving lesbians I've ever known. With her first girlfriend, she took almost a year before they were willing to try anything. "It was my fault, wasn't it? You lost that trust. I made it hard for you to be close to another person because of how badly I hurt you."

"It wasn't like that. I'm just a bit of a slut. Just when I'm single," she adds. "I'm not gonna cheat or anything, I promise."

"If you can't sleep with me, I wouldn't blame you for wanting to with someone else."

"I don't want someone else. It's so hard for me to really be with anyone else because they're not you. You're everything to me, Abigail, and I've been incomplete without you these last six years. It wasn't because you hurt me; it's because I needed you. I will always need you."

I lean my head against her, doing my best to let myself be as vulnerable as an unkillable abomination can be. I still can't believe she cares this much, especially after all this time. "I'll never leave you again. I promise."

"I believe you." She kisses my neck, as it's as about the best she can reach, and slides to the far side of the couch, guiding my head into her lap. I'm glad the guy who owned this cabin had a giant couch. Her fingers run through my fur, catching in the matted patches that I never bother to fix. I haven't cared too much about grooming beyond making sure that I'm not covered in blood in a long while. It's difficult to feel like there's anything worth presenting.

She plants a wet kiss on my forehead as her hand continues to work, caressing me and occasionally working at a tangle. It's short fine fur, just thick enough to tangle annoyingly. It's so weird to describe. With her, I can feel almost human, but with every touch, I'm reminded of how inhuman I am. At the same time, it shows just how alive she can make me feel again. "I love you," I murmur, my eyelids fluttering shut as I give in to the ecstasy of her touch.

"I love you too."

I had set up the generator, and with a great deal of effort, persuaded Ashley to lend me her laptop for the weekend, so when she decides to take a break from the petting, I set up a show for us to watch as we spend the night in each other's arms. It's the most comfortable, normal time I've had in my entire life.

❖

I didn't have the courage to go out in any sort of dress, but she talks me into dressing up a little. Rather than wearing the loosest thing imaginable, I'm wearing a high-collared purple button-up blouse with a pair of black jeans. I ordered the blouse from an undead seamstress back when I was first exploring what I was comfortable wearing with my new body once I was actually bothering with clothes.

Liz clings to my arm as we walk into the Community Center. I should've waited another week and given her more time to get used to everything. I could've let us spend more time figuring each other out again, but it's too late to take it back now. Her eyes widen once we go through the second entrance. She stares at all the stands, manned by all kinds of creatures that can scarcely be called men. She sees horns, antlers, hooves, talons, beaks, tentacles, and tails in every assortment imaginable. It was pretty overwhelming when I first saw it too, and I had the benefit of a few years seeing myself.

Her grip tightens, and her head sinks lower as she glances around, bug-eyed. "Holy shit. I mean, *holy shit*! You told me what to expect, but I didn't anticipate the scale of it. All of these mon…fiends live in Toronto?"

"Or the general area."

"I had no idea. How do they all keep hidden?"

I'd rather not answer that. Murder and slavery don't make for the best date conversation.

We pass by a stall containing various exotic weaponry, from a khopesh to a flamethrower, and several more items that are far less conventional. We stop at a bakery run by a lovely gay satyr couple. "Well now, isn't this a rare surprise," one of the two remarks. I've never been able to keep their names straight, as they look almost identical, but one is named Alika and the other is Pallab. "A human in our market."

Liz glances at me hesitantly.

"They don't eat people, and none"—I pause to sniff—"well, very few of their baked goods contain people."

"Are you sure we can't interest you in a scone made of a hanged murderer, Abigail?"

Liz's gaze turns from anxious to concerned. "You should eat it, Abby. I know how hungry you are. I heard your stomach growling all last night. You're starving. Besides, it sounds like he deserved it."

"No way." I shake my head and take a step back. "I've been off people for two years. I'm not starting up again."

"Are you sure? Maybe it'd be easier for you if you just had something in your stomach." She takes a step toward me, concern clear on her face. I know she's trying to help, but she doesn't get it.

"Liz, no. I've been there, I've eaten enough. All it ever did was make me hungrier."

"Fine, maybe I'll try it."

"No, no, no, no, no, no, no. No. You're not gonna end up like me. I'm not letting that happen." I take her hand and lead her away. "Liz, please. Don't do this. I know what I'm talking about. Let me not eat, and please don't ever try it yourself."

Her gaze drops, and she nods. "Okay. I'm sorry. I'm still new to this."

"I know. I hope I didn't scare you."

"Not at all." She stands on her tiptoes and kisses my shoulder. "Now, I really want a cupcake. Can I please go grab one?"

"Yeah, fine. I'll be right over here." I take the chance to study some weapons, looking for anything that could do a better job of protecting her. A few minutes later, she returns. I can smell a few different items in her bag, not all of them sweets, and one of them very much edible for me. I told her not to get it. I know it's just because she's worried about me, but I don't want to be around the temptation.

"They gave me a free cupcake." She grins, and I can't bring myself to be mad at her. I'll just throw it out later. Maybe I'll give it to Ashley. She's a lot less concerned about her diet.

She takes my hand and drags me to another stand, admiring the craftsmanship and beauty of the metalwork and jewelry on display. I'm always surprised by how much silver and iron is sold here—it seems like a bit of a faux pas. "This necklace is beautiful," she says, holding up a short chain containing a green jewel in the center of a fractal pattern of glass.

"Would you like it?"

She shakes her head and proceeds to buy it. I thought she didn't want it. She turns back to me, barely able to contain her glee, as she stands as tall as she can. Finally realizing what she's up to, I lean forward. It's weird to think of her wanting to buy me something. It's just wasted on me. "There, it looks beautiful. It's the color your eyes used to be, in case you've forgotten. I hope it's not too difficult a memory."

My current eyes seem to be leaking as I try to hold myself together and not weep in front of a bunch of fiends I see every week. "Thank you so much. I was starting to forget."

Resting her head on my chest, her eyes wander over the rest of the goods on display. "It's all so beautiful."

"So are you." I can still flirt. Kind of. I'm only six years out of practice.

She kisses my sleeve, and we move along, admiring stand

after stand. I so rarely shop. Eventually, we end up at Boris's. "Is that human?" she asks, pointing at a slab of meat.

"No. The kebabs over there are." I point off in the distance. They smell so good, even over the scone in her bag. I'm absolutely ravenous. I haven't been so tempted in over a year. Tasting her was a very bad idea.

"No, most of that is venison from the lovely lady who this strange human seems to be clinging to. What is happening here, Abigail? I assume you are not here to sell her."

Her eyes widen, and she stares up at me. "So they do sell people here?" I was so hoping to not have this conversation.

Boris nods, grinning enthusiastically. "Oh, of course. They sell everything: people, both living and dead, are one of the top commodities."

"There's a slave market here once a month," I say. "And other fiends often have their own victims or possessions to sell outside of that."

"Not to worry though, miss." He offers a very unconvincing smile. "You are here as a guest, and as such, you are protected by hospitality. No one will try to buy you or eat you. Especially not with that scary wendigo on your arm. Now, Abby, do tell. I thought we were friends."

"She's my girlfriend."

"Very happy for you. I had no idea you were interested in humans. Human girl, how would you like pound of silver on the house?"

"He's trying really hard to get rid of that silver." Did he run out of buyers? I guess it really isn't that popular here.

With a shrug, she holds out her hands. "I'll take it."

"Very good. Would you like a bag?"

We leave the stand with a bag full of silver in various forms. Ashley is gonna be thrilled.

Speak of the devil, and she shall appear. My phone buzzes with a message from her. *I just got here. Where are you? Is she with you? I know I've said it like eight times already, but I'm so happy for you.*

"Liz, are you ready to meet my best friend? My other best friend?" Having your old best friend pop back into your life complicates terms.

❖

We take in the cold air outside the Community Center. It's late enough that no one is likely to be hanging around outside, though this is precisely why I prefer to wear a hood. Ashley hasn't taken her eyes off Elizabeth since she first saw her, and I'm hoping her intentions are in no way culinary.

"How're you adjusting? I'm sure this all came as a pretty massive shock." Ashley takes a seat on a heavily graffitied bench as she continues to study my girlfriend.

"It was definitely surprising," Liz admits, sitting beside her. "When she told me, I thought she was crazy. Sorry, Abby," she adds, turning to me. "Also, sorry, my profession; 'crazy' is not at all an acceptable or medically relevant term."

"What do you do?" She finally starts to look more curious than hungry. I continue to keep an eye on her anyway. It's not that I don't trust Ashley, but she did fall off the wagon a month ago.

"I'm a therapist."

Ashley blinks. "That *is* interesting. Now it's really a shame that you can't come to our group. You could be a big help."

"Why can't I come?"

"Humans aren't allowed," I say. "It's dangerous for them, but it's also a temptation for everyone to give up on their diets. It's why I was a little worried about you meeting Ashley."

"Do you want to eat me, Ashley?" I have no idea how she's grown so comfortable with this idea. I guess she had to adjust quickly, dating me.

"Of course not. I think that's Abigail's job."

Is everyone I know going to make an eating out joke? "Real funny, Ashley," I mutter.

Ashley smirks. "I'll admit, she does look delicious. So, Liz, tell me the truth, have you tasted our favorite wendigo yet?"

Liz glances at me, looking far more like she's considering it than like she's asking me for help. I'd call her insatiable, but that would require I be able to attempt to satiate her in the first place. "No, though I certainly hope to soon." She turns back to Ashley with a mischievous look on her face. "Why, have you?"

Her playful response seems to throw Ashley off. She's not used to someone else taking control of the conversation. "I'm afraid that Abby and I have had to confine that to our dreams. As irresistible as she is, I tragically don't swing that way."

Liz beckons me closer, placing an arm possessively around me. She makes abstaining very difficult sometimes. "That is a shame. I suppose I'll just have to do it for the both of us, then. I'm sure Abby wouldn't mind."

"Abby very much minds." I take a step back. Her hand drifts back to her side. "Liz, I can't take that risk. I just can't."

For a second, it looks as if she's about to say something, but she nods, letting out a shaky breath. "Abby, I know I'm safe with you. You don't have to worry."

"Yes, I do. You can't understand." I need to get us to drop this topic. We can figure it out later, but I need a break from it. Holding back has already been so incredibly difficult; if she keeps telling me I don't have to, I just might give in. "So, Ashley. Any news on that front for you?"

"Well, now that I have my laptop back, my sex life is far more active, but other than that, I have had no more luck finding a cute guy. I swear, ever since Charles and I broke up, it's been impossible, but he refused to give up eating people, and I couldn't handle dealing with that. Liz, no eating people around Abigail, okay? Promise?"

I can smell the human meat in her bag. Every fiber of my being is telling me to eat it, to eat her, then maybe to eat Ashley for good measure. I take another step back, not that it in any way prevents me from being able to smell every single piece of meat.

"I guess I can do that. We're just so tasty. I mean, who could resist a piece of this." She flexes her bicep, which has grown substantially since I knew her, and glances at Ashley, who looks on the verge of salivating in agreement. "Sorry. That was messed up. I went way too far with your joke. I know better than that. I shouldn't be encouraging it. I'm sorry. Wow, I really shouldn't be allowed in your group."

"Don't worry. Ashley started it, and she can take a dose of her own medicine." I'm still trying to keep my distance. Her display hasn't made my abstention any easier, on either count. Horny, hungry cannibals make the best dates. "I'm sure it's tough to get used to."

"I've never been that big on muscle," Ashley says, still staring at Liz's. "I prefer my meat marbled. The fat just makes it so much more tender and flavorful." Her eyes look slightly more glazed over than usual as she fantasizes. "Just hold the embalming fluid. I'll eat them in a single sitting."

Liz takes my arm, watching Ashley the entire time. She isn't watching me. All I'd have to do is bend over the slightest bit, and I could finally have a meal. I pull her to me, resting my arm loosely on her shoulder and turning my gaze to Ashley. "Do you need us to go?" I'm stronger than this urge. I love her. I won't hurt her.

She waves her hand. "No. No, I'm fine. Just give me a second." She licks her lips but does the same breathing exercises I always do. "I'm okay. I'm sorry if I scared you, Liz. I promise I won't bite."

With a quick kiss to my hand, Liz moves back toward Ashley. I follow her, almost exclusively because I want to keep her safe. "I know you won't. You're stronger than you think you are. Abby told me that other than a couple dead people, you've been clean for a year. I'm not dead, so I'm not scared of you. Okay, I was for a second there, but I'm not now. Maybe I could help. I don't have a lot of experience with addicts, but I do with eating disorders, and that's kind of related to what you're going through. It's actually really common in the LGBT community, and a lot of them love coming to me. It's not my specialty, but I might be able to help you handle it."

She shakes her head. "No. I'd just rather not discuss eating with a human anymore. I thought I was stronger than I am. You're welcome to believe otherwise, but I'm gonna stick with what I know works. I made it eleven months before, and now I have a reason to stick with it. Abby's my best friend, and you're important to her, so I'm not willing to let myself eat you."

I can feel Liz releasing the breath she was holding. I can almost taste her muscles relaxing now that she knows she doesn't have to run. She really does do a great job managing her fear. I can see why her patients feel comfortable with her. She doesn't let her judgments show, and she's quite possibly the most understanding person I could have ever imagined. The rest of the night is tense, and Ashley leaves several hours before sunrise, but our time together isn't unpleasant, and we shy away from any further discussion of dinner. Once she leaves, I get to spend the entire day holding Elizabeth in my arms, secure in the knowledge that I have completely ruined her sleep schedule.

CHAPTER NINE

Elizabeth

I wake up to find Abigail staring at me. I fell asleep in her arms, practically using her as a bed. While I do miss being taller than her, having a giant girlfriend sure has its advantages. I pull myself up and kiss her softly, resting my hands on her shoulders.

She returns the kiss, but her hesitation is clearer than it was before. Her tongue stays where it is, though her hands go to the small of my back. I respond by tracing the outline of her ribs to her prominent hips and feel her shudder beneath my touch. Making a fiend purr does make you feel so powerful. I kiss down her jawline and move to her neck, her hand sliding down to my ass.

Without meaning to, I start grinding against her, and I feel her doing the same. My breath catches, and I scratch her hip as I start to slide a hand between us. Then I'm lying in an empty bed. Abigail is panting by the door to the bathroom, trying to get herself under control. "I didn't make you too hungry, did I?"

She swallows, doing her best to regain her composure. "No. I just really, desperately, madly wanted to keep going. But I know where that road leads, and I don't trust myself there."

Grumbling, I roll over, pulling myself into a sitting position. I stare into her eyes. "Then what's the problem? I want it too. I know you, Abby, and I've been waiting for this for a good decade by now. I promise, I'll be gentle."

I so love making her blush. "Liz, please."

That kills the mood. "I'm sorry. I thought you wanted it too." It's not like she's told me half a dozen times how scared she is. What the hell is wrong with me? Why would I push it? Am I really that desperate that I would ignore her wishes just so I could satisfy myself? I feel sick. "That's a lie. Fuck, I'm so sorry, Abby. I don't know what I was thinking. I do want it, but I am willing to wait until you're comfortable, even if that takes years."

"I don't know if I'll ever be ready, Liz. I've killed a lot of people, and I have to always hold myself back from doing it again. If I give in to my urges, no matter which ones they are, I'm terrified that I won't be able to stop. I'd never be able to forgive myself. I know it's not fair to you."

"It's not fair to *you*. You don't deserve that kind of pressure."

She lets out another breath and takes a seat next to me. That's a definite improvement. "I do. I'm a monster. I don't mean in the species way; I mean that I've done things that you should not be willing to forgive me for. Because of that, I have to always watch myself and make sure I can be better."

Leaning my head against her bicep, I reply in my best therapist voice. "It wasn't your fault. You were forced into it, and as soon as you gained enough control over yourself, you stopped. I know how much you beat yourself up over it, and I understand why, but you didn't choose any of this. You did what you had to do to survive, and you ended up with…I don't know what to call it, a curse?"

Her answer is only a shrug.

"You have this curse that is supposed to make you a killing machine. 'A fiend that can never stop eating.' Isn't that how you described it? Tell me, how many other wendigos have managed to stop?"

"I don't know. I've only ever heard of one, and he only lasted a couple weeks."

"And how long have you managed?"

"Two years, as of about five months ago. June twelfth."

I give her hand a reassuring squeeze, intertwining our

fingers. Looking down, I see how hers dwarf mine, the vicious claws on the end of them, and I still don't feel the slightest hint of danger. "You are the strongest person I've ever known." I can see her start to reply, but I cut her off. "Yes, you are still a person. You will always be a person. You fought against a hunger that consumes everyone it touches—that was way more poetic than I meant it to be—and after over two years fighting it, you are still here, standing strong. Abigail, there is nothing that could make me afraid of you."

"Then I need to be the one to exercise restraint. If you aren't afraid of someone who could kill and eat you before you could even move, I have to be the one who is. I am terrified of myself, and if you're not going to attempt self-preservation, I'll do it for you. I can't let myself relax for even a second. I can't have sex with you. Even sleeping with you scares the hell out of me."

"Yet I still woke up in one piece." I look up at her—my terrified, wonderful girlfriend—and smile the most defiant smile I can manage. "You are so much more powerful than your curse, more powerful than the strength of a wendigo."

She leaves a wet kiss on the crown of my head. "You might be right." So she's really starting to believe me? "But I won't take the chance. If you need to have sex, I'm okay with you finding it somewhere else. You trust me not to hurt you? Well, I trust you not to hurt me. We made it six years apart without our feelings changing, so you can sleep with someone else and still love me."

"We already discussed this. I don't want that. I just want you. Even if it means I have to learn to control myself too."

Her arms wrap around me, and I feel a tear fall on my head, followed by another. "Are you sure you can handle that?"

"Of course I am. I love you." I hold her close, inhaling the now-comforting mixture of dead flesh and floral perfumes.

"I love you too."

❖

The next morning, I wake up to her arm draped around me. I only managed a few hours of sleep; it's going to take a lot of work getting used to being nocturnal on my weekends. I watch her sleeping. Her chest doesn't seem to be moving. That really scared me the first night, but at this point, I'm pretty sure she can't die. She takes up almost the entire bed, and her legs extend a good foot and a half past the end of it. If I'm going to be doing this more often, I need to get a better bed for us. Maybe two queens in a row—that way she'd have some leg room, and I'd have space next to her.

I shrug out from under her arm and hop into her shower. The cold water helps wake me up and shed some of the lingering images from that dream. I'm a bit sad to let it go. Abby and I had so much fun in it.

I packed some clothes for work, so I throw them on and give Abby a quick kiss on the cheek as she sleeps. I grab my bag of cupcakes and head out. She made me promise not to leave them here, claiming that she doesn't like having food in her house. I think she could smell the scone I bought her. I'll message her when I get to work so she knows I didn't just run off. She's still scared of that. Not that I blame her; I'm terrified of losing her again too.

I arrive at my office at five past nine, and my first client is already waiting. It all seems so humdrum now. There are literal monsters—fiends, I need to work on that—living in this city, dealing with their own problems. Next to them, it's hard to be invested in someone who's just worried that their spouse doesn't really love them. There's no blood, no curses, no immortality, and they have regular sex.

I am, however, a professional, and I don't let my issues show. I talk them all through their problems, help them figure out ways to work through them and discuss why they believe that such-and-such must be the case. If I'm being honest, I think I'm actually a better therapist than I've ever been, even if I do feel more detached. The issue that's been gnawing at me for six years is finally settled. It's like a weight's been lifted off my shoulders, and I can just handle their issues instead. They just seem so human.

At lunch, I have one of my cupcakes. They're quite possibly the most delicious thing I've ever eaten. They may actually be magical. It's like fireworks going off in my mouth. I soon find that all of them are gone, rather than only the one I'd intended, leaving only the human scone. I have to admit, I'm a little tempted. It's probably not as good anyway; I've heard human isn't too tasty. Then again, Abby said we are.

See? Why can't my clients come in saying that they're trying to decide if it's worth having another of the most delicious pastries they've ever had if there's a chance it could turn them into a flesh-devouring fiend with an insatiable appetite?

One client does. Well, almost.

Dennis looks different. He's paler, gaunt, his cheekbones are far more prominent, and he looks like he's lost about fifty pounds when he hadn't been that big to start with. The big change, though, is the blood smeared around his lips. That's what really tips me off that he might have changed.

"I was so wrong before," he gasps, dropping his umbrella on the floor. It's not raining; the sun's out. "I don't know how I could have thought I was dead. They all must have seen me. They just didn't care. It makes so much sense. Now though, I *am* dead, and they *do* see me, and they care. At least they care when I make them."

"And how many people have you made care?" I ask, anger creeping into my tone. Some professional I am. Does silver work on vampires? My dagger is secured to my thigh, under my skirt. It's the only reason I'm wearing a skirt…well, that and I haven't had time to do the laundry. I didn't think I'd actually need it, but once we figured out a way to carry it without being so obvious, Abigail insisted.

"Just the one so far." His eyes widen as he sees the look on my face. I'm not afraid; just trying to figure out if I could draw the dagger before he bites me. "Don't be scared. I would never hurt you. You're the one person I can trust."

"I'm not scared. I don't think you should be eating people."

"What's one human? I'll live a thousand lives, and they'll be a drop in the bucket. I thought being dead was so horrible, but now that it's real. It's freeing."

"I hear there's a good art class that you might want to check out."

His expression shifts, the mad look of victory and satisfaction fading into confusion. "What do you mean?"

"My girlfriend takes a class, and she says it's mostly vampires. Maybe you should check it out. Have you been to the Community Center yet?"

He grows all the more confused, squinting at me. He must think I've lost it.

"Someone turned you and didn't bother to teach you anything about the world?"

"You're alive. What do you know?" Leaning forward, looking ready to pounce, he bares his fangs, still red from the blood of his last victim.

Great job. Piss off the vampire with Abigail a good fifty miles away out in Hamilton. "I think I have a group that'd be really good for you. There are no humans allowed, so you don't have to worry about any of us living people telling you what to do."

The confusion grows to anxiety, overwhelming the anger. I know something that I shouldn't, and he doesn't know something he should. "What kind of group?"

"It's a group where people like you get together and work to be more than the stereotypes that myths claim you are. They teach you to not need to eat people, to learn to cope with your urges without hurting others. I know it's satisfying to make people notice you, but if you go to that group, you won't have people afraid of you. You'll have a family that cares about you."

His foot taps a discordant rhythm on my floor at superhuman speed. The sound is very unnerving. "Where is it?"

"I'll give you directions. It's at the old Honeydale Mall. Will you go? At least for one session. That's your homework this week."

He bites his lip, the fangs drawing blackened blood. He is definitely not used to his body yet. "Okay. I guess I can do that, but I'm not promising to make any changes."

"Of course. That's all I can ask." I write down directions. Abby hadn't told me all of the specifics but enough that he should be able to find it. "They meet every Wednesday at midnight." I hope she won't object to my sending someone there.

"Thanks." He takes the paper from me. I don't even flinch when he travels half the room in the blink of an eye. He groans audibly. Sorry, I'm already used to it from Abby.

I'd been wondering something. I need to know. "How did he turn you? Or she."

"What do you mean?"

"What was the process like? Was it painful? Do you remember all of it?"

He swallows, wiping at his face and further smearing the blood. "I don't know. I remember him biting me, and when I was almost drained, he let me go. It finally hit me that I was really alive, and now I was dying. It was such a strange time to finally understand. I'd spent so long living a lie, and when I finally learned the truth, it was taken away from me."

"But you didn't die."

"I did. He slit his own wrist with one of his nails, and as the darkness closed in, he gave me a drink. It was the most delicious thing I've ever tasted. I've been craving it ever since. That woman's wasn't even close."

"Interesting. I've heard a similar story. I guess your first taste is always the best." Or second? She did eat her mom first.

He stares. I think he'd been hoping that I'd be a lot more

confused. Instead, I knew more than him, and I was acting like it. "Why aren't you scared of me? Everyone else is scared of me."

"Because you're not a monster. You'll always be a person, Dennis, alive or dead, and I don't have anything to fear from you."

"I could kill you. I could bite your throat and end your life."

I sit up straight, my neck readily accessible. He is so much less intimidating than Abigail. "Maybe you could, but I don't see any reason you'd want to."

He leans forward, and for a second, I think he might lunge, but he stomps his foot and is suddenly sitting on the couch again. "If you knew about this stuff, why didn't you tell me about it when I thought I was dead?"

"Would you have believed me?" I didn't know, but he needs to think that I know what I'm talking about, and five days' worth of knowledge isn't too impressive. If I seem like I'm as new to this as he is, he might not go to that group, and he might keep hurting people.

"I don't know," he mutters, resting his ankle on his knee as he bounces his foot up and down. It's like he's a kid again. I wonder if that's part of the transformation or if he just has so much energy from having just eaten someone.

"Well, you know now. The people there will help you, I promise." I really hope there's not a dead body outside. "I'm proud of you, Dennis."

"Why?"

"You're finally ready to start making changes in your life." There we go. That proud look on his face, as if he was given a gold star on an exam. I'm pretty sure he's going to go to Abby's group.

Once he leaves, I drop the bravado and let out a shaky breath. Maybe I was a little scared. Only because I didn't have a stake. Why is everyone I interact with an undead fiend capable of ripping me apart before I can even move? Even weirder, why do I seem to prefer it that way?

CHAPTER TEN

Abigail

I managed to convince Liz to stay at her place tonight. It's not that I don't want to spend every waking moment with her. it's just that she slept maybe eight hours this entire weekend, and I want her to be awake when she's with me. She sends me a few messages before bed, and they're amazing to wake up to, even if it's not quite the same as having her in my arms.

I'm going to bed, so it's your last chance to change your mind. I love you, Abby. I'll see you tomorrow, okay? Her other message was a little less wholesome. *Just broke out my vibrator for the first time in a while. Would having phone sex sometime be too tempting for you?* I've been rather focused on that idea for the last twenty minutes or so, and I think I've come to the conclusion that I might be up for trying it. I just wish I could try more with her without having to worry.

My phone rings, and I give up on figuring out how to use my likely atrophied genitals. "Hey, James." Well, he is certainly the appropriate person to ask about a lot of this stuff. It just feels weird asking a guy for sex advice.

"Hey. I heard Ashley got to meet your girlfriend. When am I going to get to?" There's some symphonic metal playing loud enough wherever he is that I could hear every note even if I was still human.

"Turn that down, and maybe I'll let you."

"Fine." He clicks a button, the springs in a chair squeaking beneath him as he shifts. The music stops, and his foot hits the floor, causing a sudden cessation of the squeaking. He's the king of annoying noises today. "When can I meet her? I mean, this is the first person you've dated since I've known you. She has to be like the most beautiful woman in the world to distract you from your obvious vow of celibacy."

"She is, and maybe I won't let you meet her."

"I'll turn the music back on."

"You are the absolute worst."

Another *thunk* as he sets his feet on his desk. "I wouldn't make a move on her. I don't eat people anymore, remember? Let me live vicariously through you. You can still have sex."

Oh, if only. "No, I really can't."

"Why not?"

I growl. I can hear him gulp. I wasn't even trying to threaten him. "If I give in like that, I'm going to end up hurting her or going all the way and eating her, like you said. I can't trust myself. If I have a taste, I might take a bite. If I finger her, it might result in internal bleeding."

"There are other ways to have sex."

"I am not having 'the talk' with you."

His laugh is so strange. Like, it's almost too perfect. It's somehow more intimidating than anything else about him. I guess you can take the demon out of Hell, but you can't take Hell out of the demon. If that is where he came from; he's stubbornly coy about it. "Come on, I wanted to do some shopping anyway. I'll show you a few things."

Is he going to help me buy a strap-on? Would a strap-on work? This is such a terrible idea. I guess it doesn't hurt to have one, and maybe a vibrator would help with phone sex. God, I can't believe I'm really considering this.

I start to grab a hoodie, but I resist. I'm trying to be better for Liz. I keep hurting her with what I'm not capable of. I can at least do everything I *am* capable of. I'm still wearing the green necklace—I finally took off my cross—and I decide to complement it with a green skirt. It's been so long since I last wore a skirt. I bought it when I was feeling my most disgusting and awful, and I thought it'd make me feel better, but it only made it worse. But thinking of the way she looks at me, I almost feel human again. Even knowing how I look in a skirt can't change that. I match it with a blue long-sleeved top that covers most of my fur. I don't have any mirrors, and I have no desire to check, but I feel like I might look decent. If you squint.

By the time I arrive at the Community Center, James is already there. He whistles appreciatively as I approach. "You clean up good."

I roll my eyes. It's not that I don't appreciate him complimenting me in one of the most insulting ways he could manage, I just know that he's only doing it to make me feel better. I know exactly how awful I look. We head inside, and he leads me to a section that I never really bothered to explore. There're some more esoteric items that require being immortal to be able to survive them during sex, but most of the goods are fairly mundane. Though they do tend to have much higher power settings than the human variety. A few are even name brand. I had no idea we were a demographic worth targeting. I guess a bunch of lonely wendigos and ghouls have uses for them. I groan. "This is so embarrassing."

"Have you never bought one before? This is all pretty normal." He eyes a device that seems to shove blades inside a male orifice. "Nothing I haven't seen before, at least."

"No, I haven't, okay? I was still pretty closeted when I was human, and I was only twenty-one at the time."

"Straight people buy sex toys too. A friend never took you shopping? Not even Liz?"

I shake my head. "No, now will you help me?"

A horrifying smile appears on his face, his eyes looking increasingly demented as they begin to glow red. "Oh, you are in for a treat. I'm going to show you everything you could possibly need to know."

"How about just the basics that would let me not hurt her?"

"Well, if you don't want to risk biting her, there's always this." He gestures toward a strangely shaped item.

I have to lean forward to figure out what it is. "Industrial-strength ball gags?" I am in so far over my head. What part is industrial-strength? "I don't think I want to do anything kinky. I just want to be able to be intimate with her. Maybe eventually we could look into something exciting, but right now, I was mostly thinking a vibrator, maybe a strap-on if I could be really sure I wouldn't get too excited."

"They have restraints that can hold an ogre. With that ball gag, you wouldn't be able to hurt her."

I walk away from the table. This is all too much. What am I even doing here? "I don't want to have to do that," I cry as he catches up to me, concern clear in his still-glowing eyes. "There's no intimacy if she has to tie me up like an animal before we can even try anything."

"Speak for yourself. I've always found it very intimate. Besides, it lets you do what you want to do, even if it might not be quite to your preference."

"I don't care about getting to feel good. I just want to be able to hold her, kiss her, please her, and do all those things I've been dreaming of doing with her since I was sixteen." Cold tears stream down my face, stopping only when they hit the necklace now that my fur is so much better groomed. Wow, it already sounds like I'm her pet. Why not just let her hog-tie me? It's just never how I pictured things.

"You'll still be a lot closer to your teenage dreams than most people ever get. Though I did have that Bacchanalia where we were all covered in beer, and a freshly waxed man fed me roasted pork belly. Gods, I miss the Roman Empire."

"Why am I even talking to you?" I can't do it. I can't. I'll try phone sex, and maybe after that, we can figure out some more things. Even if I was tied up, I'd still smell her, I'd still taste her, and I'd still be so hungry. How can this ever change? We're gonna keep having this issue as long as our relationship lasts, assuming it's not the death of it right away.

James draws a handkerchief from his pocket and offers it to me. I wipe my eyes and fur. "Okay, clearly this is all moving too fast for you," he says. "How about we find you a nice toy to use, and maybe you could call Liz up and surprise her when you get home?"

If I call when she'd have to wake up anyway, it's not like I'm depriving her of sleep. I guess I could do that. "Okay."

"Will you at least talk to her about the other stuff?"

"Like the industrial-strength ball gag?"

Rolling glowing eyes are one of the few things that I can honestly say still disconcert me. "Yes. It's not ridiculous. it's exactly what your jaws call for."

"It sounds absurd."

"You're a wendigo dating a human. Things are going to sound ridiculous. Suck it up, and get used to it." He turns back to the stand. Still trying to think of a response, I follow him. "Here, one of my favorite brands makes this for particularly sturdy undead and very durable demons. I'll buy it for you. If this can't get the deed done, nothing can." He pauses, the wand still in his grasp. "Wait, you haven't gotten off in six years?"

I think I might actually hate him. "No, I haven't. Thank you so much for telling the cashier."

"Oh, Lawrence is cool."

"Hi," the clerk says.

"Hi, Lawrence." This is so stupid.

"Maybe you'll finally be able to relax," James says. "Who knows, maybe it'll finally satisfy that hunger. I doubt too many wendigoag have tried."

I take the stupid fucking sex toy and leave. When he follows me, I just mutter *thanks*.

"Abby, wait."

I turn, my teeth bared. I don't know if I could digest him, but I'm tempted to find out. "You made a fool of me in front of everyone for no reason."

"I'm sorry. You know I don't really have much of a concept of inappropriate. Sex is what I am, and especially now that I'm not doing it, I get a little bawdy."

"It's no excuse."

"I just want to help. Please?"

As I bare my fangs, he takes a step back. "Why should I listen to you? Anything I say, you'll just use as ammo to make fun of me.' Oh, Abby's never used a vibrator; Abby's scared of a ball gag; Abby's never had sex before.' I'm sick of it."

His jaw drops. Unlike Ashley that one time, it stays attached. "I had no idea. You mean *ever*? Not just as a wendigo?"

I fold my arms over my chest. I want to run away, but I really do need the advice. "I don't know. What counts as sex? Like, I had a girl touch me before, but she didn't put a finger in or anything. I did come from it, though, I think, but it was just the one time. It felt weird. I was already in love with Liz, and I thought she didn't feel the same way, but it seemed wrong trying to make myself be with someone else."

James blows out a breath, taking a seat on the ground and resting his head in his hands as he stares up at me. "Wow. I'm sorry. I knew you were a little uncomfortable with the subject, but I thought it'd just been a while. You're really crazy about this girl."

"I have been my whole life."

"Well then, I'm going to help you figure out how to make everything perfect for her. It's the least I can do after how I acted. I really am sorry."

"I guess I can forgive you. I know it's just how you are." I blink away more tears. I've never told anyone that. Not even Ashley, and she's supposed to be my best friend. Not even Liz.

"I know some really interesting people. Even if I have to break my diet, I'm going to see if anyone has any tips on wendigo sex. Preferably without resorting to vore."

"I have no idea what that is."

"That's for the best." He stands and rolls his shoulders. "I'll talk to you tomorrow. Go call your girlfriend."

"Thank you. I will." After a few minutes collecting myself, I decide to do some more shopping to kill time. Maybe by the time he has that advice for me, my place could be a bit more livable for Liz.

❖

My hands are shaking, and my heart is doing the closest thing to thundering it can manage as I lie in my new bed, waiting for her to answer my call. "Morning, Abby. You just about to go to sleep?"

I had to buy some fuel for my generator to make sure it could power this thing. My first ever sex toy lies on the bed next to me, staring judgmentally. "I was going to. I was just wondering if maybe you, um, would like to…" I swallow what feels almost exactly like a femur lodged in my throat. "Do that thing you suggested last night?"

"Oh. Are you sure? It won't make you too hungry or anything?" She sounds almost as nervous as I am.

"I don't know. I mean, even if it does, there's nothing to eat here, and I doubt it'll be as bad as when you cut your tongue, and I was able to resist then." I know I'm not worrying over nothing, but part of me is starting to believe her. Maybe I really can manage.

"We could just talk and play with our toys. Or do you use your hands? We don't have to do anything you're not ready for. It'd be nice to hear you. I've fantasized about it so many times, and I've always wondered what you actually sound like. But if you're not ready, it's fine. I can wait. Even if I do keep pushing for it."

How can she possibly still want me the way she does? I've

changed so much from the girl she knew, and yet it doesn't seem to have changed how she feels in the slightest. I'm the luckiest woman in the world. "I don't want to wait. I wish I'd thought of this sooner. It's so much less scary. And I just bought a toy for the occasion."

"Really? It any good?"

"I haven't tried it out yet." I take in a deep breath. I should tell her. It feels weird having James know something so private about me that even Liz doesn't know. "I've never tried anything before."

She takes a moment to reply. "Huh. You always seemed so much more experienced. So you've never used a toy?"

"I've never done anything. I mean, I fooled around once, but that was it. I put on an act because I thought you weren't interested, and I didn't want you to know that I didn't want to be with anyone else. You seemed okay with being with others, so I just kept up the act."

"I'm an idiot." She lets out a pained laugh. "I should've told you how I felt back when we were practicing kissing as kids. I've always loved you, Abby."

I giggle like a nervous schoolgirl. Behold the mighty wendigo and tremble.

"So I'm kinda your first. I can live with that. Why don't you try out your new toy?"

I do. The motor is almost deafening, but when I place it against parts that just this morning I had given up hope on ever using again, I can barely contain myself. I scream loud enough that I can hear animals around the cabin running away for half a mile.

"Wow. That was really hot." How could she possibly have liked that? I'm sure her ears must be bleeding. "I may need to turn the volume down a little, but that was beautiful. I take it your new toy works. You came?"

I let out a throaty sigh, mewling in pleasure. "Yes. Oh my God, yes."

"Good." I hear a buzzing noise, which is soon muffled and joined by a slick sound. I can hear her shaking against the bed. "Oh fuck, I wish you were right here. I want you to feel this. I want your hands on me. I want to look into your eyes. I want you to hold me as I break again and again."

I'm already close all over again. I may have to thank James later. "I want that too. More than you could possibly imagine. I'm trying, Liz, I am. I won't make you wait forever." I don't know if I'm tearing up from arousal or emotion, but I can barely bother to care as the wand brings me to the edge.

"I'm so close."

"I am too."

"You are?" The machine picks up speed, and I can hear the faint vibrations of her hand pressing against her. "Think about me on top of you, looking down at you, my hand between us, teasing at you as I grind against you. Me kissing you as my finger slides in."

"Elizabeth!" I cry as I fall over the edge.

She gasps, and I can hear her thumb swishing against her as she joins me, panting breathlessly. "That was amazing. Hell, that was better than most sex I've had."

"Same here. Not that that's saying much."

She giggles, breathing heavily as she shifts in the bed. "I can't wait to do it again, but I should get up and get ready. I'm running late now."

"You should, and I should sleep. I love you, Liz."

"I love you too, Abby. You're amazing. That was the sexiest thing I've ever heard."

"Monster fetishist," I tease. I don't know how to take a compliment.

"Just an Abby fetishist. Sweet dreams, honey. Can I come over tonight?"

I try not to bite my lip as I fret over that decision. I want to do this again, and if she's here, I don't know if I'll be able to put it off much longer, and that's a terrible idea, but I really want to hold her, kiss her, show her how much I've changed the place and, if I'm lucky, maybe try out James's advice. "Yeah. I'll see you tonight. I need to run a couple errands first, so ten or eleven? Have a great day at work."

"It's a date."

I dream of nothing but her. I only even eat her in one of them.

Chapter Eleven

Elizabeth

I have some time to kill after work, and after everything that Abby confessed to me this morning, I feel like I owe someone else their own explanation. This is going to hurt so much. Well, if she tries to kill me, at least I'm armed. I've switched to jeans and have my dagger secured to the small of my back this time to avoid having to wear a skirt. It made sitting in my chair for eight hours a little annoying, but it was worth it to be able to look all confident and butch when I have to deal with my ex. It's also way quicker to draw. I guess that could be important too.

I knock on Carol's door, my heart hammering a million beats a second as I wait for her to answer. She should be home by now. It's almost six. I guess she could be out somewhere. Hell, maybe she has a date. I should've called first. Just as I turn back to my car, the door opens, and she walks out, wearing a bathrobe, her hair a mess for the first time in her entire life and her eyes puffy and bloodshot. Shit. It's been almost two weeks. How is she not over me?

"Lizzy?"

What am I thinking being here? "Hey, Carol," I say nonchalantly. If I die, tell Abby she can eat my body.

"What are you doing here?" She wipes her eyes with a sleeve of her robe.

"There was something I wanted to tell you. It's not that

important, though. It can wait. I'll get out of your hair." I didn't realize how badly I'd hurt her. She doesn't deserve to suffer more.

"No, come in. Please. I could put some tea on if you'd like."

"I won't be staying long." I follow her inside. She hasn't bothered cleaning in a while. There are pizza boxes and a pile of blankets on the floor and some used tissues scattered around the wastebasket. She tosses a pillow off the couch and motions for me to take a seat.

I do, and she sits next to me. "So how have you been?" Her fingers comb through her hair as she looks at me, unblinking.

"I've been really great, actually."

"Oh." The smile she's plastered on her face vanishes in an instant, but she manages to replace it quickly. "I've been great too. Everything has been wonderful. I actually got a promotion, and there's this new girl I've been talking to." She brushes her hair behind her shoulders, straightening her back and only sniffling a little. I should just let her have this.

"That's great. I'm really happy for you. It sounds like we're both a lot better off now."

Swallowing, her jaw tightens and she nods about as convincingly as a fifties animatronic would.

"I should get out of your hair. I'm really glad that you're doing so well." I hate that I did this to her. I won't ever hurt Abby like this. I won't ever hurt anyone like this again. When I got off the phone with her last time, I was relieved because it meant I could get a burrito. I am the absolute worst.

She clutches my hand. "Wait. You said you had something you wanted to tell me."

Shaking my head, I pull away and stand, taking a few steps toward the door. "It really wasn't important. You have a good evening."

"No." Her hand falls from her hair, and her nails dig into the couch. "Tell me what you wanted to say. Clearly, it wasn't anything good. Have you come back to remind me how little you cared about me? It's not like I didn't know. I just thought maybe you'd come around. For fuck's sake, who goes an entire year without telling their partner that they love them? I just kept waiting, expecting you to say it, but you never did. Then I finally say it, and you dump me like I'm nothing."

"Did you want me to lie to you?" I'm letting her drag me into this. I came to give her closure, and that was wrong. Let her have her victory; she's more than earned it.

"I wanted you to be a decent girlfriend!" She jumps to her feet, stomping toward me, her index finger outstretched.

"Well, I wasn't." She falters. "I'm sorry. That's all I wanted to let you know. I'm sorry I was so awful to you. You deserve better, and I hope you find it."

Her eyes fill with tears, and she tries to blink them away.

"Have a good life, Carol." I open the door and head back to my car. She doesn't try to follow. God, that was a terrible idea.

❖

"I talked to Carol." I sit curled up in my car on the side of the road, my knees tucked under my chin. It hit me harder than I thought it would. "I was such a terrible girlfriend to her, and I never even cared. How was I so broken that I could treat her like that?"

"You're the therapist; you tell me." Sandra's familiar voice fills my car.

"Narcissistic personality disorder?"

"You're not a narcissist." Her voice is calm and soothing. "You were awful to her, but from the sound of it, you're being so much better with Abby—who you still haven't let me see, by the way—and based on the fact that you actually care now, it sounds like you've really grown."

I throw my head back, smacking it against the headrest. Why would Abby possibly want me? She deserves so much better. "I just made Carol cry more. I'm clearly not that much better if it didn't occur to me that going there would make things worse for her. She's so miserable. I don't think she's left the house in the last two weeks. I've been off with Abby almost every day, and the girl I was dating just two weeks ago is barely holding it together."

"Abigail disappearing did quite a number on your ability to get close to people. Now you know why she did it, and you're managing to move past that, but your behavior was perfectly reasonable."

"That sure doesn't sound like what you said last week. Weren't you mad at me for dumping her? And what if now she ends up just as messed up as I was? I hurt her as badly as Abby hurt me, and I didn't even have a good excuse."

Sandra sighs. "Liz, you're being too hard on yourself. You and Abigail had something special. You and Carol didn't. You were a terrible girlfriend, and she knows it. She'll get over you. She just needs a bit more time."

"Thanks." My reply is only a little bitter. I know I was terrible, and that she's right, but it still sucks to think of myself that way. I'd been convinced that I was fun, laid back, and just not that into commitment. Now that I'm with Abigail, I'd commit in a second. I wasn't just enjoying my twenties or whatever other bullshit I told myself. I was using other women and leaving a path of destruction in my wake. Even committing to doing better is so meaningless since now I'm with someone who I actually love, and there's no reason for me to act like that again. "You really don't think I'm an unrepentant monster who doesn't deserve the happiness I've managed to find?"

"If you were any of those things, you wouldn't be beating yourself up right now."

I manage a half-smile. "I guess that's a fair point."

"Abigail is good for you. She's finally made you the person I always knew you could be...the person you were back when we first met."

"Well, I'm glad I'm regressing, then." We met when I was a kid. I sure hope I'm not regressing that far.

It's a little past six. I should probably grab some food and start getting ready for tonight before too long. Though I still have plenty of time. "I do think she's good for me, though," I finally add.

"Yeah?"

I nibble on my lip. She'll never believe we haven't had sex yet. "She's been really scared to have sex after everything she's been through, but we're planning on doing it tonight, and it's everything I've been dreaming of for so long, and I am so incredibly excited."

"Finally getting to do something you're good at?"

"Excuse me? You mean something I'm *amazing* at."

"I'm really happy for you." She chuckles. "That's fantastic. I've been waiting for this moment for a decade, and it's finally come." She sniffles dramatically. "This must be what it's like to be a mother. I'm so proud of you."

"Thanks, Mom. Just so you know, I'm gonna break curfew."

"That's my girl."

My legs drift back down to the floor. Talking about Abby always makes me feel so much better. Well, it does now. It certainly didn't a few weeks ago. "I'll make sure to give her one for you too."

"Give her two just to be sure. Oh, guess what? I had a date this weekend, and the guy was actually a real charmer, and we're seeing each other again tomorrow!"

"You didn't give me time to guess." I glare at the display in my car, feigning offense. "That's amazing, though. Anyone I know?"

"Just a guy I was talking to on this website. I met his dog. He has this cute yellow Lab. It was just the sweetest thing. It wanted me to rub its belly for hours."

"You went to his place? Did you get up to some more rubbing?"

"I have no idea what you're talking about." I'd know that tone anywhere. She just got laid.

"You slut."

"Hey, it's been a while. Not all of us had a menagerie of beautiful women to help us get through waiting for Mr. or Ms. Right to sweep us off our feet."

"First off, I sweep her off *her* feet." God, she would love that. I wish I actually had powers too. Then I could swoop her up in my arms and hold her or have my way with her. I'd see where the mood took us. "Second off, did you *want* a menagerie of women?"

"Beggars can't be choosers. At least then I wouldn't have had to deal with all the dicks I dealt with."

I try very hard not to laugh. I do not succeed. "If you were dealing with so many dicks, you clearly weren't having that bad a time."

She's glaring at me. I can feel it even twenty miles away. "You know what I mean."

"Of course. You had a menagerie of your own."

"Christ, I wish. Hey, Peter is practically a menagerie all his own. That man's an animal."

"Straight sex is horrifying. I don't want to hear any more."

Her laugh echoes through my speakers. I turn the volume down until I can barely hear her. "Oh, you're going to hear more. He and I…" I turn it down to zero and take a moment to watch the cars pass by. There're a few pedestrians on the street, and I look closely, trying to see if any of them might be fiends. I hope that Dennis really does go to that group. I'll have to ask Abby about it. I really liked helping him. It doesn't seem like there's anyone else willing to, at least not any humans. I turn the volume back up. "And then he grabbed a towel."

"Sounds like a great time, Sandra." Okay, I still have a little bit of growing up to do.

CHAPTER TWELVE

Abigail

I am, as ever, absolutely terrified. Are Liz and I really going to…I mean I *want* to, but what if it's not safe? I need to hear back from James. He's taking his sweet time. Surely someone somewhere decided to have sex with a wendigo and came up with a good way to keep themselves safe. I spend the next hour thinking of all the possible ways this could go wrong. I know I can back out, and I probably will, but I really want to be able to do this with her. This morning was magical, and if it's anything like that in real life, it will be absolute perfection. I hope.

He finally calls. I answer before it finishes the first ring. "James, hey, hi, what did you learn?"

"Simmer down, Abby. Isn't she not getting there for, like, four more hours?"

My phone claims that it's seven o'clock. "Three or four."

"You have time."

"And you have something useful?"

His weirdly symphonic laughter crackles right into my ear. "I have so much info for you. Where should I start?"

"What're my options?" I sit on my new bed. It's way softer than the old one. The salesman claimed it's made of basilisk feathers, but I'm pretty sure he's full of shit. It smells like goose. Real or not, it was worth the price; it's like lying on a cloud. I even have an actual headboard, gold with an inlaid ivy design. I thought it worked for a cabin in the middle of the woods.

"Well, again, there's no wendigo in the world with your restraint, so you are probably safe. I think a strap-on is a great idea. It wouldn't be as sharp as you, and it prevents you from tasting her, which for some reason, seems like a good idea to you."

"For some reason? Maybe you should bring that up at group."

"For a perfectly understandable reason."

"Better." I stretch my legs. It's weird not having my feet on the floor. There's even a little extra room. A pound of gold was a bargain. "So what else?"

"I assume anything with more direct contact is out? Tribbing would likely be safe. Unless that's sharp too. I've never personally been with a wendigo. Not exactly my type. I mean, you're very pretty. I certainly wouldn't object. Liz is a very lucky girl."

Is there something about being a few millennia old that turns you into a complete tactless asshole? "You're not my type either, James."

"I'm everyone's type."

"That's why you're walking me through lesbian sex, I suppose."

"And I'm very happy to do so. See, I'm a great friend. You could use a dental dam. You wouldn't be able to taste her, and you could still take advantage of your horrific-transformation-given gifts. I'm sure she'd enjoy it. I could get some that were made for a palis. I'm sure that'd suit you. Or you could use a condom."

"What's a dental dam? Wait, like, use a condom on my tongue?"

"Believe me, the taste would certainly ruin your appetite."

I scratch at the bedding as I think. The blanket is supposedly spun from the fur of some ancient monster that could only be cut by a powerful magical sword, so my talons can't pierce it. I'm gonna have to do some serious hunting to make back all the money I spent, but it is nice not tearing open all my blankets when I'm nervous. "Okay, I'll keep it in mind. Seriously, though, what's a dental dam?"

"It's a piece of latex that you put over her when you eat her out."

"Oh. So same as the condom, basically. Okay, anything else? So far, it's mostly just stuff I could've found googling lesbian sex." After I sifted through all the porn.

"All right, you want me to get to the more interesting stuff? I can do that." He proceeds to outline how to use an assortment of devices, what a sex machine is, the best angles for mutual masturbation, the erogenous zones of a female wendigo—that one is really good to know—and the use of cocaine to numb my taste buds and sense of smell. Never mind all the damage that a coked-up wendigo could cause. Upon prompting, he sighs exasperatedly and gives me "less fun" substances to use for a similar effect. When he's finally done, I have quite a shopping list to go through.

"Thank you." He spent two entire hours detailing all the ways that Liz and I might be able to have sex.

"Be sure to tell me every sordid detail."

"No."

"I do not get you, Abigail. Well, you two crazy kids have fun. If there's anything more I can do, don't hesitate to let me know."

"Want to go buy me all of that stuff?"

"I'm afraid you're on your own there. I already spent all of my paycheck."

I stare at my phone. "What paycheck? You don't have a job."

"Hey, conning people out of money is still a paycheck as long as they use a check. I still can't believe I actually managed to sell that woman a bridge. It wasn't even a nice bridge."

"You're a terrible person."

"I'm a terrible *demon*."

Groaning, I hop out of bed. "I'm gonna get going. Have fun with your ill-gotten gains." Once we hang up, I throw on some clothes and make a dash to the Community Center. I only have an hour, but running at top speed, I can make it there and back in time. It's still too early for most of the shops to be open, so my options are limited, but I can't exactly go to a normal store without causing a commotion, and delivery could have some unfortunate complications even if I had the time for it. I only manage to buy a few of his suggestions. Apparently, the big sex toy vendor doesn't get there until one.

Once I'm home again, I have time to consider how insane this is. I need to back out. I smell her approaching, hear the familiar tracks of her car on the dirt road. I can do this. That smell is only eliciting wholesome lust.

❖

I answer the door with a nervous smile. She hasn't seen the place since I redecorated. I really want her to not feel as if she's squatting in some monster's den. She makes me feel human, and I'd like to do the same for her at the very least.

After I point it out, she drops her car keys on a little table I set in the foyer and wraps her arms around me. "I missed you last night. Though this morning did almost make up for it." Pulling back, a lascivious grin on her lips, she stands on her tiptoes. "Kiss me already."

I comply, bending down the foot and a half she needs and threading my hand through her hair and cleanly around her head.

Her smile seems far more innocent as she pulls away and closes the door before taking off her coat. "We should get a heater for this place." She stops in her tracks, heading toward the couch. Her gaze sweeps over the room. "Or maybe you already did. Holy shit, you really changed the place. And I thought the table was impressive."

"It's not too much?" I didn't think to get a heater. Not feeling temperature sucks. That was dumb of me. I can't believe I thought a TV was more important than a heater. I can't even get cable.

"I like it." The couch has been replaced with an even larger one that is less full of holes, the last few pieces of hunting memorabilia from the previous owner have all been removed, there's carpet that doesn't even have an animal head attached, and most importantly, I've added a fridge and a microwave. She notices this last part and seems to understand the implication. "You're sure you're okay with me eating around you?"

No. "I'll be fine. I just want to stop holding you back. You have sacrificed so much for me in this relationship." I approach slowly, in as non-predatory a manner as I can, and pull her to me, resting my hand on her lower back. "I want to give you everything. At least, everything I can."

"Abby," she murmurs, clinging to me, blinking away tears. "You give me everything I need. I don't want you to even begin to think that you're not enough for me. You're perfect, Abigail." She cups my cheek, looking right into my hideous, misshapen, fuzzy face. "I love you."

No accounting for taste. "I love you too. It's why I want you here more. I'm not saying move in with me—I know it's not practical—but I can give you a drawer, or as many as you want, and you can keep food here and whatever else you need. I'm not sure if there's a way for me to set up a washer and dryer—I just hand wash my stuff—but if it's possible, I'll do that too. I want this to be another home for you."

"I want that too." She lets out a shaky breath. "There's actually a way that could be a bit more possible too. Not that I'm moving in just yet." She chuckles, a slight blush on her cheeks, which she promptly hides by resting her head on my chest. "I was wondering if you thought the Community Center could use a therapist? I saw a fiend the other day, and it made me realize that you guys aren't really having those needs met. I could probably halve my hours and stop taking new clients. Then I could spend around half the week here without it messing up my sleep schedule too much or having to drive an hour and a half every day."

I have been feeling a little guilty about all that. Even if I actually can be good for her, which I'm still not entirely convinced of, I'm definitely bad for her schedule. "That's an amazing idea, actually. I'm not sure how well it would be received since humans aren't all that welcome there, but I'm sure a lot of us could use it. It'd probably do all those vampires in the art class some good too."

"I'm already one vampire's therapist," she squeals. "So I have credentials."

I stare. "How? I mean, you said you had a fiend client already, but a vampire? I know they can mingle in society pretty easily, but they're really rare."

"They are? You'd mentioned them before, so I assumed they were as common in real life as they are in fiction."

I shake my head and realize she probably can't see it. "No. I'm not close to too many, but from what I know, they're kind of endangered."

"Oh. Huh." She considers this for a few seconds, toying with the fur under my shirt. "He was just turned. I guess they're making conservation efforts. Good for them."

She handles this stuff so well. I was more thrown by everything when I first learned about it, and I was already part of it. "Yeah. Who'd want undead creatures that feed on humans to die off?"

She tugs at my fur. "I certainly wouldn't," she insists, her voice firm and commanding as she pulls away, glaring. "I won't have you talking that way. You're perfect just the way you are, and you certainly shouldn't want people like you to die off."

"Sorry."

"Wanna watch anything on your new TV?"

"Maybe. I bought some DVDs of shows that I never got to finish."

"That sounds amazing. I don't have any other plans this weekend. I'll grab some microwave popcorn, and we can curl up on the couch and binge a whole season. Did you buy any?"

"I did, actually." It was one of the only food things I thought to get. I smile. "I can't eat the popcorn, but that sounds amazing. Well, if you wanted to do that this weekend, maybe we should do something else tonight?" I'm so subtle.

Seductively licking her lips, she takes a step toward me, her hand running down my back again. "And just what did you have in mind?"

I can do this. I won't attack her. We'll be okay. "I…" I swallow and inhale and exhale slowly, trying to gather myself. "This morning gave me a few ideas. Maybe we could…well, you know."

One of her hands drifts over my hip, sliding down to my thigh. "I don't know. What were you thinking of?"

Her hand slips under my waistband, touching just beside my…fuck, I'm so inexperienced I don't even know what word to use. I guess labia, but that's so technical and doesn't sound sexy. Lips? "I don't really know what I'm doing."

Her laughing against my chest is not exactly making me feel more sexy or comfortable.

"Liz," I whine.

"I'll take the lead. I *do* know what I'm doing. Let's go up to the bedroom."

I nod. "Okay. I bought a few things that James—another friend of mine—said could make this easier for us and won't have me in biting range."

"I suppose I can live without biting."

"Liz! This is really hard for me."

Sighing, she looks up, looking almost ashamed of herself. "I'm sorry. I know." She scrunches her eyes shut and blows out a harsh breath. "Okay. Grab the toys and meet me upstairs."

I can do that.

When I open the door to the bedroom, she's already lying in my new bed, naked and bared to the world, to me, with only a leather strap around her belly. The ice inside me feels like it's melting, perhaps literally, as warmth spreads through me from between my legs. I'd always imagined this, and it's so much better than I could have pictured. Her smile melts me all the more as I approach. Without thinking, I run my hand along her smooth tanned thigh, careful not to let a talon scrape her. My gaze travels down her body, her short black hair, her warm, marbled brown eyes taking me in and actually wanting me, her inviting smile, powerful shoulders, tantalizing breasts that only partially make me want to bite them in a non-sexual way, and the curve of her belly and hips leading down to those beckoning thighs on her long legs. She really does want me. I don't know how or why, but I would do anything to keep seeing that look in her eyes. "God, you're beautiful."

Her eyes trail over me, and I do my best not to flee. "Let me see you too. Please," she adds.

With a quick nod, I pull my shirt off, revealing my stretched chest with barely any fat or muscle left, my exaggerated shoulders and flat belly. At least I have one trait I wanted when I was alive.

"Wow." Her breath catches as she takes me in. "Keep going."

The sweats join their brethren on the floor, and I close my eyes. No one has ever seen me like this and lived. My legs are almost bones, with barely enough flesh to cover them, and my hips protrude out even farther than my shoulders, with fur thick enough to hide my—um—the thing she's gonna be touching.

I hear her slide forward on the bed and feel her hands on my hips, moving down, rubbing my thighs with one slipping between them. "Abby?"

Slowly opening my eyes, I nod hesitantly. How can she want this? "Are you sure?"

"I think that's my line. I am so very sure." Her breath puffs warmly against my pelvis as she takes me in, a finger grazing my lips. I shudder, bucking against her. "Are you?"

"I'm sure. Oh…" I set the stuff on the bed. "Did you need any of this?" I'm not trying to delay. I don't think I am, at least. I just want to be helpful.

She glances at the items. "I don't. You're welcome to use that strap-on on me. I wasn't expecting that. I just want to do this myself, to feel you and taste you." I know that feeling. "Lie down." She stands, gesturing toward the bed.

I do as she suggests, lying on the bed, very happy with the increased length, or maybe a shorter bed would've made things easier for this. "Is this good?" I ask, forcing myself to keep my legs apart no matter how badly I want to cover myself. I can handle this. I know I can.

"It's perfect." The bed shifts as she climbs on, crawling toward me. I look down to see her grinning, her mouth just over me. I shut my eyes, and I let out a low moan as she plants a soft kiss on my less-damaged set of lips, her tongue grazing them before she lifts her head up again. "I love your taste, and I love those moans you make. Don't hold back, okay?"

I'm always holding back. "Okay. I just don't want to scare you."

"I might need a pair of earplugs, but I actually brought some. Give me a second." She grabs a small bag from her pants on the floor next to mine. "Trust me, I really love the noise. I just want to be able to keep hearing it." Her lips wrap around my already engorged clit, and she absolutely needs those earplugs. I scream. Loud enough to shake the house.

"Oh God, Liz, please." I hold my hands to my side. I had always imagined running my fingers through her hair as she did this, but that seems like a good way to scalp her when I can barely control my movements. I hold my feet to the side as they're not any less sharp, but they're past hers anyway. "That feels amazing."

"I'm glad," she says, her tongue flicking against me as she forms the words. Even as deadened as my nerves are, she's still getting to me.

As a finger slides inside me, I start to lose myself. I shake my head. I can't lose myself; that's too dangerous. I don't want to come to and find that I ate her in the middle of us having sex. She keeps going, but I'm holding back too much. I'm too scared to let things happen. I want this so badly. "Liz?"

She glances up, a few strands of fur stuck to her lips, along with a blueish ichor. Is that me? "Yes, my love?" Her eyes are half-lidded, and I can feel her panting against me, her gaze still trained between my legs.

"Could I try? I mean, not this, it's too dangerous, but could I try the strap-on?"

"You don't want me to keep going?" The pained look on her face absolutely destroys me. She always has to give up so much for me. It's not fair.

"I do. I really do. I am just so scared that I'll lose control."

Sighing, she rises, climbing over my leg. "Okay. Let's try that." She sounds so disappointed.

She helps me into the harness, swinging her arm clear of my foot at the last second, and pulls the straps as tight as they go. It actually fits all right. Looking down, it's so weird to see the red phallus protruding from me. I wasn't sure what size to get, but the succubus working there was very helpful. It wasn't the place where James bought my toy, but they had a few toys in addition to a number of illicit drugs and accessories. I think you can actually smoke out of this dildo.

Liz leans back on the bed, hands intertwining behind her head as she leans against a pile of pillows. "Come on."

How? "Could you try a different position? If I'm on top of you like that, my mouth would be right in your face and…" I trail off, hating myself so much for all of these requests.

She nods and, without a word, moves the pile of pillows to the middle of the bed, leaning against them so that her legs fall off the side. It's almost the same way I always slept. So that actually would have been helpful. I was right.

It slides in with no resistance and elicits a sharp cry from her. "Are you okay?" I ask.

"I'm fucking fantastic. Keep going. Could you…" She glances down at my hands. "Never mind, this is perfect."

I keep going, the awkwardness dying down a little with each thrust, her eyes watering as her hands move haphazardly around the bed. The toy presses against my clit, and I find myself whimpering too. This is more than I could have ever asked for.

She looks up at me, lust in her eyes, her hands scratching lightly at the skin and fur on my belly. Then she pulls herself up, whimpering sharply with the motion, and pulls me into a kiss as she falls into her orgasm. I can smell her all the stronger. Every inch of her seems so delicious. I want to just… I pull away and stare down at her, panting. She's okay. I didn't bite.

I tear off the harness as I pull out, my claw accidentally slicing through it, and turn from her. "I can't. Liz, I can't. I'm sorry."

"Wait!" She chases me, running down the stairs.

"Liz, I am so fucking hungry." I turn to look at the incredibly beautiful and incredibly naked human woman staring at me. "If I let myself go for even a second, I don't know what I'll do. I want this so badly. I thought maybe I could actually manage, but I just can't. This morning with you was amazing, and I'm happy to do that anytime, but I don't think I can ever do anything further."

She walks out the front door, heading naked into the snow. Is she leaving? Before I can collapse to the floor in a self-hating heap, she walks back in, holding a paper bag. I can smell the human in it. "Then eat."

"What?"

"If you're starving, eat. I'll go buy you more. Hell, I'll buy you an entire dead person, ten if you need, just eat. You won't need to hold yourself back if you're not starving. Then I can be with you."

Shaking my head in disbelief, I stare. I find myself taking an unbidden step toward the food. "You don't understand."

"You won't give me the chance. You always hold everything

back. Well, I'm tired of you always thinking you have to protect me. You don't. I'm a big girl. This is what you need to eat to survive. Just do it. He was a murderer; it's fine. Just eat." Tears stream down her cheeks as she holds the bag out to me. "Please."

I take another step, reaching out for it. I shut my eyes and wrench my hand back, clutching it to my chest. "No. It won't help. I won't. I can't."

"Then I will." She pulls the scone out and lets the bag fall to the floor, fire burning in her eyes as she stares at me.

"What?"

"If I'm a wendigo, then you won't have to hold back anymore." She holds it up to her mouth.

It probably wouldn't actually work, but I can't take that chance. I won't have her become like me. I snatch it away. She reaches for it. If I throw it, she'll grab it and eat it anyway, and it smells so good. Before I know what I'm doing, it's in my mouth. I've bitten down, eating the entire thing in a single bite. I've swallowed. It's inside me. I ate a human. It tasted amazing. I smell more food. I need it. I want it. I crave it.

I turn toward Liz, my teeth bared, clutching at her. She ducks under my hand, but I'm on her again in an instant, pulling her to me. I can smell her fear, the adrenaline pumping through her body, and the mouthwatering tender meat that comprises her. I open my mouth, leaning forward, desperate for another taste of flesh and feel a sudden burning in my abdomen.

Almost-black blood drips down from a gash cut across my belly. I stare, trying to figure out where it came from before looking back to my prey and seeing the silver dagger in her hand. "Liz?" What am I doing?

Before I can say anything more, she's gone. Her car starts, and I hear it tearing down the dirt road. I could catch her. I could still have another meal. I manage to hold back, collapsing to my knees, tears falling onto the floor. I've ruined everything.

CHAPTER THIRTEEN

Elizabeth

I drive for what feels like hours but must only be a few minutes. The stars and trees fly by. I must be speeding, but no one stops me. I find myself at a Tim Hortons with no real idea of how I got there as I wait in the drive-through. I've already ordered or else I pulled past the speaker without remembering to do so. I grab my credit card from my purse in the passenger seat and pay for what was apparently two coffees and a dozen doughnuts. The cashier stares at me, his mouth hanging open. I'm not sure why. I blink back at him, and he looks away, then hands my card back. It looks like he's about to say something, but I drive off rather than waiting to hear it.

A short time later, I'm in the parking lot of Sandra's apartment. With a coffee in each hand and the box of doughnuts resting on my forearms, I clamber up the stairs and kick at her door. After a few minutes, I call her name, and lights turn on in a building behind me. Before anyone starts yelling, or at least before I notice, the door opens, and a very sleepy Sandra wearing flannel pajamas stares back at me. "Liz?" She rubs her eyes and blinks as if unsure of what she's seeing. "Why are you naked? Come inside before someone sees you."

I'm naked? Oh. I look down, clearly seeing how cold I should be. "Sorry," I murmur.

She pulls me inside. "Peter is here. He's still sleeping, but let me get you some clothes." She comes back an indeterminable amount of time later. I haven't moved an inch. She pries the coffees from my hands, sets the doughnuts on the table, and hands me clothes.

I look at them, trying to remember how this is supposed to work. It only takes me a second, and I throw the shirt on, then put on her oversized underwear and pants. They're not falling off me, so she seems satisfied enough.

"What happened?" She sips the coffee. I should've ordered three.

I take the other one, and it goes down without my even tasting it. I look up to find Sandra shoving a doughnut in my face.

"Eat and drink. You clearly need it. Then tell me everything."

I barely taste the chocolate and cream as I eat a couple of doughnuts. At some point, Sandra moved me to her couch. I rest my eyes on the coffee table, occasionally remembering to blink. My coffee cup is empty, so I let it fall out of my hand.

"Liz, you're really scaring me."

"Sorry," I mutter, checking my hands and the table for my coffee. I'm still thirsty.

"Did something happen with Abby? Are you okay? Why weren't you wearing clothes?" Her voice sounds almost calm, as if she's asked this so many times, there's barely any emotion left for it.

"Oh, I didn't say?"

I'm still staring at the table. She takes a few seconds to respond. "No. No, you haven't. You've just been sitting in my living room for an hour sipping coffee and eating half a dozen doughnuts. What happened?"

"Sorry. She tried to eat me." I lean back in my seat, the memory replaying. I see her moving toward me, hunger in her eyes. I see my knife cutting into her, her faltering, saying my name, and my trip to the car, all in slow motion, in agonizing detail. I even see myself picking the keys up off the table rather than listening to her. "I think I really hurt her. I ruined everything."

"What do you mean she tried to eat you?" She sounds frantic again.

I glance at the clock. Holy shit, how did it get so late? It's almost eight. "I need to go."

"What? Liz, no. Talk to me. You can't just show up at my apartment naked at six in the morning and leave without explaining yourself."

I showed up at six? How long was I at Tim Hortons? What else did I do? "I'll explain later. I have to get to work."

"You're in no condition to work right now. Liz, please, this is insane. I'm worried about you."

"Don't be. I'm fine."

"No. No, you're not. That is fucking absurd. You are anything but fine, and you're staying right here."

I walk past her to the door. It's only when my feet touch the snow that I realize I'm not wearing shoes. I'll grab some from home on the way to the office. If I go back inside to borrow a pair, she'll never let me leave.

❖

I am only a few minutes late. I get there at 9:05 with a very annoyed client waiting for me. I know we went to my office, he started talking, and after that, I don't recall anything more. I hope I was helpful. I'm sitting in my chair with new appointments on my calendar, files full of notes on my clients, and several open tabs on wendigos, vampires, ghouls, and a handful of other fiends. I don't remember doing any of this. Okay, maybe I'm not fine.

I go back to Sandra's—I still remember promising that, at least—and find her frantic and waiting for me. "There you are. It's almost 6:30. Don't you normally get out at five?"

Shit.

"I went out and bought dinner, so you're lucky your timing is so good. It's still hot."

We sit at her table with a bucket of steaming fried chicken between us. I grab a leg, and as I bite into it, I find myself imagining that it's human. I savor the taste.

Sandra watches me tear into the food. She doesn't say a word, just picks at her own chicken as I savage mine, ripping it apart with my teeth.

When I'm finally done, she hands me a mug of coffee. I consider eating her as well, but the chicken did fill me up. I'm not sure I have the stomach for more. "Thanks," I murmur, finding my throat dry.

Nodding shakily, she makes her way back to her seat, her own cup of coffee in hand. "Liz, please. I need to know what happened."

"It was nothing. Just a misunderstanding. I'll clear it up tonight. It'll be fine."

"Liz, you promised."

I sigh. I guess it's not an issue if I end up eating her. "Abby's a wendigo, we had sex, and she tried to eat me, and I ended up cutting her and running away. I can still remember that hurt look in her eyes when she came to, realizing what she'd done, and what I'd done. I can't believe I just ran. I should've stayed."

"The hell you should've," she shouts. "What are you even talking about? Abby tried to hurt you? You cut her? What happened?"

"She couldn't resist it anymore. She's wanted to for so long, and she's been holding back, and I taunted her, giving her food and insisting over and over that she eat. She gave in, and it was too much. She couldn't stop." I really am a monster. I didn't understand. I didn't listen. She made it clear she couldn't eat anymore, and yet I tried to force it on her.

"You egged her on? Liz, it's not your fault. It's never your fault when someone you love hurts you. You can't blame yourself for her fucked-up behavior."

I find her grabbing my hand, and I pull away. "No, it *is* my fault. She didn't want to hurt me. I made her."

She's crying. Tears are streaming down her face, and I can hear her sobbing. "Liz, listen to me. You're a therapist; you know better. Being abused is not your fault."

"She's not abusive." My voice is flat. Maybe it comes off as confident. Abby is as far from abusive as possible. She's done nothing wrong.

"That's what they all say. Abby hurt you, really badly from the sound of it. I don't understand the rest, but I know you need to stay away from her. Please, I'm worried about you. This is all my fault. I'm the one that made you call her. I've been wanting you two to get together since I've known you. How could she have changed so much? She never seemed the type."

"Thank you. I'm so glad you did. I don't know what I would've done without her. She's everything to me."

"Liz, will you listen to yourself?" Now she's shaking me, her hands on my shoulders, her forearm so close to my mouth, I could bite it. "This is not okay. Maybe I should see about getting you to a hospital. We can cancel your appointments for the rest of the week. You need some time off. You need to be away from her. You need to recover, Liz. This is terrifying."

I stare. It takes a minute for her words to reach me. She wants to take me away from Abby. "No. I'm not going anywhere."

"Okay, no hospitals, but you're staying here tonight. You can have my bed. I'll take the couch."

I start to come back to myself. I need to have my wits about me. She can't put me in a hospital. I won't let her. There's nothing wrong with me. "No. You take the bed. I don't want to sleep in your gross straight-sex bed." That sounds like me, right? "I'll sleep on the couch. I'll be fine."

She studies me. She wouldn't be able to take me to the hospital if I ate her. Then I could finally be with Abby without fear. Why am I holding back? There's no reason not to. Everything would be so much better. "Okay. Just promise that you're not gonna do anything stupid. I'm so worried about you, Liz."

"Of course, Sand," I offer, my smile as genuine as I can

manage. "I would never. I'll look after myself. I know what I have to do."

Finally releasing me, she pulls away, biting her lip as she nods. I wonder how it tastes. "Okay. Christ, I thought Abigail would be good for you. How did this happen?"

I'm bad for her. That's the only problem. I have to fix it. I have to fix me. This is the only way. "I'm gonna go to sleep now. I'm really tired."

She swallows, still watching me. It's only seven, but I didn't get any sleep last night, so it should be believable. "Okay. I'll try to keep it down. You get some rest."

I fall asleep the second my head hits the pillow. I guess it wasn't a lie. I am completely exhausted.

❖

All my dreams are of Abigail. I wake up, terrified that I overslept. It's almost midnight. I'm fine. I'm still wearing shoes, so I get ready to rush to the car only to find my keys missing. Damn it, Sandra. I scour the apartment, throwing open every door, checking under every surface, feeling the underside of the coffee table and dining table. She must have them on her.

I sneak into her bedroom, opening the door without a sound. She didn't lock it. Good. She's not too paranoid, then. Just paranoid enough to steal my keys. So I wasn't too unconvincing. I check the nightstand and find it empty. I don't want to have to check her pockets. There's no way she'd sleep through it. Fortunately, I find them in the drawer in the far nightstand. I snatch them and walk as quietly as I can out of the room and make my way down to my car. I actually feel the winter air this time. The wind has picked up and is tossing snow all over. It's still early. There's plenty of time.

I drive carefully out to Etobicoke, parking in front of the once-abandoned mall. There are hardly any other cars here. I'm not sure where most of them park or if they even have cars, but it's not like it matters. I beep the doors locked and head inside, passing through the façade to find the living, breathing world within. Lights and colors surround me. Crowds of every imaginable shape and form emerge to either side. I feel so much less crazy here. This is the world I belong in, and I'm going to make it permanent.

I look around for familiar faces and don't see any. It's Wednesday night, so that makes sense. I browse the stalls, looking for anyone interesting. I don't know if there are artifacts that could do what I seek, but I doubt I can find them on my own. Some of my research from earlier comes back. I remember why. I was trying to find out what can turn me. Ghouls are out, I've heard mixed things about wendigoag—apparently, that's the actual plural—but I found a few creatures that could do it. I don't know if any of them are real, except for vampires. I know exactly how it works for them. They may be rare, but I can find one. Even if not today, I know exactly where one will be on Monday.

Nevertheless, I am still going to try. I can't wait. I need to fix things. I know what I'm looking for, and while I continue to search the stalls, very little of my attention is on the merchandise; most of it is on the customers.

I watch for anyone too human looking to fit in. Eventually, I approach a girl. She must be one. She looks perfectly human. "Hi," I offer. I did not think this through.

"Oh, hi." Her voice is throaty, like an old jazz singer. It pulls me in.

"Hi," I say again, my goal slowly fading from my mind.

"Hi." She laughs, a beautiful smile taking over her features. "Do I know you?"

"Unfortunately, I don't think you do." I take a step toward her. What was I looking for again?

She lets out a low murmur, somewhere between amused and aroused. "A human, here? You look like you could be so much fun."

"Oh, I can be, I promise."

"Are you here as a guest?"

That sounds familiar. What am I trying to think of? I know I was asked that before. "Yes." That was the answer. Why?

"Of whom?" The sultriness in her voice is amplified. She sounds almost hungry.

Hungry. Right. I remember. "Abigail Lester. I'm her girlfriend."

She blinks, taking a nervous step back. "Oh." She clears her throat, the sultriness all but gone. "I'm sorry. I didn't mean anything by it."

Is she scared of Abby? "Do you know Abby?"

"Not well. Just that she's a wendigo and could rip me apart for trying to seduce her girlfriend. I'm sorry. I really didn't mean to at first. I didn't know you were human, but when it worked, I couldn't help myself."

I stare, not quite knowing what she's talking about, only that she made me stop thinking about Abby for a few brief seconds. That thought makes me mad. No one should be able to take Abby from me.

"I'm a siren. I can lure people in, make them desperate for me. I really did want to play with you. My apologies, you're under the hospitality of this place. I'd rather not be thrown out, so you'll have to look elsewhere if you're after some fun," she says hurriedly, her voice higher, more awkward. It's like she's actively working to be less attractive. I suppose she is.

"Wait." I'm myself again, maybe even more than when I entered, but I still have a mission. It's the only way I can be with Abby.

"What?" She eyes me, looking suspicious and confused.

"Do you know any vampires? Ones that might be here."

She shakes her head and backs up again. "I don't know what trouble you're after, but I'm going to stay out of it. Tell Abigail that Caris sends her regards and bears her no ill will."

She runs, actually runs, shoving her way through the crowd to find anyplace else to be. What the hell was that about? I hope whatever vampire I find doesn't react the same way. Maybe Dennis really is my best option. I wonder if he's here.

I stop to grab a cupcake and shove it in my face to make myself feel better, and I don't even pretend that it's a person. I could try to eat a person scone again, but I'm not sure it'd work. When I was researching, it said that it had to be in a time of famine, and I'm not even all that hungry. What if I had eaten Sandra? Would I have killed my best friend for nothing?

I guess that siren breaking her spell broke whatever trance I was in. Time seems to be moving normally now. I'm not blacking out. I wonder if I could get her to help my dissociative clients.

At least the cupcake is delicious. It's the first thing I've actually tasted all day.

"You look like you've had a rough day," one of the satyrs says. "Need another one?"

I shake my head.

"All right. Oh, how did Abby like her scone? Did you manage to get her to eat it?"

Tears fill my eyes as I nod. "It didn't go as planned," I manage, my voice breaking.

"I'm sorry, honey." He rests a surprisingly human hand on my shoulder. "I know it would hurt my sales, but you need to listen to her. She doesn't want to eat people anymore."

I brush his hand aside. She clearly does. That's the issue. "You sell blood-filled doughnuts." I point at the display next to the human scones. "Has anyone bought any today?" I know exactly what Abby would say if I listened to her, and it's just not enough. I can't keep forcing her to make so many sacrifices for me. It's so hard for her. I can give up this one thing, my humanity, so that we can be happy together.

His woolly eyebrows knit together as he looks me up and down. "Why do you ask?"

"It's for Abby. Please. I promise, I won't try to feed her any more scones."

His hoof stomps once on the ground. "Okay. I guess I can

tell you. That guy over there just bought four of them." He points at a black-haired man looking through a collection of old books at another table. "Before you even think about it, don't. Abby wouldn't want you to change."

I'm really not subtle, am I? "Thank you." I chase the vampire, ignoring the clerk's warning. It's the only way she and I can be together. I have to do it. I tap him on the shoulder, and he turns.

I never would have guessed he was a vampire. He looks barely any paler than me, and he's wearing a perfectly ordinary T-shirt and jeans. He doesn't even have a widow's peak. "Yes?" No accent either. Not like Dennis has any of those things either. Am I being racist?

"Hi. My name's Elizabeth Rosseau, I'm looking to be a therapist here, and I was wondering if I could ask you a few questions about what sort of needs your people might have. You're a vampire, right?" I hadn't even planned that. It just rolled off my tongue. I had only thought up to the "hi."

"I am." He inhales sharply. "You're human. What exactly are you doing here?"

"Like I said, I'm looking to be a therapist. Could I borrow you for a few minutes? I'd just like to talk outside." The rules wouldn't apply there, right? He won't be violating hospitality if he bites me. Even if he tries to kill me, it's worth the risk. I have my dagger. I'll cut him and drink his blood if I have to. He'll never see that coming.

He hesitates for a moment but eventually holds up his index finger, signaling for me to wait. "All right, you have my curiosity piqued, ma'am. Just let me pay for my books, and I'll accompany you."

I lead him outside without an issue, promptly finding a secluded spot where no one will see a thing, and I enact my plan.

Chapter Fourteen

Abigail

I walk into group with my head hanging low. I can't believe I'm going to have to tell them. I can't believe I did this. When everyone is seated, I stand. "I really need to talk. I know I used up a bunch of time the last two weeks, but something really bad happened last night."

Ben, composed as ever, nods, his eyes radiating warmth. "Of course, Abby. What happened?"

"Let me start by saying I did not eat Liz; she's okay. But I did eat the scone she bought me. I tasted human for the first time in years, and I needed more." I wipe tears from my eyes. The previous night replays. I hate myself. "I was so hungry that I could only see her as food. I'd bought her a silver dagger for if something like this happened, and she used it on me. She ran away. I think we're over. I don't know what to do."

"Do you want to eat right now?" he asks.

I shake my head. Food is the farthest thing from my mind for the first time in six years. "No. I don't. At all. I just want to show her how sorry I am, to hold her again, to have her back. I just want to still have her in my life, even if we can't be together anymore. She means everything to me." Tears stream down my face, and I let out a high-pitched whimper that could almost crack glass. "I'm so scared."

"That's interesting," James muses. Asshole. "So you're not hungry?"

With a heaving shrug, I turn to him. "I don't know. I can't even feel it right now. It's like the hollow pit inside me has been devoured by heartache."

Ashley pulls my arm to her, resting her head against it. "I'm so sorry, Abby. I smelled that scone in her bag. I knew it was a bad idea. I should've talked to her."

"It's not your fault. I knew it was there too."

"So you were around already-dead human meat that was bought as a gift for you, and you weren't eating it?" James seems so focused on this.

Why does it even matter? Nothing matters anymore. "No, I wasn't. I only ate it because she said if I didn't, she would."

A collective gasp goes through the room. "Why would she do that?" Robert asks. "She's a human. It's not like it would taste good."

Sighing, I gulp back another sob and clear my throat. "She thought it'd make her a wendigo. I don't think it would've, but I couldn't take that risk. I wouldn't change her for the world, no matter how much easier it'd make things for me."

James pats my shoulder. "I'm sorry, Abby."

"That's so beautiful." Ashley wipes her tears on my forearm.

"That's really impressive," Ben says. "Even now, you still have that much restraint."

"It's easy to say it when I see what it cost me. I gave in to the hunger for maybe a minute, and it lost me the only thing I've ever wanted. Nothing is worth that. I already didn't want to eat anymore, but now just the thought of it makes me see that terrified look in her eyes again. I thought about eating more once she left. I thought about hunting someone down or buying a corpse, but I couldn't do it. The idea makes me as sick as eating anything else would."

"Huh." Ashley looks up from my arm. "I can't even imagine. The last time I fell off the wagon, I ate for days. You had a bite and don't want more?"

"Maybe it won't last, but I can't imagine eating anyone now."

Ben stands and crosses the few feet to me, his small green hand patting my massive black-furred one. "This is amazing. You've actually conditioned yourself to associate human meat with something so negative. Don't get so cocky that you think you don't have cravings anymore, but this is an amazing sign. I'm just sorry it came at such a high price."

I nod. That price was far too high.

Kara weeps a few feet away. "That's true love," she sobs, wiping at seal-eyes with a flipper. She is not going to make the mistake of taking her pelt off again.

"That's all I wanted to say. I just needed to get it off my chest. It happened last night, and I've been going crazy since. I think I cried for so long that there might not be any deer to hunt around my cabin for a long while. I could hear them all scurrying off." I let out a pained chuckle. "Not like it matters. I don't have anything to spend money on now anyway." What have I even been saving for? I just earn money because that's what you do. I pay my phone bill, occasionally buy gas for my generator, and that's it. I buy the odd luxury, but what do I really need? I guess I'll just spend a lonely eternity in my cabin now that I have no one to share it with. "Thanks. All of you." I wipe at my eyes as the tears continue falling. I'm lost without her.

"Huh, kinda reminds me of my therapist," a new guy muses. "You said she wanted to become a wendigo? My therapist was asking about how to become a vampire. It had just happened to me, so I guess it wasn't an unreasonable question, but she seemed really into it."

My eyes narrow. This must be the client she said she referred, but that was just the other day. Could it really be the same person? Why would Liz want that? "When was this?"

"Monday. Why?"

I'm not sure if that would violate confidentiality. Does it go both ways? "It's not important. What did she say?" I can scarcely breathe. Had her trying to eat the scone not been a sudden impulse? Was this something she already wanted? Is she trying to do it for me?

"She just asked me how it had happened. I told her I didn't remember a lot, but she pressed me for details. I assumed she was trying to help me process it and maybe she had some morbid curiosity. She seemed the type. She was so understanding of my death, my old one back when I thought I was dead, not now that I actually am dead. Then she told me to come here. Now that I think about it, she did say she had a girlfriend here. Is that you? Did you try to eat my therapist? That's hilarious. If she wasn't such a good therapist, I probably would've done so myself."

I manage to refrain from tearing him limb from limb. "Real funny. But you think she wanted to be a vampire?"

He shrugs. "I don't know. Maybe. She could've asked me to turn her. I owe her a lot. I would've done it. She didn't, though, so she probably was just being a good therapist, right? Or maybe my turning her would be unethical. I'm not really sure. Is that what a dual relationship is?"

I'm not even listening. With him talking about her, I can almost smell her. Wait, that's not my imagination. I *can* smell her. She's here. I look around, my nose raised, trying to find her. Her scent trail is all over the next room. How did I miss it until now? "I have to go." I stand, walking past the rest of the group, practically having to climb over the vampire on my way out. She's here. Why is she here? I have to find her.

❖

I prowl the stands, following her trail, everyone parting for the big scary wendigo on the hunt. She went outside, but the scent is fresh; she just left. She might still be nearby. I shove open the door and see her car, but her scent leads away from it. I follow it around the side of the building to a dark alcove with a red emergency exit door, and a vampire sinking his teeth into her neck.

I shove him aside, my own fangs bared. "Stay the hell away from her," I bellow, my voice its natural horrifying basso.

His eyes widen. So few people see an angry wendigo and live to tell the tale. Now I've made it two. He flees without a word. I turn back to Liz. There's no blood on her mouth, but her neck is spraying everywhere. I must've torn it when I ripped the vamp off her. "Liz?" I can barely breathe. She's gonna die right here, isn't she? It's all my fault. I need that vampire to come back. I press my hand to her neck, trying to stop the bleeding.

"Abby?" Tears well up in her eyes. "I'm so sorry."

Pulling her close to my chest, I shake my head. "You didn't do anything wrong. I'm the one who tried to eat you."

"I forced you into that position, I hurt you. I didn't understand anything. I'm sorry."

"Don't talk. We need to get you to a hospital."

"I'll be fine." She winces. "How bad's the bleeding?"

I take my hand away, seeing the chunk of reddened, torn-open flesh. I don't even want a bite. "It's not great."

Her eyes squeeze shut. "Shit. I was just trying to be better for you. If I wasn't human anymore, everything would be so much easier."

"I don't want you to change, Liz. I just want you to be you. I love you." I plant a soft kiss on her lips, pressing on the wound just enough to stop the bleeding without choking her. What am I going to do? "I'm gonna take you inside. Maybe someone can help."

"I love you too," she murmurs, her eyes staying closed. I don't know what I'll do if she dies. I can't take it. She has to be okay.

In less than a second, I'm pushing back through the doors, clutching Liz tightly. Every eye in the building turns to me. That's what happens when you hold out a bleeding human to a bunch of fiends. "Can anyone help?" I sob. "She's hurt."

Everyone moves at once. I have no idea where Ashley comes from, but she's reaching out, trying to take Liz. I pull her back. I can't let go I have to look after her. "She needs to go to the hospital," Ashley insists.

"I can't take her." I can't stop crying. "I can't leave her alone. Isn't there anyone here who can treat her?" Normally, the vet's on call. I'm not sure I'd trust her with this, but anyone's better than nothing.

Boris shoves his way through the crowd. "I have bandages, but she will need to go to doctor. Remove hand, please?" I uncover it for a fraction of a second before placing pressure on the wound again. "She may bleed out if she is not seen quickly. Let me wrap her up, then you can take her."

I shake my head but lower Liz enough that he can work on her. What am I going to do? Can I just run her to the hospital and drop her off? What if that hurts her? What if someone sees me? There'd be so many people there. Could someone else take her? Her car's right there, but who can I possibly trust?

I want to take her so badly. She's my girlfriend—holy shit, she's still my girlfriend—it's my job to look after her. I shouldn't have to rely on someone else.

The remaining members of my diet group file out of our conference room and into the crowd of onlookers. It's useful being able to see over everyone. Dennis makes his way to the front. "Ms. Rosseau," he breathes, taking the last few steps toward me.

Boris glares at him.

"Let me help her!" Dennis insists, looking up at me, pleading. "I can turn her, then you won't need to worry. She won't even have to go to the hospital."

It's what she wanted. Who am I to deny her? I already ruined it once already, assuming that was going as planned; he may have been trying to kill her. Then she and I could spend eternity together.

As monsters. She doesn't deserve that fate. "No." I force the word out, almost choking on it.

He takes another step toward us, his voice a panicked plea, "Please. Abby, right? It's the only way. She wants to be a vampire. Let me help her. Let me save her."

It's so tempting. I want to give in, to know that she and I can live happily ever after, but I won't rob her of her life. I can't. "No. I won't let you."

"Then let me help. I can take her to the hospital."

That's a possibility. Can I trust him? He'd be alone with Liz. As she's bleeding out. Even through the bandage, he'd smell it clear as day—night—and I don't know if he could resist it. Until today, I didn't think I'd be able to resist that kind of wound myself, and I'm not even a vampire. Plus, he might turn her, and while it would rob me of some of the responsibility, I have to do everything I can to stop it. If, when, things are all sorted out, and we're happy and growing old together, she still wants it, then it's her choice, but when she's bleeding and on the verge of death, I won't let it happen to her. I can't.

But who can I trust? Boris can pass as a human if he wears a hat, but it's not like he's the most trustworthy sort. He rips me off every week, but he's saving her life at no cost. He might sell her. I like him okay, and he likes me, but he's not a friend. He's not someone I trust.

Ashley? She can't pass as human, even if she might be slightly better about it than me, and she's hungry. She'll want to eat Liz. She's already said as much. I can trust her, but I don't know that she can trust herself, and that puts me right back at the same point.

Kara can pass as human, and I'm still not sure why she's in the group. Selkies don't normally eat people, but that's all the more reason I can't trust her. I don't know what she's after. Who else do I even know? What can I do?

"Oh, honey," a new person calls, taking a step closer to Liz. I start to pull her away and receive a silent reprimand from Boris. I finally recognize Caris, a siren I met early on in my time here. "I guess she found that vampire she was looking for." She glances at me. "I'm sorry, Abigail. I told her I wouldn't help, but I didn't think this would happen. I should've watched after her."

"You know her?" I'm still trying to wrap my head around everything. I may be processing a bit slowly. In my defense, the love of my life is almost dead.

"I met her today. She seemed desperate."

"I'm desperate now. Can you help her?" She doesn't eat people, she can pass as human, and she feels as if she already failed Liz once. She's perfect. "Please take her to the hospital. Her car keys should be in her pocket. Her car is right outside. Please. I'm trusting you. I can't do this myself."

She nods. "Okay."

Trust, but verify. I don't want her to go alone. "Vampire boy."

"Yes?" He looks up, hunger still clear in his eyes.

"Go with her. If Liz starts to die before you get there, do it. And look after her, okay?" If I let both of them go, there's almost no way they'll betray me. I just wish I could tell Caris to stake him if he tries anything. Damn vampire hearing, it's almost as good as mine. I lock eyes with her, willing the message to her, hoping that she understands my silent, madly desperate plea. *Look after her. Don't let anyone hurt her.*

She nods. I think she understands.

Boris stands up, admiring his work. "It's not perfect, but it should keep. As long as you don't toss her around, she should survive the drive. I'll take the fee out of your next haul, Abby." I hate him.

"I'll keep her safe," Caris whispers, hugging and grabbing my precious cargo. I look down as Liz is taken from me. Her eyes are still closed. How long has she been unconscious? That's not a good sign.

Dennis fishes the keys out of her pocket. "I'll drive." Probably a good idea since I'm not sure if Caris even knows how. Besides, it makes it easier for her to watch Liz while he's busy driving.

They run off. I'd be faster. I should be the one taking her. I feel a pull at my elbow and spin on whoever's disturbing me when Liz is in so much danger only to find Ashley. "I'm so sorry, Abby."

With a nod, I find a nearby bench and collapse onto it. "I need to be there for her."

Taking a seat next to me, she rests her hand on my knee, looking up through tear-filled milky eyes. "You've done everything you can."

"Then I should be able to do more."

"I know, but we're not so lucky. You saved her life, now let the two of them finish the job. She's lucky to have you."

My eyes narrow, my mouth opening as I stare, not able to comprehend how that could be. "How? All I see is the damage I've caused. She's hurt because of me. She wants to stop being human because of me. Hell, I almost ate her yesterday, so she runs here and almost gets herself killed."

Patting my knee, she shakes her head sadly. "Look at it from her perspective. How amazing must you be to be worth all that? She loves you so much. She was willing to give up everything to be with you. It's the most romantic thing I've ever heard. I'm kinda jealous. If a guy was willing to do that for me, I wouldn't be beating myself up. I'd be letting him, I'd be marrying him, and I'd be spending eternity with him. Instead, look at you. You try to save her from herself and everyone else. You're the best person I've ever known, Abby, and you completely deserve that girl's utterly insane adoration."

I'm not sure I agree, but it's nice to hear it. I wrap my arms around Ashley, pulling her into a hug as my tears fall onto her back. "I'm so scared."

"She'll be okay, Abby. She'll either come back as a human or a vampire, but she *will* be okay."

I try to blink away the tears, but they keep coming. I don't know if I'll be able to stop crying until I hear from her. I need her to make it. I need her to keep being her. I need her.

CHAPTER FIFTEEN

Elizabeth

The last thing I remember, I was in Abby's arms. So she isn't mad at me? We're okay? Oh, thank God. Looking around, I find myself in a hospital with an incredible pain in my neck as I turn. Fuck. I shut my eyes, leaning back in bed. "Abby?" I call. Did she bring me here?

"Fortunately for you, that bitch isn't here," a voice says. It takes me a second to place it. Sandra? How did she find out where I was? "You just got out of surgery. They called me when you got in. I'm still on file as your emergency contact."

"What time is it?" I check my pockets for my phone, but I'm in a hospital gown. I glance around the room again, wincing in pain, trying to find my clothes. It should be in my pocket or maybe my purse.

"It's a little before eight a.m. I have your phone, and I canceled all of your appointments for the rest of the week. You need to recover." Her voice is firm, almost cold. I think she might be pissed at me.

"Give it to me." I reach toward her, doing my best to ignore the pain. "I need to tell Abby I'm okay."

"No. She doesn't need to know anything. She's been hurting you, and it's clearly escalated. Just look at yourself." She glares at me. I turn my head and try to ignore her. I need to let Abby know I'm all right. She sounded so scared when she found me.

"She didn't do this. I did this to myself."

"Just listen to yourself. Making excuses for that monster."

They prefer "fiend." I hold in the laughter. I don't feel like explaining it to her.

"You need some time to get your head on straight. You promised me you weren't going out. I trusted you. Clearly, I can't do that, so you're going to take your time and recover. Forget about her. You'll find someone better."

"You're not my mom, and I'm not a child." God, that sounds childish. "Give me my phone."

"You can have it back once you've started to be reasonable again. I've already messaged her. She won't be bothering you now." Sandra stands, rubbing her eyes. She looks exhausted. Has she been here all night? "I'm going to tell a nurse you're awake. Don't even think about running off."

I glower, useless and impotent in my hospital bed. What did she tell her? Did she pretend to be me? Did she claim I was breaking up with Abby? I wouldn't have thought she was capable of it, but she's never acted like this before. I'm actually a little scared of her now, more than I've ever been of Abby. I kick the foot of the bed, the motion causing a shock wave to spiral from my neck. I swear it didn't hurt this badly last night.

A few minutes later, someone in scrubs comes in, accompanied by Sandra. "Hey, Doc, am I good to go yet?" I ask. A girl can dream.

He checks my chart. "I'm your nurse, so we'll have to wait for your doctor to say anything, but I'm pretty sure we're going to want to keep you for observation. Can you tell me what happened? Your friend says your partner attacked you."

"She didn't. I was being dumb." I try to think of how to explain this, but whatever cocktail of drugs they pumped me full of seems to be slowing my planning capabilities, and they weren't remarkable to begin with. "I was bitten by a dog," I offer. It sounds so dumb.

"That would make sense with the injury." What? That

worked? "There's not really any way I can think of for a person to cause that kind of damage, not without some pretty powerful jaws. I could be wrong, but I certainly wouldn't guess it was from a person. Does her girlfriend have very sharp teeth?" he asks Sandra. I'm not sure if he's serious or joking, but I laugh anyway. She does. I cut my tongue on them once. I find myself laughing harder. Yeah, I've been drugged.

Sandra lets out an irritated sigh. "She didn't when I knew her, though who knows what weird things she might be up to now."

"I'm doubting it's that, then, though you're welcome to wait for the doctor to give her opinion."

"Her girlfriend is abusing her, and then she shows up in the hospital with that injury? It doesn't take a genius to put two and two together." She waves before crossing her arms and glaring. "What do they pay you people for? You're supposed to be keeping her safe, not just throwing her back to the wolves."

"Well, it looks like it might've been a wolf. Miss, is your girlfriend abusing you?"

"Nope." I shake my head, trying not to giggle, though fortunately, the pain makes it not so funny. Did he turn up the drugs, or are they just kicking in? Does morphine even do this? What if it's a drug from the vampire bite? Do vampires inject venom or something?

"That settles that. There weren't any other bruises remarked upon, and I can't see any signs. The giddiness should be a side effect of the medication. You lost a lot of blood, so you're gonna be here for a while. You're on an IV. Give it some time, and you should be okay. We've replaced most of it, but you lost almost two liters. You're lucky to be alive." He sifts through the pages as he reports.

I wasn't trying to be alive. I was trying to be undead, but I guess that isn't so pressing now that Abby seems to have forgiven me. Assuming Sandra didn't ruin that. "How much have you put back in me?" What a weird question. I laugh again.

"You're on your second liter right now. You lost some more blood in surgery, so we're getting you another half-liter, but at this point, the signs are good. No signs of infection. Give it a few more hours, and you should have a full tank again. Then we have to make sure there aren't any complications from the surgery. The bite was bad, but it missed your carotid, though it ripped two of your jugular veins." He lets out a low whistle. "You must've gotten here just in time. At this point, it looks like you'll be okay, but you shouldn't be making plans to head anywhere yet."

I need to see Abby. "Sandra, can I please have my phone? I need to let her know I'm okay. She didn't do this."

"We'll see what the doctor says," she grumbles. "I'm going to the vending machine. Don't let her leave," she adds, turning to my nurse.

When the door closes, he smiles. "You can call me Kevin, by the way."

"I'm Liz. Is there any way you can make her give me my stuff back?"

He sighs sympathetically. "She's just worried about you. If you'd like, I can get you an outside line, and you could try calling her."

"Yes, please. I need to talk to her."

He hits a few buttons on the phone, and I give him the number. I'm glad I had it memorized since I was fourteen. He holds the phone to my head for me. I can do it myself, but he's being so nice that I don't want to fight about it. I'm already doing enough of that with Sandra.

"Liz?" Her voice is as calm as ever, but I know she's frantic. She answered before the first ring even finished.

"Hey, Abby. I don't know what Sandra messaged you, but it's not true. I'm okay, and I love you."

A whistling breath sounds through the phone. I'm really starting to think that's cute. "Oh thank God. I was so worried. The message she sent, you sounded furious. So that really wasn't you?"

That fucking bitch. "No. It wasn't me."

"Okay. Good. Did they say how long you'll be there? I want to see you so badly, but I can't."

"I know, honey." I close my eyes, imagining her next to me. I can almost feel her hand stretching from my shoulder to my elbow. "It sounds like it'll be a few days, but I'll try to keep you up to date."

"Thank you."

"Abby, I just want you to know, I never blamed you for the other night."

"You didn't?"

"No. I'm the one who messed up. I should've listened to you. I'm sorry."

"I'm sorry too. For that, obviously, that was awful, and you have every right to be mad at me for it, but mainly for making it all so tough for you. It was scary, but I didn't actually freak out for any of it. I just thought I would. Well, except when I had that scone." She pauses, accompanied by another whistle. "James had a suggestion that I really didn't like, but it would probably solve our problems. Maybe a muzzle instead of a gag, though. If you still even want to do anything, I mean. I think I can handle it now. I can't imagine wanting to eat you anymore, but I just want to be careful. It's not important right now. Your recovery is what matters. I'm sorry, I shouldn't be bringing this up. I've just been running through that night over and over again, thinking of all the different ways it could've gone. Maybe I could get one specially made."

"You don't need it."

"Yes, I do, just to be safe."

"Fine. I'm too high to fight. I would still love to do that with you, so if that's what it takes, then sure. They might have time to make it too. Who knows how long my recovery will actually take."

"Okay. I love you."

"I love you too." I can feel the smile tugging at my lips. I feel so much better now that she knows I'm okay, and we even worked through the elephant in the room while we were at it. I can handle the rest of my stay here. "Sandra should be back any minute. I should probably get going, and you should get to sleep."

"Okay. You take care of yourself. Can I call this number?"

I look at my nurse, still standing calmly over me, holding the phone. "Kevin, would she call this number?"

"I think so. If she needs the room number, it's 341."

"Sounds like it, but it's room 341 if that doesn't work. What hospital?"

"St. Joseph's."

"I'm at St. Joseph's." We bid our farewells, and hopefully, she actually goes to sleep. She must need it as badly as I did. Sandra walks in and continues insulting Abby to Kevin and me for as long as we'll listen, but at least I know that Abby doesn't believe her anymore. I'll deal with Sandra when I've recovered.

❖

Three days in the hospital is far too long. Fortunately, they finally release me. I was tempted to release myself, but I've been in no rush to spend more time recovering at Sandra's house. I want to be at Abby's.

Unfortunately, Sandra seems to have other plans. It's a Saturday, so she doesn't have to go into work. She hasn't left my side all day, and we're waiting for my release to go through. Then I'll be out of here and stuck with her bitching and trying to keep me from seeing my girlfriend. She still hasn't given me my phone back, and now I won't have the room phone to rely on either. Never thought I'd miss people having home phones.

Kevin drops in with my paperwork. "It looks like you're ready to go. Try not to hang out with any more pit bulls for a while, and you should be fine."

"Thank you." I don't know what I would've done without him. He helped me wrangle Sandra and let me call Abigail whenever I could. I hated waking her up, but talking to her all day while Sandra was at work was a vital part of my recovery. I thought about trying to ban Sandra from my room, but she still had all my stuff, and it seemed like it would be more work than it's worth.

We make it back to her apartment, and she tries to help me up the stairs. "I have stitches in my neck, not my leg. I'm fine." I tug my arm away and make the climb on my own.

She huffs but doesn't try again, opening the door without a word.

I'm wearing a new pair of clothes she bought. My car keys were nowhere to be found in my old clothes and neither was my phone, thanks to Sandra. Abby explained that my car was back at her place, but she didn't have any way to bring it to me. She could maybe fit in a car if she curled up in the back seat. The height is bad enough, especially for my sedan, but she's too bulky. I wonder what kind of cars basketball players drive. They're a bit shorter than her, but that'd probably work.

Sandra sets some things on the counter, and I plop down on the couch. I'm sick of this. I just want my phone. "Are you going to let me go home?"

"I want to keep an eye on you over the weekend. I don't want you running back to her."

"I kind of need to get my car. Gonna be pretty tough to go to work without it."

"I could get it for you. What's her address?"

Slumping back, I place my feet on her coffee table. "Never mind."

"Then I'll drop you off at work on Monday."

This is kidnapping, right? "Are you going to do this forever?"

"Only until you get your shit together. You know this isn't okay, right? You showed up here, buck naked with a dagger strapped to your back, shaking and terrified, and then you try to run back to her."

Okay, that is pretty hard to explain. I didn't think she'd noticed the dagger. So I don't bother trying. "Give me my phone."

I can almost hear her rolling her eyes. "I'm going to go get us dinner. What do you want?"

Great. I'm actually hungry. "A burger and poutine? I'm tired of hospital food. I want something gloriously unhealthy."

"Fine. I'll be right back."

As soon as I hear her car roll out of the parking lot, I dash to the kitchen, checking the assortment of items from the hospital, desperate to find my phone. It's not there. Does she seriously still have it on her? How crazy is she? I grab her laptop from under her bed and manage to sign in. She hasn't changed her password since college. I use a website to call my phone and don't hear anything. That means she has it, it's dead, or both.

I log in to my mobile carrier's website and check my messages. No fucking way. Sandra, you are quite literally the worst person I've ever met, and at this point, most of my friends used to eat people. I find the messages she wrote: *I can't do this anymore, not after everything you've done to me. I thought this would be a dream, but it's been a nightmare. Stay away from me. I don't want anything to do with you. We're done.* The responses are a series of increasingly confused and worried messages from Abby, all of which she ignored. Who the fuck does this? Who dumps their friend's girlfriend for them?

I use the site to message Abby. *I'm out of the hospital, but Sandra won't let me leave her place.* I hesitate. Should I give her Sandra's address? It's a terrible idea, but I'm not sure I have a better one. Maybe I could try a taxi, but I don't have my purse. I don't want to give any human friend Abby's address. It'd require too much explaining. I give in. It's the only choice. I send the message quickly and close the window, trying to switch to something more innocent in case Sandra returns. Wow, she has a lot of porn tabs open. I slam the thing shut and put it back under her bed. Abby will save me. I just have to sit tight and put up with my friend who has clearly gone off the deep end. Maybe I *should* have eaten her.

Chapter Sixteen

Abigail

What am I going to do? She's not in any danger, right? Or is she? She hasn't responded to my last three messages. I can't run through town, though. Should I see if someone else can help?

I stare at her message again. She gave me the address. She must want me there. If I bundle up really well and avoid letting anyone see me too closely, it should be okay. I can run away if there's an issue.

Can I handle being around all those people? Ben said that I can't count on the idea that I don't want to eat anymore.

It's worth the risk. For her, I can handle it. I have to. She needs my help. Before I have time to rethink my decision or come up with an actual plan, I throw on a hoodie and sweats, and run to the address. I'm so glad phones have GPS.

It takes me over an hour to get there, and by the time I do, the sun's already down. Hopefully, I won't stand out too much. I climb the stairs in two strides and find the door to the apartment. What am I doing? This doesn't make any sense. I should leave. I can come get her when Sandra's asleep. I didn't think this through at all. I should have at least brought the muzzle.

I can smell so many people. It's terrifying. I still feel that same familiar hunger, but all it stirs within me is the image of her, terrified, dagger in hand, running away from me. I won't let it happen again. I steady my breathing and listen to the apartment complex. Conversations filter out from every building. It takes a moment, but I manage to place one of the voices as Sandra's. I still remember it. And there's Liz. She's so close. I want to hold her and take her away from this, but how can I do it without revealing myself?

"What the hell were you thinking?" Sandra's all but screaming.

"I don't know what you're talking about." Liz is fighting to stay calm. She doesn't want to give away any more than Sandra already knows.

"You gave that psycho my address."

"She's not a psycho!" There's a thump. Sandra takes a step toward her. Liz's breath catches. "The only psycho here is you."

What is she doing to her? I have to help. I feel every muscle in my body tense, only held in inaction by the fear of showing myself.

"I just want to keep you safe." Sandra's so close to her, their breathing is almost mixed. "What the hell is your problem?" I can smell the adrenaline. Was that thump her hitting Liz? She wouldn't.

I hear another loud thump, and I can't wait anymore. I have to act. I knock the door down without breaking stride, and in a second, Liz is in my arms as Sandra's fist slams against a wall. Not the wall Liz was pressed against.

She wasn't hitting her.

Sandra stops and turns, agonizingly slowly and yet so fast I haven't even moved. Her eyes widen, her mouth dropping open. She screams.

I should've just grabbed Liz and run. I had time. What the hell is wrong with me? "Sandra," I try, but I have no idea where to go from there.

Liz coughs, rubbing at her neck. "Well, Sandra, this is Abby. I know you've met, but it's been a while."

Thanks, Liz. Real helpful. "Hi." I hold up one long-clawed hand and wave casually. This may be the most awkward situation I've ever been in.

"Could you set me down?" Liz asks. "I need a second. Moving like that kinda..." She falters as her feet hit the ground, almost falling. "I don't breathe as well as I used to."

I had thought it was the phone before, but her voice is different too. That's my fault. The vampire wouldn't have done so much damage if I hadn't ripped him off of her along with all that skin. "I'm sorry."

"So this is who hurt you!" Sandra brandishes Liz's dagger. "What are you? You're not Abby. Do you have her under some kind of spell?"

"So that's where my dagger went." Liz collapses on the couch. "She didn't hurt me. It was a vampire. She saved me. I'd gotten in over my head."

"What?" Sandra's eyes turn to Liz, the blade still pointed at me.

"Oh for fuck's sake." I snatch the weapon out of her hand and drop her on the couch next to Liz and sit cross-legged on the floor before them. "How about we have a talk like civilized adults? You already kidnapped my girlfriend. You don't need to go and threaten me with a knife too."

"Kidnapped? Me? You're the monster here. Don't try to change things. I was trying to look after her."

"They prefer 'fiends,' actually," Liz explains, her hand resting on her injured neck. "Be nice to her." She's breathing slowly, trying to steady herself. "Just give me a second, and I'll explain everything."

"How about this *thing* explains? Are you even Abby? You have her voice, but that's about it." She stares up and down my massive form. "You sure as hell don't look like her."

"I have everyone's voice," I grumble back in her own voice. "I do, however, have my memories, my feelings, and my life. I haven't done anything to Liz other than love her and try to be as good for her as I can despite my"—I gesture at myself—"limitations."

"Limitations? You're a giant monstrous freak."

Liz glares at her. "She isn't a monster, and she's not a freak." She rises and walks toward me, her steps more stable than they were a moment ago. She drops into my lap, draping an arm over me as she rests her head on my chest. "She's the love of my life. I don't care what form she takes. It'll always be true."

I place the softest kiss I can manage on the top of her head. "I'm sorry about the door, but I thought you were going to hurt her."

"I would never." Her eyes are wide again, now burning with outrage rather than fear.

"You *did* kidnap me and break up with my girlfriend over text."

"I—"

"And you were yelling at her and hitting a wall," I add.

"Well—"

"Plus, Kevin said you were stopping some people from seeing me."

"I didn't know who they were." She stares, horror clear on her face again.

I wrap an arm around Liz. "I know you wanted to keep her safe, but you were treating her like a prisoner."

"I didn't want her to go back to you. You didn't see what she was like the other night. She was terrified and completely out of her mind, and that's because of you. If you weren't going to keep her safe, someone had to. She's my best friend. I've been worried sick about her." She wipes her eyes as she takes a shuddering breath, tears sprinkling her blouse. "Liz, what was I supposed to think? You wouldn't tell me anything. I wasn't allowed to see Abby. You kept defending her despite looking more and more scared and sleep-deprived."

"Okay, she does deprive me of sleep," Liz says, her lips trailing up my neck.

"You and..." She points in my direction. "That thing! You had...how? Why? What?"

"How? Do you need a demonstration?" Liz asks.

"Jealous?" I suppose I never could resist fucking with Sandra.

She rolls her eyes. "Okay, you two are still you. I believe it now. No one other than Elizabeth Rosseau and Abigail Lester could drive me half this crazy."

"You were crazy when I met you," Liz says.

That seems to have defused the tension, at least. Sandra's still terrified and angry, but she seems more disturbed than horrified at this point. "How did this happen? What are you now?"

Liz and I tell the story, each filling in parts the other leaves out, though not going into too much detail on my eating my parents. Some things are a bit too much. We also completely skip over any mention of killing after that. We are trying to make me look good, after all. "Holy fuck."

Sandra covers her mouth, fresh tears streaming down her cheeks. "That's all possible? Monsters are real? She's really a wendigo? You weren't kidding? And you're okay with all this?"

"Yes, I told you, the term's 'fiend.' I told you that on Wednesday. I was not kidding, and yes, I am so okay with it. She's brought a whole new world to me, one that's far more interesting than I ever thought possible. One that's full of people who could really use a good therapist." She chuckles. It sounds so much drier than it used to, as if she's picked up a decade of smoking in the past week. "This is all I want. I love her." Her fingers intertwine with mine, and she closes her eyes. "Now that we have all that sorted out, if you call her anything like that again, I'm uninviting you from our wedding."

What? Our what? My mouth drops open, but I promptly close it, not wanting to show my fangs. "Liz?"

She squeezes me tightly. "Our *eventual* wedding. Don't go freaking out just yet."

Right. Okay. That makes sense. We're really gonna get married? I tear up a little picturing us at the altar.

Sandra deflates, nodding solemnly. "I'm sorry."

"Thank you. Now, please don't tell anyone about her." Liz

leans forward, desperation seeping into her voice. We've risked a lot sharing all of this.

Sandra sucks her teeth. Liz has just asked an impossible favor of her, and she's been through a lot already. I'm still mad, but I can empathize. "Will she pay for my door?"

"Will you give Liz her phone back and stop trying to control her?"

With a sigh, she produces the device from her pocket and takes a few hesitant steps toward me. Far enough away that she has to lean over and fully extend her arm to Liz. I could still snatch her in an instant. All she's doing is setting herself off balance. "Here."

"Fine, then I'll pay for it."

Liz takes the phone and glares at me. "Are you serious? After everything she's done? You're going to pay for that door?"

I shrug. "It's fine."

Liz rolls her eyes. "Well, I guess that's all sorted out." She stands, wincing and massaging her neck. "Will you carry me back to your place?"

I slowly rise, trying not to look any more intimidating than necessary, but Sandra holds her hand up. "Now wait just a second."

I finish standing but stare at her, my head scraping the ceiling as I wait for her to continue.

"You could barely breathe after she carried you a few feet. Let me drive you."

"Oh." Liz's eyebrows scrunch up. She clearly hates the idea but doesn't have a better one. "Fine, but if any mobs of angry villagers with torches and pitchforks end up there, I know who to blame."

"They won't, I promise." She seems to mean it. Maybe she's actually starting to come around. Hopefully, that means no more kidnapping.

I make the way on foot, and they drive. I probably could've

managed to stuff myself in her car, but I'd rather not have to pay for any more damage to Sandra's property.

❖

Liz and I collapse onto my couch as we hear Sandra's car pull away. She didn't seem interested in coming inside, not that we invited her. I carefully cup Liz's cheek, sifting through her hair to avoid cutting her. I was scared that I'd never hold her again. I thought she left me, then she almost died, and then I thought she'd dumped me again. I just want to soak in this moment, her in my arms with no pressure, no problem, and the chance to just relax.

Her lips meet mine, her arms wrapping around me. I give in, allowing my tongue to explore her mouth, holding nothing back. Her tongue stays in her mouth, but that's the only concession we make to my diet. Tonight is ours, and ours alone.

After a few moments, she has to come up for air, stroking the fur on the back of my neck. "This is perfect," she whispers. It seems a crime to break the silence.

I play with her hair, nodding.

"I'm sorry for everything that happened this week. I shouldn't have put so much pressure on you. You're already everything I want, and I don't want to push you for anything you're not ready for."

Leaving a soft kiss on her forehead, I smile. Her smile back is so pure and beautiful. She really isn't scared of me in the slightest. "I was putting pressure on myself too, but I was so much in my own head that I wasn't letting myself enjoy it. Now I have that muzzle, and I think it'll really make things a lot easier." Are we going to try again already? I was content just cuddling on the couch. Weren't we supposed to be watching TV this weekend?

"You don't need the muzzle. I trust you."

"I know you do, but I don't trust myself. It's not because I think I'll try to eat you. It's so I know for a fact that I can't. There's no risk of my losing myself, and I can enjoy the moment without fear. It's not too weird for you, right? I'd understand if that would be kind of uncomfortable. It's why I was desperate to avoid it at first."

She toys with the zipper of my hoodie, sliding it down, allowing her access. Her lips meet my neck, my clavicle, my chest, and then she pulls back, her bright eyes looking up at me. "I'm fine with it if it's something you really need. I want you to be comfortable."

"Thank you." I want to scratch at her back, but that seems like a good way to send her back to the hospital, so I stroke a slow circle, lightly massaging her. "I love you, Liz. I just want to know that we're safe."

Her lips return to my neck, and I shudder, gripping her tighter. "Then get the muzzle."

I stare. "Are you sure? You're still recovering. I don't want to tear your stitches."

"Then you'll have to be careful, won't you?" Her nibbling on my earlobe convinces me.

"All right, I'll get it." I grab the nylon-mesh strap from the bag on the counter, securing it over my mouth. As much as it makes me feel like a freak and all the more like a cannibal thanks to a few classic movies, it makes me feel safe. I know that I can trust myself as long as this is on. I know I won't hurt her.

I find her in my bed, her gorgeous tan body already on display. This time, I don't hesitate to join her. I don't think I'll ever stop hating my body, but she makes it so much harder. That same awe as before shows in her eyes as she looks at me. Her fingers run along my chest. "There's no scar."

"I heal pretty well." My voice is only slightly muffled.

She kisses near to where the cut was. I think she's pretty much dead on. "Well, I'm still sorry. I love you more than anything, and I never want to hurt you. Now, does that thing stop your tongue?"

I try it. It takes some maneuvering, but two feet of pure muscle makes a lot of things possible. This is an added bonus I hadn't considered. I can actually please her without having to worry about wanting to eat her. I can be closer to her than I'd ever dreamed possible. "I guess it doesn't."

She stares at me, unblinking. "I did not realize how long it was. Holy shit."

I grin. There is one trait I'm proud of, even if I was pretty sure I'd never get to do anything with it.

"Put it in me."

She doesn't have to ask twice. I have to adjust the angle a bit, but I still end up with perfect access to her, winding my tongue around her lips, circling her, not quite touching.

"You tease." She grips my fur, pulling lightly, trying to guide me where she wants me. I give in. I tongue her clit, and she bucks against me, her grip tightening. "Oh fuck. Oh, Abby, that's amazing, please, please keep going."

I lap at her, exploring her folds, teasing her but flicking her most sensitive area every time she starts to get restless. She tastes amazing, and all I want to do is please her. I feel none of the urges I'd feared—I just want to make the woman I love happy. I could spend an eternity down here. My tongue slides inside her, and she gasps, her hips thrusting repeatedly against me, riding my tongue, guiding it to just the right spot.

Her hand slides down to her clit, playing with it as my tongue continues its work. She screams, madly, desperately, her hips and hand never stopping. I thrust in and out, flicking my tongue against her walls, probing for every last weakness, picking up speed each time she moans. I wrap my arms around her, drawing her close, despite it not being necessary. I fill her up with my tongue, savoring her taste, taking her. "I'm gonna come, Abby... right there, please."

I keep going, evening out the pace as I beat against that same spot, her fingers continuing their frantic work in front of my eyes. I taste, smell, and feel her climax, the flood of endorphins, her body rocking as the waves travel through her, clutching desperately to me as if she's terrified that she'll be cast adrift in the ocean that's taking her. Never stopping, I work at her until the last ounce washes over her, and she's completely spent.

Only then do I rise and lie with her, clutching her to my chest. She plants kisses against me, savoring the euphoric glow. "That was fucking amazing. Best I've ever had. God, Abby, you were so worth the wait."

Resting my forehead against hers, I murmur in agreement. "That was everything I ever wished it would be and more."

We lie like that for quite a while, basking in each other's presence and the endorphins. "Let me take care of you," she mumbles sleepily once she's finally come back to her senses.

I shake my head, resting a hand firmly against her hip to hold her in place. "No. You're hurt. You can have your turn when you're recovered. I can wait."

"But I wanna." She sighs, her eyelids drifting closed.

I let her rest, safe in my arms, while I dream of the life before us.

CHAPTER SEVENTEEN

Elizabeth

We've been together for a few months now, and I've pretty much moved in. The place has changed a lot. Not only do we keep food in the fridge, but we managed to install an oven. It's amazing what you can get people to do when you have a bag of gold. A new painting of the two of us together hangs over the fireplace. I tried to convince her to paint herself as she is now, but she isn't ready. She did, however, agree to put a mirror up in the bathroom so I can look at least somewhat presentable for work. I still keep a few things at my apartment—at least until the lease ends next month—but I only go to my office on Mondays, and I have another therapist that I share it with the rest of the week. It's still not easy to convince fiends that I'm someone they can turn to in order to discuss their troubles, but Abby and Ashley have been doing their best to drum up business, and it seems to be working.

I'm sitting in my office at the Community Center. It was once a perfume store, and it still smells faintly, but it gives me a nice spacious area with plenty of room for my desk and clients. Some of them really need the room. Running five minutes late, my most recent referral walks in.

At first, I'm not quite sure what I'm seeing. When it clicks, I realize I'm looking at a mirror image of myself wearing the same outfit. When she sits, a fox tail wraps around her leg to rest in her lap. God, I love this job.

"Good morning," I say.

"I suppose two a.m. counts as morning."

Small talk was never my area of expertise anyway. "What brings you here?"

She looks at herself, then up at me as if only now realizing we're wearing the same skin. Awkward. One of us should change. "You, I suppose."

That's the downside of dealing with immortal clients. They take their time with everything. "Go on."

"I've heard good things about you. I thought perhaps I'd try you out, see if they were true. I don't think I quite understand. You seem to be a good fit for me in theory, but I'm not sure what more you could offer." She looks to the ticking clock on the far wall. "I'm sorry, what were you here to see me for?"

That's interesting. "You're here to see me, Ms. Watanabe."

"Not anymore. Is it not Ms. Rosseau now?"

As much as I have dreamed of this, I thought both of me would be a bit saner. Not that I'm one to talk. "Is that what you're here about? Are you having trouble remembering who you are?"

Her eyes light up, her mouth widening to reveal jagged fox teeth as she nods. "Yes, that's right. Oh, you are good."

It is nice being complimented by myself for once. "Do you remember who you used to be?"

Her eyes lose focus, her mouth shutting partway. Her eyebrows knit together, and a muscle in her jaw twitches as she stares at my knee. "Oh, right...I was a fox."

I could've guessed that. "Right." I tap a few buttons on my laptop. I have to rely on demonology texts more often than the DSM-5 these days. "A kitsune?"

"Yes. I'm glad you've heard of me."

"So you know who you are?"

An inhuman chuckle leaves her throat. "Oh, my mind does get away from me sometimes. I'm sorry, I keep thinking that I'm your therapist, and it all gets so convoluted. I know that I'm a kitsune; that's not the issue. It's not who I am. I've lost something integral to me. I've spent so long being a wife or a husband, a father, a daughter, a friend, or an enemy to everyone that it's all starting to fade together. I'm not taking identities anymore. They're taking me, and they all fall apart, dragging my mind along with them. I'm not at all sure what to do. I need to remember who I am."

These clients just don't get boring. "Well, I'm glad we've figured out the problem. That's a huge first step. When you say that who you are isn't a kitsune, what do you mean by that? Is who you are any different from who you're pretending to be at the time?"

Her head tilts. "I'm not pretending. I always am who I am. I used to be able to keep track of it better."

"So you're not concerned so much with who you are in a metaphysical sense as keeping track of your identity?"

Her hands slide through her hair, twine through it, follow it down, and then stop in midair as if shocked by how short my hair is. "I want to be able to keep things straight."

"Okay." I type a few notes. "I think I'm starting to understand. Who would you say you are right now?"

"I'm you. I'm Elizabeth Rosseau, therapist to fiend-kind, lover of wendigoag, and romantic extraordinaire. The human who decided that fiends were so much more interesting than her own kind. Who decided that she had to help them. That's who I am."

"I only love one wendigo, not all of them." Most of them are fucking terrifying. I had one as a client a few weeks back, and I had to have Abby keep him off me if I wanted to keep my flesh attached to my bones. I'm so glad she was nearby. "And I'm not that much of a romantic." Wait, this is about her, not me. "Well, who were you before now?"

Her eyes shut, and her body shimmers, cold fire unraveling from somewhere deep within her. It consumes her and just as quickly fades, leaving a tall, muscular redhead wearing a brand-new outfit: a cold-shoulder top and a pencil skirt. "Vivienne McCain. I'm a journalist."

For a second, I thought she might set the room on fire. I've never seen anything like that before. It takes me a few seconds longer than I'd like to admit to formulate a reply. "So you're not having trouble sorting that out?"

Her eyes narrow, and I swear I see flames in them. She winces, and her body begins to change again but rights itself, maintaining the journalist's form but looking fainter. "Almost. It's like there's too much memory in my head, and I can't process everything. I'm sorry, have we met?"

Fuck. Her issues might be a bit more than just psychological. I'm going to have to talk to the apothecary and see what we can do. I'm never going to get used to that word. "Does that mean you're having memory problems as well?"

Suddenly, there's a fox curled up in her chair. There wasn't even another burst of fire. It rests its head on its front paws. "Nothing works right anymore."

I was not trained for this. "Miss?"

I'm sitting before me again. "I'm sorry. So do you think you can help?"

"The identity problems are stuff we can work through, but the memory issues may be neurological. There's a veterinary hospital not too far that we've made arrangements with. They have an MRI machine, and I'd like you to be checked out. I'm going to write you a referral. Is that okay?"

She nods. "If you think it'll help."

"I don't suppose there's any chance you have brain scans of a healthy kitsune?"

"My brother is the one who recommended I see you. Maybe I could talk her into going with me, and she could be tested too?"

The pronouns are the least confusing part of this conversation. "Sure. That sounds like a great plan. She's not having these issues too, is she?"

"No. He's not."

"Great. Then you two go together. I'll write a second referral. Come back to me with the results. This seems kind of urgent." I check my calendar. "I actually have an opening tonight at midnight if you think you can get the MRI done before then."

With a vigorous nod, she stands and extends her hand. "Yes, thank you, that'll be perfect. I'll see you then."

I shake it. "It's no problem."

"I'm sorry, what do I owe you?"

Hey, I'm not doing this for charity. "A hundred dollars for the session."

She hands me a bag of diamonds and charges out of the room. I guess I'll put this toward her future appointments as well.

❖

"Looks like you got an interesting one," Ashley says, walking through the open door. After the wendigo incident, I've made sure to always have a guard posted nearby, even if it does cut into my paycheck.

"You know I can't talk about it." I rise and stretch. I have two hours without another appointment, more than enough time for the shopping trip I've planned with Ashley.

"Business has really been picking up. Plus, I haven't had to beat anybody up."

"I still can't believe he acted that way. I thought violence wasn't allowed here."

Grabbing my hand to drag me along, she replies, "Yeah, and that's why he's not allowed back. So are we doing this or not?"

I try my best to look coy, but I'm too excited, and my grin overwhelms me. "Fine. Let's go look for rings before Abby starts to wonder what we're up to."

"Yes!" She pumps her arm and leads the way to a far-off section of the marketplace. "I know they're kind of expensive here, but the quality is so much better." Her gaze falls to a shimmering diamond. "Oh my God. If someone were to get me that, I would absolutely melt. Hell, I'd marry them on the spot, no questions asked."

I do not understand straight girls. "Okay, Ashley. The thing is, we're looking for something that *Abby* would like."

"What's not to like?" She gestures madly at the glittering ring. "It's beautiful!"

The jewel is huge, it's way too expensive, and it's gaudy. I mean, maybe something big would work on her fingers, but they're not fat, just long. "Let's keep looking."

"But I love it."

"I'm not marrying you."

That shuts her up. She grumbles, but we continue our search. I find a cute ruby ring. It's tiny, but the quality is outstanding, and it wouldn't snag on anything. "I like this one."

"You're going to propose with a ruby?"

"Maybe keep it down and don't announce this when my girlfriend has super hearing."

Her eyes narrow. "Fine, but a ruby is still a bad idea."

I roll my eyes. It would clash with her necklace anyway. Maybe something green.

"What about this one?" She points toward the back of a case at a ring with a spidery silver band studded with tiny diamonds and a heart-shaped sapphire in the center.

"So sapphire is okay but ruby isn't?"

"It's so pretty!"

"Doesn't giving her a silver ring seem a little rude? I know that just touching it doesn't hurt her, but it's like proposing to a vampire with a wooden ring. Or proposing to you with a silver ring, now that I think about it." Is there a human equivalent? "Proposing to me with an anthrax ring?"

"Even touching anthrax is bad for you."

"Fair point."

"I would be totally okay with this ring. Who cares that it's silver? It's perfect. I just love it. It still has the diamonds, which are an absolute necessity, but the sapphire is so pretty."

"Ashley, is there something I should know?" I rest my hand on my hip, feeling like a judgmental mom.

"What do you mean?" She takes a step back, pulling away and narrowing her eyes.

"Why are you looking for a ring for you? Is there someone you're hoping will propose? It's not me or Abby, right? 'Cause I'm pretty sure we've made it clear that we're both taken."

"Ew, no." She lets out an exasperated gasp and turns on her heel. "I've just spent a long time fantasizing about this." Her fingers scrape the case as she bends down to stare longingly at the ring.

It strikes me that there's something quite important that I don't know about Ashley. "How long?"

She looks up. If she was capable of crying, I think she would be. "My whole life."

Still not the answer I'm looking for. "And how long has that been?"

Her gaze turns back to the ring, her hand pressing against the glass. "A while. Don't worry about it. I'll find someone. You don't need to propose to make me feel better or anything."

I sling my arm through hers, tugging her back to her feet. "I wasn't planning on it. I'm sorry."

Her eyes stay on that ring. "It's okay. You're right. It's a tacky ring anyway."

I wasn't going to say it. "How about we pick out a cute outfit after we find the ring? Something that'll bring those boys running."

With a deep breath, she manages to tear her eyes away from the object of her desires and give me a quick nod. "All right. That sounds great. Now, let's find that ring. Oh, Abby is gonna flip. So you want something smaller, sleeker. You people, I swear." I'll let it slide. "So, what about something like that?" Her gnarled finger extends in the direction of a little slip of a ring with a split band in the back and a cute but flawless diamond in its base. I try picturing it on Abby's hand and blush.

"That could work. Tough, I had been kind of considering an emerald." I bite my lip. I do really like it. It would look so good on her.

"Why an emerald?" She holds up her hands as if to say "right, sorry, it's her ring," and leads me to a section that's all emeralds. "Maybe one that still has diamonds on it?"

I scour the case, drifting over each and every ring. I see it. My jaw drops. It's perfect. In the very center of the middle shelf lies a nestled emerald ring, exactly the same shade as her necklace. It has a gold band with a semicircle around the two gems. It'll look beautiful on her. "Could I see this one?" I ask the clerk.

The antlered attendant comes out of what was either a meditative trance or hibernation and looks straight into my eyes. "Of course." She grabs the ring from its spot on the shelf without even checking which one I meant and hands it to me. It's heavier than I'd thought.

"Wow."

Ashley peers over my shoulder. "All right, I guess I get it. That is gorgeous."

I love it. "I'll take it. Could you resize it to a size ten?" I may have measured Abby's hands when she was sleeping. It's not creepy if it's to keep my proposal a surprise.

"Of course. It'll be ready for pickup tomorrow. That'll be two thousand dollars, payable on pickup."

That's only a little more than I was hoping to spend. "All right. I'll see you tomorrow." The second I say this, Ashley grabs my hand again and all but drags me across the market. I guess she didn't forget about my offer. I spend the remaining hour shopping with her before my next appointment.

Chapter Eighteen

Abigail

A few weeks ago, a new butcher came to town. She was offering me twice what Boris was for my deer, averaging a thousand bucks per haul, if you'll pardon the pun. Now, Boris and I go way back, so I offered him one chance to beat her offer before I switched. That's why I'm now walking away from his table with twelve hundred dollars.

I see Liz's short black hair in the crowd and head toward her. "Hey, honey."

She turns to me, blinking slowly before she seems to recognize me. "Oh, Abby!" She throws her arms around me and tries to lean in for a kiss, but I don't lean down.

She doesn't smell right. I also don't recall her having a tail. "You're not Liz."

She pulls back, blinking. "I'm not?"

I shake my head.

"Oh." She stares at my feet. I shuffle them awkwardly. "Right, sorry. I'm not. I forgot."

"You forgot that you weren't Liz?"

"Yeah." She smiles. She seems very proud of herself for figuring that out. "I'm on my way to an appointment with her. She's helping me get over this. I have so much trouble sorting out who I am and who I'm not. Thank you for the reminder. You've been a huge help, Abby." Her hand moves to the back of my neck, and she tries to pull me into a kiss again.

"You're not my girlfriend."

"Right. I wasn't thinking." She pulls back. "Well, it should all be in the MRI. We're working on it. You have fun at group."

Do kitsune even get people's memories? Liz has her work cut out for her there. With the Liz impostor gone, I weave through the crowd to the conference room. I'm actually early for once. They're just setting up the chairs. I help out, and we finish in only a few seconds.

"Hey, Abby," Ben says quietly. The doors are still open while we're waiting for everyone else, and he's never been too big on announcing who's here. He thinks it's rude. "Getting used to the live-in girlfriend?"

I bare my teeth in a massive grin. "I'm well past used to it now. It's practically heaven." Way better than back when she was my roommate. That was far closer to hell. Between her dates, hiding my feelings, and everything else, I don't know what I was thinking doing it for so long.

"I'm glad. Still no desire to eat her?"

"Nope. I'm pretty good, and I think the muzzle helps a lot."

He laughs, his green face splitting open in a friendly smile. "Whatever it takes. Keep fighting the good fight."

The chairs fill in as we all take our seats. James is absent for once. What the hell does he have to do ever? He's an incubus who gave up sex. I suppose that's hardly fair from the wendigo who gave up cannibalism. I'm sure he has something weird to get to.

Once the group begins, Ashley raises her hand. "Hi. Um. Shit. I'm Ashley, I've been in the program for ten years, and I haven't eaten people in"—she checks the time on her phone—"almost twenty minutes."

"The fuck, Ashley?" I do my absolute best not to yell. "Again?"

"It's not as bad as it sounds."

"When you joined, you said you were giving up corpses as

well," Ben says. "Our big thing is avoiding killing, but you were pretty particular."

"It's those scones. They're just so good. You know what I mean, right, Abby?"

My eyes narrow. "Yeah. I remember the absolute worst night of my life, the only night I'm more traumatized by than when I first turned. Thanks."

She bares her teeth, laughing awkwardly. "This cute guy bought me one. I couldn't just say no. He bought it for me, and I gave him my number. I wasn't going to *not* eat it. They're baked with all the love that wonderful gay couple can shove into them. Okay, that makes them sound less appealing. They're really good!"

"That's not an excuse, Ashley." Ben huffs. "I suppose it's at least better than you going hunting. Are you going to stay on your diet, or are you going to keep eating and going on dates with him?"

"And more importantly, who's the guy?" I ask, earning a glare from Ben.

"You wouldn't know him." She ducks her head pitifully, sinking into the chair. "He's just this really cool gargoyle." She's mumbling so badly I can barely make out what she's saying. "He has nice wings, okay? I'm not sure if I'm gonna eat more with him. I don't think he eats humans. He was just buying a cinnamon roll. So it probably won't come up again, and I'll be fine, and he and I can live happily ever after."

I roll my eyes. Fucking hell, Ashley. I swear she'd do anything if a guy asked her to. "Just promise me you'll take care of yourself, okay?"

"Of course. I mean, I have to be in good enough shape to make it to your wedding."

Her face goes as still as rock. Just like her new boyfriend. "My wedding, huh? Who's to say the two of you won't beat us? I'm sure you'd be walking down the aisle already if he asked."

"Why? Do you think he will? Did he say something to you? Tell me everything you know!" She grips the collar of my blouse tightly, pulling me toward her. "His name's Will. Have you met him? You have, haven't you? I bet he asked about me."

"Oh my God, Ashley. I don't know any gargoyles."

"A likely story."

"Can I speak?" The anthropophage from the night that Liz first called me raises his hand. He only comes to group a once or twice a month. I think he must live pretty far away. "I haven't talked much before."

Ashley shuts her mouth, and Ben gestures for him to continue.

"I wasn't sure if I could do it. I've been really scared, but I've gone over four months without eating anyone. I know for a lot of you, that isn't the biggest deal."

"It's always a big deal," I reply. "Every day counts."

"We're so proud of you," Ben adds.

Robert pats him on the back.

"Thank you." He leans forward. I'd call it hiding his face, but it's in his torso and pretty well hidden already. "I just want to keep it up. I've been so lucky to have Nora as my sponsor."

A small—relatively speaking—bunyip smiles, showing its enormous tusks. So her name's Nora. I never caught it. I don't think she's said a word in the almost three years I've been coming.

"She talked me through some tough times." He swallows. I think. His shirt moves around where a human stomach would be, so that's probably what swallowing looks like. "I'm just really proud of myself for making it this far, and I wanted to share it with everyone."

We all clap. Even Nora pounds her hooves together. How does she use a phone? I mean, I know we're all fiends and everything, but there are some things that I still don't understand.

A young man who I don't recognize goes next. "I'm Huey." His voice is a strange singsong with a certain power to it. "I've been eating humans for a few millennia now, and a couple hundred years ago, I had to stop cold turkey. It was pretty difficult, but I've been managing. Finally. I like to sit in on these groups when I get the chance and see other people dealing with the same struggle. Does it feel like it costs you? Like you're weaker, like you can't fight back the darkness anymore?"

Ben gives him a warning look. "Most of us give up a lot for it. We try to encourage each other not to look at the downsides but the upsides. We're not hurting people. We're able to be part of society without causing damage, without making people hunting us more likely, and we're able to help make a good impression on humanity."

"I'm just still hungry, even after all this time."

"Believe me, I know," I say. Ben eats plenty of non-human things; he can't relate. "It's a huge sacrifice, and it hurts every day." Of course, I feel the same if I do eat; only then, I'm even bigger. "I'm glad you came. It sounds like you're at a down point right now. We all go through those sometimes. You just have to accept that it's for the greater good."

"But how can I be sure? What if I need to find a way to start eating again?"

"You don't. The strength it takes to give it up is far more than you could ever gain from eating even a thousand people. We can be part of society rather than a predator picking them apart one at a time."

He nods. "I suppose I'm just feeling nostalgic. Back when I ate, I felt needed. Now I feel like I don't belong anywhere."

"You always belong here." Ben takes a few steps toward him and hands him a business card. "Call me anytime. I can help you through these dark patches."

"Thanks." He takes the card and stares at it. "I'm sure all of you are right. I've made it this long. I can keep going."

Kara raises her flipper. "Hey, I've been coming here for a while, and I think a lot of you, especially you, Abby"—she doesn't wink, I'm surprised—"have really helped me understand humans a lot more. I was so hateful for so long after what one of them did to me. He's the one I ate. That's why I started coming here and seeing why I shouldn't do it again, and it's really meant a lot. I really appreciate that none of you have ever given me a hard time for being a selkie. I know I'm not exactly a normal fit. We don't typically eat people, but I did, and I really needed this. It's now been a year to the day since I gave it up. Well, a year and four days, but we didn't have group on Saturday."

We all applaud again. I don't know if I still need this group now that I have Liz, but I think I'm still needed. Besides, they're my family. I love it, and I wouldn't be able to have the life I've been dreaming of if they hadn't helped me reach it.

Kara grins back with that goofy seal smile. The meeting devolves into casual conversation and catching up, and I stick around for a while to talk to a few people. Liz has clients until four, so I have time to kill.

❖

I remember when smelling bacon cooking in the morning was a nice thing. I feel slightly queasy as I wake up, clutching my stomach. Liz is nowhere to be found, but unless someone else broke into my house—our house—to cook breakfast, I'm pretty sure I know where she is. I can stand being around her when she eats, though meat is always a little tougher, but the smell of it cooking is too much. I can almost taste it, and the taste of anything that isn't human makes me sick. God, being a wendigo sucks.

I decide to take my time in the shower. Liz helped me have it remodeled, so I now have a waterfall faucet, which means a lot less hunching over. I don't know why I never thought of it before. There are plenty of fiends perfectly capable of renovation work. I guess it never mattered enough. When I can't be hurt and have to bend over almost everywhere I go, it's not that big an issue. I love that she decided to make it a priority. It makes the place feel a lot more like home.

By the time I'm done and have dried my fur to the best of my ability, there's only a slight lingering scent of bacon, nowhere near enough to overwhelm me. I don't bother throwing anything on since I need to air-dry and head down to see my girlfriend.

The sun is already low, and the only light in the place is the TV. I guess Liz is fully on my schedule now if she's having breakfast at eight at night. "Morning, honey," I say.

"Good morning!" She grins, looking up from her book, her eyes exploring my body. Okay, there may be a second reason I didn't throw anything on. A girl likes to feel pretty sometimes, and she definitely makes me feel it. She pats the spot next to her on the couch. "I bought a new movie yesterday. Wanna watch it?"

I take the seat and drape an arm around her, pulling her head to my chest. "Sure."

She wraps her arm around my belly, snuggling in. "I have to put it in the Blu-ray player."

"No deal. I like you here." I cup her chin and kiss her. I promptly feel her hand cupping my ass.

She takes advantage of my surprise to pry herself free and sticks her tongue out at me before grabbing the case from the mantel and popping the disk into the player. She takes her seat next to me, remote in hand. "Now we can cuddle."

I lean against her shoulder. "Fine. You win. Now, will you tell me what the movie is?"

"You'll see in a second."

A set of bright colorful images flashes on the screen. I have to say, I was not expecting a ten-hour superhero movie marathon. She tricked me.

She grins. "I haven't been to the theater in a while, and someone was selling this collection on a single disk with perfect quality. I wasn't going to just say no."

"Did you have to sell your soul for it?"

Pursing her lips, she considers this. "No, just fifteen bucks."

"I guess it's worth it, then."

"Damn right it is." She slides to the side of the couch and

guides my head into her lap, her fingers playing at the soft fur on my head.

I promptly give in. I could watch thirty hours of action movies if she keeps doing that. It feels so good.

I don't even fall asleep, despite how comfy I am. The movies manage to keep my interest all right, but I'd be lying if I said I wasn't mostly staying awake to feel her fingers and her occasional reactions to the films. She winces at every good fight, jumps high enough that I have to move with her when an alien pops out, and throws potpourri at the screen when the hero and damsel end up making out in the end. I guess it was the only thing she had on hand.

"Having fun?" I ask after she returns from a quick bathroom break at the end of the third movie.

"I am. I love cuddling with you. There's nothing quite like spending a lazy weekend at home with your girlfriend."

I stretch, sitting up, my arm almost hitting the ceiling. "Then come cuddle some more, and we can finish the marathon."

A mischievous grin spreads across her face, and she doesn't step toward me. "Oh, I had something better in mind."

How is she not still spent from last night? "Really?" I hide my lascivious grin behind my bicep. I hate showing my teeth to her. It always feels so threatening, even though I know she likes it.

"Not that. We can save that for when we get home."

My eyebrows shoot up. "Where are we going?"

"You'll find out when we get there." It's only now that I notice she's not wearing pajamas anymore. How did I miss that? I normally can't take my eyes off her when she's wearing a shirt and slacks.

"So we're going to the Community Center."

"Nope." Her grin only widens. "Go get dressed."

"There's literally no place else we can go. What, is there some fancy new fiend club I'm not aware of?"

"Maybe. You'll find out when we get there."

Why is everything a surprise today? "I really wanted to stay in tonight and just relax and cuddle."

Her lower lip protrudes in a pout. "I promise you'll love it, Abby. It'll be amazing."

I can't say no to her. "Fine. Will you at least tell me what I should dress for? Are there gonna be people? Should I grab a hoodie?"

"Nope." She slaps my ass, pushing me toward the stairs. "Go throw on a cute dress or something. We're going on a date."

I haven't had the chance to do that in ages. It'll be nice to have a normal date with her. What can that even entail, though? I can't eat, and we can't go anywhere. Well, I guess she has something in mind. I climb the stairs and sort through every single outfit I have to find something I would be willing to be seen in. It takes a while.

CHAPTER NINETEEN

Elizabeth

Taking a wendigo someplace as a surprise is a lot harder than I was thinking it would be. She can barely fit in my car, and I know that even curled in the back, she can smell and hear every single thing in our path. There's almost no way she doesn't know where we're going. It's okay. She still doesn't know what I have planned.

I pull over in front of the University of Toronto and climb out. It takes Abby a moment to unfurl in such a way that she can escape. "There is no way on earth that I'm riding back."

"That's fine." I break into a smile I've been barely holding back.

"Why are we at our old school?"

"I'd like you to break us into this building."

Her eyes narrow, but I suppose she must trust me because she doesn't ask any questions. Maybe she's accepted that I'm hell-bent on making this a surprise, and nothing she does will change it. We walk through the building, the empty halls strangely silent. In my mind, they're always so crowded. Fortunately for her, the ceilings are high enough that she can stand to her full height, and she takes advantage of this fact. "I was stuffed back there like a sardine for over an hour."

"I know, honey, but I promise it was worth it."

"You could have told me to meet you at the University of Toronto."

"That would ruin the surprise," I grumble and lead on.

I think it's now that she finally realizes where we're heading. She stops waiting for me to lead and instead, approaches the door to the dance room. "This was your diabolical plan?"

Nodding vigorously, I gesture at the door.

She rolls her eyes and kicks it open. I feel a little bad doing all this damage to our alma mater. Maybe we should leave some money.

I set my messenger bag on the ground, shrug off my heavy winter coat, and begin rifling through the bag.

"I knew you had to be up to something. You've used the same purse since you were nineteen, and that's not it," she says.

"I assumed the 'it's a surprise' already suggested I was up to something. A purse would hardly change that."

She shrugs, then stares as I pulled out a Bluetooth speaker and my phone and set them on the counter. "You're joking."

"I told you. I'm giving us a real date."

"Liz—"

I put on an old-fashioned waltz. "I trust you still remember how? I thought I'd start off with something easy." I hold my hand out, beckoning her to join me.

"You know if I step on your toes this time, they might come off."

"Steel-toed boots."

"You think of everything." She laces her fingers with mine, careful not to cut me, and places her other hand on my shoulder. I rest my hand on her hip and lead her through a few practice steps. I'm really rusty. "I know how much you liked the class back in college. I thought it'd be fun."

A soft chuckle erupts from above my head. It's weird leading someone two feet taller than me. "I only signed up because you did. You were the one who was all into it. I just wanted to spend time with you, and if I'm being honest, to hold you like this."

I try to stare, managing to gape at her chin. "What do you

mean? You told me you loved it. I thought this would be really special."

Her grip tightens on me but loosens immediately. "I'm sorry. I do love it. I just love it because of you."

Damn it. "I thought this would be like the most romantic thing ever." I dance sulkily.

"It *is* romantic." We're starting to get back into the swing of things, our steps matching, my boots becoming less necessary, and the movements becoming so much more natural. I do my best to dip her, but it's quite a feat. She smiles, keeping herself aloft with the hand that had been on my shoulder. "It's the most romantic thing anyone's ever done for me. I didn't think I'd ever have a real date again."

That mollifies me a bit. She looks so beautiful. I focus again on the dance, leading her through two numbers. She smiles—her teeth showing without her even trying to hide them—swooping along beside me, her skirt flowing to the music. After the third song, she freezes. I can feel her staring. "I didn't say it was all waltzes."

Chuckling nervously, she resumes following my lead, our bodies closer now as we attempt to remember our old Latin dancing lessons. We salsa as best we can. By the second song, it's not coming as naturally as the waltz, but we do seem to be recalling the steps.

Once I've managed to relearn how to samba, I've worked up a bit of a sweat. I haven't danced in a while, and steel-toed boots are not the best footwear for it. Abigail, however, hasn't begun to slow. She seems as if she could go all night. I do my best to keep up with her. I don't want this to end.

I was a little worried that I wouldn't be able to get her to dance, that it would be too awkward or that it had been too long, so I included a few sillier songs at the end of the playlist. We make it through every song, so by the time we've finished "YMCA," "La Macarena," "The Chicken Dance," and "The Time Warp,"

I've finally run out of music, and I feel like I'm ready to collapse on the hardwood floor. "Damn wendigo stamina," I say as I do just that.

"You didn't seem to mind it the other night."

"Wendigo tongue stamina is excluded from all complaints."

She giggles, sitting down beside me. "Thank you, Liz. This has been perfect."

I manage to gather enough energy to lift my head off the ground and onto her thigh. "It's not over. There's more I want to do."

"And what's that?" That smile, uncovered, unashamed, and so very beautiful, manages to give me a second wind.

I force myself to my feet and extend a hand, helping her up. I know she doesn't need it, but I thought it'd be cute. "Let's go for a walk."

We head back outside, leaving a couple hundred to pay for the broken doors, and walk through the snow. I have to stop holding her hand and stuff mine in the pocket of my heavy coat. Toronto winter at three a.m. may look idyllic, but it's not the best time to go for a walk. I'll manage. It's worth it for her.

We see the park bench where we used to eat lunch during the summer and smoke pot back when we had roommates who weren't each other. We walk by the cafeteria where we ate every meal of our first year with our meal plans. We pass a thousand memories: classes, study groups, other romances and failures, helping each other through breakups—which was mostly her helping me—and the life we spent in our first years as adults, our first years alone and a whole half hour away from our parents. Looking at her, I can see that she's seeing the same things.

I lead her by our old dorm and spin her around so she can see the snow-covered landscape marked only by our footprints. We're right by the place where we first confessed our love for each other without a sign of another living soul having ever touched it. I reach into my bag and, with some effort, pull out a small canvas and an easel. "I grabbed some of your paints and stuff too. I'm sure these aren't the best conditions for it, but I thought maybe, since it's so nostalgic, you might want to paint it?" I offer it all to her, feeling completely ridiculous. I planned out this big, heart-wrenchingly romantic date, but in reality, it all seems so silly.

"I never really painted landscapes."

"Right. Yeah. I should've known that. I'm sorry." Just like I didn't know that she wasn't that into dancing. I'm ruining everything.

"But I'd love to try. This…" She gestures at the snowy grounds. "It's all so wonderful. I haven't been anywhere so human in such a long time. Aside from that issue with Sandra, at least. I love it. It's getting late, though, so I think just an outline, and I'll finish painting it at home. I don't want you to freeze."

I let out a sigh of relief. "Sure. That sounds amazing."

I stand there, watching as she's completely lost in her work. She's so cute when she's working. She keeps having to stop herself from biting her lip. I wonder how long it took for her to master that grip so she has such precise control of the brush without her claws getting in the way.

It only takes her half an hour before she looks up from the painting and smiles. "I got a little carried away, but that'll do for now. I covered all the important stuff. I can fill in the rest later."

I take a few pictures from a couple angles with my phone. "Will these help?"

"They might." She giggles, fingers wrapping around my forearm, gently tugging me to her. "Let's head home."

"Not quite yet. There was just one more thing I wanted to do."

Eyeing me suspiciously, she asks, "Yeah, and what's that?"

"Come on." I drag her along. We're almost there. Here. This is it, the exact spot. I point at a third-floor window. "That was our room our third year in college, right?"

She looks up, tilting her head and squinting. Fortunately, no one is looking back. "I think so."

"I remember looking out of it, right to this spot, whenever I was staring into space. I can still picture it perfectly, and even covered in snow, this is it."

"Okay?" She turns her gaze back to me as if trying to unravel whatever strange mysteries may be playing in my mind.

"Six years ago, right up there, we confessed our love for each other before leaving for winter break." I thought I'd be seeing her since we lived right by each other, so it wasn't the big dramatic gesture it sounds like so as much as asking out a cute girl, but I play it up. "So I wanted to do this here."

"Do what?"

I stick my hand in my pocket and come out with a small box, bending down on one knee. "Abigail Lester." I pop the black velvet case open, revealing the emerald ring. "Will you marry me?"

Her hand clasps over her mouth as she nods. "Oh my God! Of course, Liz! Of course I will." She pulls me from the ground, sweeping me into a kiss, her arms wrapping tight around me. I meet her lips, tasting her tongue, feeling her against me, running my hands down her back. She pulls back and nods again. "I can't believe it. I love you, Liz."

"I love you too." I slide the ring onto her finger, and she stares at it, her charcoal eyes alight with wonder.

"It's beautiful."

"Not as beautiful as you." I know it's cheesy, but now seems the perfect time for that kind of line. "My wife."

"Your fiancée," she retorts. "You're gonna have to actually follow through to make me your wife."

"Oh, I will. There's nothing I want more."

After we properly celebrate back home, we start working out the details. I can scarcely believe it. We're planning our wedding!

❖

"You're serious?" Sandra asks, dropping her menu on the table. I wait for her to insult Abby, call her a monster, any of the things she'd have done without question a couple months ago. "You're actually getting married? You?"

"No, I'm lying, I just proposed to the love of my life as some elaborate con for sex." Fuck, I wouldn't even blame me; the things she can do with that tongue. "Of course I'm marrying her. You've been telling me it'd happen since we were eighteen."

"Yeah, but that was back when you had feelings and treated women with respect."

"I treat Abby with respect." Does she really have to remind me of how awful I've been? "And I apologized to Carol. I've changed. I can actually be in a healthy relationship now. Especially if someone doesn't kidnap me."

She glares. "That was one time. You had a pattern, while I made a single mistake."

"Kidnapping is hardly a mistake."

"I thought she was abusing you."

"Well, she wasn't."

"I know that *now*." Folding her arms over her chest, she stares at the menu. I haven't gone out to eat in ages. It's kind of a nice novelty.

"Does that mean you don't want to be my maid of honor?" Abby and I talked about it earlier in the hypothetical. I am not looking forward to telling her about this.

Sandra's gaze flies back up to me, her eyes wide. "Wait, are you serious? I didn't think…after everything…we hardly even talk anymore."

"I know, but you were always the one trying to get us together, and I wouldn't have called her if you hadn't pushed me to." And I don't have anyone else I can ask. I haven't talked to any of my human friends in months, and Ashley is obviously going to be Abby's. "Please?"

"Of course I will." She clasps my hand. "I swear to you. I

will be the greatest maid of honor the world has ever known. You will want for nothing. Your wedding will go off without a hitch."

Maybe she can keep James in line. I had him renewing his credentials last week to make sure he could conduct our ceremony. He did manage to hook us up with this gorgeous chapel on the upper floor of the Community Center, and he's been working to renovate it with a few contractors. For an incubus, he's kind of terrible at lying, so I had to keep him away from Abby. I know I should've waited for her to say yes, but I wanted to make everything perfect for her. "Thank you. It might need it."

"When is it?"

"Well, we haven't finalized the date yet, but I was hoping for about two months from now. I'm already having the venue set up. I wanted to make sure that was out of the way so we could plan everything else."

She stares into my eyes, taking a deep breath. "Okay, one more important question. Can I bring Peter?"

I let out a sigh. "No. No, you cannot. You know this. You haven't told him about fiends, right?"

"Well, no."

"You and I will be the only humans there. He can't come."

"You hardly count as human."

I grin. "Thank you. That's so nice of you."

"My point exactly." She rolls her eyes, returning her attention to the menu. "Fine. I'll be the only normal person there. That's how much I love you, Liz. I'm willing to go into monster land just for your wedding."

"Sandra." My voice is firm, almost deadly. "What did I say?"

"Shit, I'm sorry, I forgot, I didn't mean anything by it. *Fiend* land."

"Better."

"Am I uninvited?"

Grumbling, I shake my head. "No. You're not."

"Good."

The waiter arrives, and she orders a prime rib dip. I get a steak and a glass of wine. We don't have a grill, and Abby doesn't drink. I've missed it. "So I was thinking about going shopping after this."

Just as I expected, she squeals, and her eyes light up. "For a wedding dress? Oh my God, I get to help, right? We have to pick out my dress too. This is so exciting!"

"I was planning on wearing a suit. I haven't worn a dress since college."

Her face falls, and she gapes at me, looking as if I told her she wasn't invited to Disney World. "You can't do this to me."

"It's *my* wedding." She sounds like Ashley. Straight girls, I swear.

"Yes, it's your *wedding*. You can't wear a suit. This is the day you've been dreaming of since you were a child. We have to find you the perfect dress. It'll be magical. You're going to love it. I promise. If you hate it, I'll pay for your tux."

I raise an eyebrow. "If you can't find a dress I love, you'll pay for my tux? That's the deal?" Free tux, yes!

"That's the deal."

"All right." I extend my hand. "You have yourself a bet."

She grins as she takes it. "So can we go now? I can get my sandwich in a doggy bag."

"No, I'm hungry."

"But dresses!"

"But steak."

She stays and looks at dresses on her phone the entire time. I guess it's a fair compromise. My steak is absolutely amazing. Perfectly seasoned and grilled, medium rare. Having to deal with my own culinary skills is the worst part about living so far from anything resembling a decent restaurant. I've missed food.

"Oh my God, look at this one." She almost knocks her uneaten sandwich onto the floor as she shoves her phone in my face.

I'm loath to admit it, but it's the most beautiful dress I've ever seen and would suit me perfectly. I grit my teeth and glower. "I love it."

"I thought you would. Oh my God, it's perfect for you. Abby is going to go crazy. Wait, will she actually? Like, if she sees your cleavage in this, is she going to eat everyone in the front row or something?"

"No, Sandra." She will love it, though. The nice swooping neckline to show me off, the somewhat excessive train, the hoop-skirt that'll make me look like some distressed Victorian maiden. I've seen some of the books she reads. She's going to lose her mind. "All right. I'll get it."

"Yes!" She sends me the link and finally starts eating.

"I don't know my measurements."

"We'll take them back at my place. Now finish your food so we can go."

"You've barely even started yours, and I'm almost done." I shove another bite of steak into my mouth. I hate how much I love that dress. It's so girly. I never dreamed of my wedding. I dreamed of spending my life with Abby. I didn't think this wedding was actually going to be such a big deal. Hell, we're having it where I work. It should be a cute little thing where we kiss in front of a handful of our friends and then I take her home and have my way with her. Why is it becoming such a thing? Maybe Ashley's possessed me. Can ghouls do that? It's the only logical explanation.

Looking up, I find that Sandra has finished her sandwich. I shouldn't be surprised. Sandwiches are the second most important thing to her after weddings. "There's a bridal shop nearby that has that exact dress. Let's see if their model fits, and we can take your measurements there, and we can pick out my bridesmaid dress. I've been thinking red. It's pretty standard, right? Besides, I look so good in it, so how could we *not* go with red?"

I wonder if red attracts vampires. "Fine, red, whatever you want. I don't care."

"You will. Come on, they close in two hours. Let's hurry."

I follow her, and we head to the little bridal shop.

❖

The dress fits. It'll need a few alterations, but it looks amazing. The modern sleeveless top with its swooping neckline shows off my biceps and my cleavage, as Sandra promised, but once it's taken in, it'll cling to my waist above the skirt. I'm not terribly out of shape, but I didn't expect any dress to look this good on me. A nice suit, on the other hand…well, I've already committed. I'm not sure I could imagine wearing anything but this dress. Its blend of old and new should be more jarring, more anachronistic, more off-putting in some way, but it comes together perfectly, and it's genuinely the first time I've ever liked how I look in a dress. It doesn't even clash with my short hair. My heavily emphasized biceps save that, giving it just the slightest bit of dapper on top of the mountains of femme the skirt and lace provide.

"Let me see," Sandra says.

I walk out of the changing room and twirl for her. "Happy?"

Her jaw drops. "Oh wow. This is the happiest moment of my life. You look so beautiful. Can I give you away? I mean, your parents aren't coming, right?"

I blink. I haven't thought about them in ages. Should I invite them? It seems like it'd be rude not to, but we're not exactly close, and they don't know about fiends. It would be weird.

"Liz? You there?"

"Sorry. I…" I blow out a breath. "I haven't talked to them in a while."

"Maybe you should call them? You don't have to invite them or anything, just let them know."

I nod. I wonder if the store would mind if I wore this for a little longer. It makes me feel more confident. "Yeah, I might as well. You pick out your dress, I'm going to do this while I still have the courage to."

She doesn't even try to insist that I look with her. It's a miracle.

The phone rings a few times before my mother picks up and asks in a concerned voice, "Liz? Are you okay? Do you need money?"

"I haven't borrowed money from you in years." I cover my mouth. I do not need to be yelling at my mother in the middle of a dress shop. It sounds too much like my childhood.

"Well, it's not Mother's Day or my birthday, so excuse me for being a little surprised."

I throw myself into a nearby chair. I hope I don't damage the dress. My head bangs on the wall as I try to make it through a single conversation with my mother. "Can't I call you without it being a big thing?"

"Well, I'm sure you could, but it would certainly be a first."

"Fine, I guess it's a big thing."

"Are you okay?" She sounds panicked. "Did you get an STD? Are you in the hospital?"

How big a slut do they think I am? Okay, I might deserve it. I'm just amazed she knows lesbians can get STDs. "No, Abby and I are getting married."

There's only silence on the other end of the line.

"Mom?"

"Could you repeat that?"

Rolling my eyes, I say, "Abby and I are getting married."

"So you finally found her again?"

"Yeah, it's a long story."

"Well, when's the wedding? I can't wait."

"We're eloping, Mom. It's just gonna be her, me, and a judge." I was always going to lie to keep her away no matter what happened, but I actually have a good excuse now that it's happening for real.

She snorts. "Fine, we'll just send you a gift in the mail. I can't believe I won't get to see my own daughter's wedding. Will you at least send me photos?"

"Sure." Another lie, but it'll get her off the phone quicker. "Can I talk to Dad? I want to tell him too."

"Oh, all right. I just wanted to ask you about everything. How long have you two been back together? What happened with her? Will you at least tell her that I'm mad at her for sending you into a crippling depression from which you're only now recovering?"

"No. I will not say that. That sounds terrible. Please give me to Dad."

With a derisive snort, she hands me over. "It's your daughter. She has big news that she wants to tell you."

"Thank you, Catalina." Static crackles over the phone as he takes it from her. "Hey, kiddo."

I look at my reflection again. I really do look amazing in this dress. "Hey, Dad."

"So what's the big news?"

"Well, I finally got together with Abby a few months ago, and now we're getting married. That's all. You have a good day."

"Wait just a second. So you two are really doing it?"

I've told them all I wanted to say. Can't I just hang up now? "Yep."

"You know it's not really marriage."

"Nope, totally is, more real than yours."

"And just what do you mean by that?"

I groan. "Nothing, Dad. Have a good day. I'm gonna go." He was actually the easier parent to talk to. He wasn't even bothered by my being gay, just the marriage thing. My mom was the one who freaked out.

"All right. I love you."

"You too, tell the same to Mom. Bye." I hang up. There, at

least that's over with, and they don't know where the wedding is, so they can't try to crash it.

"How do I look?"

I turn to find Sandra in a floor-length red dress that clings to the edge of immodesty. "I know it's a bit much, but you gotta admit, I look good in it."

"Trying to pick up a new guy? I'm sure you could find someone pretty interesting."

"I'm sticking with my own species, thanks."

I give her another look. She does look pretty good. Though not quite as good as me. I think that's the general rule for weddings. "Fine, whatever, get it. I really don't care."

She kneels in front of me, places her hand on my chin, and tilts my head up. "What happened? Did the phone call go okay?"

"It went like I figured it would. I'm not that upset. I just am not capable of putting any more emotion into dresses than I already have today."

She pats my back as she stands. "I understand. Go change back into that T-shirt and jeans. I'll pay for the dresses."

I stare up at her, utterly confused. "But I lost the bet."

"Yeah, and I talked you into dealing with your parents. It'll count as my wedding present. Go get changed, and I'll meet you at the front."

I'll talk to my parents again if it means she'll spend another few grand on me. "Thank you." I change back and feel a lot more like myself.

Once I make it back out to the front, she's finished paying. The alterations will be done within the week, which gives us more than enough time for the wedding. I lean against her shoulder as we walk out. It was a long day and so far out of my comfort zone, but it's worth it if it means I'm marrying Abby. With her, even a wedding is fun.

CHAPTER TWENTY

Abigail

"She proposed! Ashley, I can't believe it. I never thought it would really happen. I'm gonna get married." I stare at the ring. I've barely been able to take my eyes off it since she placed it on me. "Can you believe it?"

Ashley bares her teeth. "Yeah. I had no idea. That's great. The ring is so pretty. It's even prettier than a diamond ring would be." She pokes it with her finger.

That's not like her. She thinks pretty much all other gemstones are tacky. "Really? I mean, I certainly think so. Plus, it matches my necklace." I wish it still matched my eyes. "But what's going on with you?"

"I have no idea what you're talking about. I think it's a very nice ring. Not everything has to be diamonds, and I adore the double design. They look amazing together. I love it." She leans over, almost falling off her bed as I show it off.

That much makes sense. She loves ornate rings. When I borrowed her computer, half of her bookmarks were wedding and engagement pages. I didn't know there were that many different designs of rings. There was also a lot of porn, but I'd expected that. "Ashley, I appreciate that you're putting me first for once, but you're acting really suspicious."

Her eyes widen. "No, I'm not. I don't know what you're talking about."

I glare.

"Okay, fine. She told me, and I helped her pick out the ring. It really is beautiful, though. I tried to talk her into a diamond, but you always wear that necklace, and it looks so pretty on you, and she's totally right, and I love it. Please don't hate me for not telling you."

So that's why she was talking about Liz and me getting married at group. I can be so dumb. I pull her to me, hugging the life out of an undead girl. "Thank you."

"What?" She pushes against my chest, giving her enough space to stare. "Why?"

"I'm glad the two of you are finally becoming friends. She hasn't tried to steal you away as her maid of honor, has she?"

Her awkward smile finally fades into a genuine one. "No. I saved that for you."

"Will you?"

"Do I get a ring?"

"No. That doesn't even make sense."

With a big sigh and her lower lip protruding in the most pitiful pout imaginable, she leans back against her bedpost. "I guess I'll still do it. Only because I love you."

"You can bring your gargoyle friend."

Her face lights up, and she pulls herself forward. "I can? But we just met. I don't know if he'll even want to come. Do you think he'll want to come?"

"Who wouldn't want to go to a wedding with you? Have you two had your date yet?"

Fidgeting with her blanket, she looks away. "I haven't had the nerve to call him."

My mouth drops. "What do you mean you haven't called him? You were freaking out about him giving you his number. It's been four days. What are you doing? You're wasting time. Do you not want to have a date to take to my wedding?"

"No, I do." She lets out a deep sigh, her eyes turning back to me. "I'm just scared. What if he doesn't want me? I mean, why would he? I'm…" She gestures at her body. "Just look at me. Who could possibly want this?"

Planting a light kiss on her forehead, I place my hands on her shoulders. "Any guy would be lucky to have you. Now, call him. When you're done, we can go meet Liz at the Community Center."

"Will you call?"

"I'm not the one talking to him."

"Please." She squeezes my forearm, panic clear in her eyes. "Just call and put it on speaker? You don't need to say anything. I just need you to do it for me."

With an exasperated groan, I take her phone and place the call. I set the phone on the bed and sit on the coffin.

"Hello?" a gruff voice says.

"Hi." Her voice is shaky, tentative, not at all the perky girl I know. "It's Ashley. The girl you bought the scone for on Wednesday."

"Oh. Hi, Ashley. I was starting to worry you wouldn't call."

"You know how it is. A girl has to have some mystery about her, right? I can't just give it all away immediately." Of course not. She has to wait until the first date for that. "So I was wondering if maybe you'd like to meet up tomorrow? I'd say today, but I have some important things I have to do with my best friend."

"Sounds exciting. I would love to see you tomorrow. I'm sorry about the scone. I heard you were in that weird group thing. I swear I didn't know. I think it's cool."

Her smile takes up her entire face. "Thank you. Yeah, I've been in it for ages. I probably shouldn't have had that scone, but it's not your fault. You were just being a gentleman."

"That's all I try to do."

"Well, if you are such a gentleman, pick me up at my place. Tomorrow? Around one?"

"It's a date."

She puts her hand to her mouth to cover her squeal. "I'll see you then."

"I can't wait."

She clicks the end call button and throws her arms around me, squealing at the top of her lungs. My ears ring for a solid minute before I can understand what she's saying.

It's just more squealing. "Oh my God, I'm so excited. I have a real date. With a real live man. It's going to be amazing!"

I grin, gently rubbing her back. "I'm proud of you."

"Thank you." She clings tighter to me. "I couldn't have done it without you. Thank you so much."

"Anytime. Now, can we get going? I told Liz we'd be there at eleven."

"Yeah. Of course." One last squeeze and she releases me. "Just let me text him my address and throw on something cute just in case. You never know, he might be there."

❖

Liz wraps her arms around me. "My fiancée," she murmurs, staring at my ring.

"Should I buy you one so you'll stop ogling mine all the time?" I run my fingers through her hair, holding her close as she holds my hand before her.

"I wouldn't say no, but you can save it for the wedding. So did you ask her?" She gestures toward Ashley.

Ashley squeals and joins in the hug. She squeals a lot. "She did. I'm so excited for you two. I might even have a plus one to bring. She told me how it went. It sounds like it was just as you planned. You two are the cutest couple. You're like my goals."

Liz pecks my neck quickly before pulling away. "I have another surprise for you. Come with me."

We follow her. I didn't even know there was a second floor. I have to practically walk on all fours to avoid hitting my head on the stairs. I grumble as they lead the way. I can't believe Liz wanted to be a wendigo. There is literally no good part.

Once we arrive at the second-floor landing, I can finally

stand straight again. Liz rushes through the door. Ashley and I catch up without issue and head toward loud hammering coming down the hall. How did I miss that noise until now? How good is the insulation here? Liz stops in front of the door where all the noises are coming from. There's a stained-glass window above it. "What's this?" I ask.

"I found a venue for our wedding."

"You want to marry a corpse in a church?" I know it's not the nicest thing to say about myself, but it seems appropriate.

"You're not a corpse, Abby. You're going to be my wife. I figured we'd get rid of some of the religious iconography, since it makes a few of the fiends uncomfortable, but it's really beautiful, and I wanted to give you a proper normal wedding. I'm sorry. I know I should've asked first. We can pick someplace else if you want. I've just been exploring the building between appointments, and I thought it'd be perfect."

She opens the door, and I peer through. There're half a dozen people working away restoring it. Including James. Is this where he's been all week? "How the hell did you set all of this up?"

"I'm very persuasive."

"So money, then?"

"Not for James, actually. He just wanted to do a nice thing for you. He said he still felt bad about something and felt like he owed you. He also said that he's an ordained minister and wants to officiate our wedding. If that's okay with you?" She smiles wide as if pleading with me to be okay with all of this.

"What's he a minister of? Are we getting married through some sex cult?"

"I have to admit, I was a little scared to ask."

I can't blame her. "All right, let's take a look around. We'll see if it's as perfect as you say it is."

We all head inside. I barely have to duck under the door frame. Within, I find James, four fiends I barely know, and Sandra. I don't think my brain can process her being here. I'm just going to assume it's that crazy kitsune. That makes so much more sense than her being in the fucking Community Center. "Please tell me you didn't tell Sandra about this place. There's no way that's a good idea."

"She's going to be my maid of honor. You said it was okay. She kinda had to know."

"We said we were still considering it," I scream, as quietly as one can scream. She absolutely heard me.

Liz sighs and stares at her feet, making the exact same look she made when her mom caught us stealing cookies that she'd made for a bake sale. "I'm sorry. I meant to tell you earlier, but I wanted this all to be a surprise, and I guess it slipped my mind."

I groan, and almost everyone in the room steps back. But Liz doesn't. Even when I'm irritated with her, she's still not afraid of me. She trusts me. I should trust her. "Are you sure about this? I'm sure Ashley would be more than happy to go off the wagon again if it stops Sandra from spreading the word about this place."

"She's my best friend."

"After what she—"

"Please, Abby?" She pouts, staring pitifully up at me. I already wasn't going to say no, but I sure as hell can't now.

With a heavy sigh and a shrug, I nod. "Okay. Fine. She can stay in the wedding, and no one eats her. So long as she keeps it a secret."

"She'll do that."

I hear Sandra gulp. I turn to her and act as if we weren't discussing murdering her. "Hi, Sandra." Kidnap any girls lately?

Another gulp and a nervous chuckle. She hesitantly approaches me, taking a half step back before closing the last couple feet. "Hi, Abby. The killing me thing was a joke, right? Please say it was a joke."

"Of course." I offer a smile that I'm certain shows off my fangs.

She looks relieved. And scared. "Well, if you're done with

that, we still need to figure out dresses for you two. We already have ours paid for."

I stare at Liz, looking her up and down. "You're going to wear a dress? I haven't seen you in one in ages. I can't picture it."

"Well, you'll get to see it soon enough." She tugs on my skirt, slipping closer. I still feel so weird wearing one. I wasn't exactly femme to start with, but she makes me feel pretty in them. "I can't wait to see you in yours."

Well, I guess that's settled. I have to get a wedding dress. I hadn't even thought about it. "So we're actually having a big ceremony?"

Her eyes widen. "We don't have to. I'm fine with the four of us. I just thought it'd be nice. Shit, I'm doing it again, aren't I? I'm just making all of the decisions for us and jumping into things and making assumptions without bothering to check with you. We're getting married. I thought I was better now."

"Do you want a big wedding?"

She shrugs. "I don't know. Sandra wants a big wedding." She drags Sandra in front of her.

"Liz, I'm serious."

"I want to marry you. If there are a billion people there, that's fine, and it's also fine if there's no one there. What do *you* want? I've made too many decisions without you. You decide."

I look around, taking in the space. I picture us in front of a crowd of everyone we know, pledging our love to each other. "I would sort of like to be able to invite everyone from my group. I mean, they're practically family."

"Well, I don't want to invite my family, but I'm happy to join yours. So you want people here, then?"

I sigh, hunching my shoulders and in general failing to be any smaller than a giant monster can be. "I think so. It doesn't need to be huge or anything, maybe twenty people."

"That sounds perfect."

"You're going to say, 'because you'll be there,' aren't you?"

She blushes. "Of course not. That would be corny."

"You'd never be corny." I kiss her cheek. "So, Sandra, and now that I think about it, Ashley, I assume you have a billion dress ideas already? Ashley, don't lie. I've seen your bookmarks."

We spend a few hours fixing up the chapel and going over wedding ideas. Ashley and Sandra seem set on a particular flower while Liz and I both want a different kind. For some reason, this is a standstill. You'd think our wishes would win out, but they're so much more passionate about it. It's flowers. It is literally the least important detail except for the streamers. They also argue about the streamers. Liz drags me aside while they're bickering, pulling me into a kiss before whispering, "Should we just let them plan it?"

"Is that an option?"

She blows out a breath. "Maybe, but they also might make everything super tacky, over the top, and straight out of a romcom."

"There are good romcoms."

She rolls her eyes. "Fine. So, we'll let them plan it, then."

I seriously consider the idea. "It's *our* wedding."

"Do they know that?"

"Almost certainly not."

"Then let's go remind them."

We let them keep the streamers but insist on our flowers, and we go back to planning. We have time, but this will take a lot of work if we're really going as all-out as we seem to be. I was always rather focused on who I was marrying, but I'd be lying if I said there wasn't a part of me that wanted something like this. At the time I was fantasizing about it, I probably wanted the monsters too. Little kid me will be sad that Dracula isn't coming.

The planning takes so long that Sandra has to call in sick for work. I'll admit, that does give me a certain satisfaction, though not as much as if she'd gone to work. I've still got a bit of a grudge.

There's plenty more to be done, but we manage to make a good dent, and the venue is looking much more presentable. We have time.

Our wedding is going to be perfect.

CHAPTER TWENTY-ONE

Elizabeth

"You still haven't seen her dress, right?" Sandra asks, attempting to do something—God knows what—with my hair in my makeshift dressing room that was once a beauty salon. "You are going to love it. Just try not to rip it off her in the middle of the church, okay? That's kind of frowned upon. Unless that's normal for fiends. Do fiends have big orgies at their weddings? I guess if I'm not allowed to tell Peter anyway, then he won't know if I have a little fun."

"What happened to you thinking being with a fiend is weird?" I ask, gritting my teeth as she tugs at my hair. It's too short for this. There is nothing fancy she can do. What is she trying?

"I didn't know how sexy some of them were. Just because you went for the terrifying monster type—"

"I don't care that it's in half an hour, I will still uninvite your ass."

"I'm just saying, that preacher is pretty good-looking. You know if he swings my way?" Her reflection grins. It had taken her so long to clean that mirror enough that we could see anything in it.

"He swings every way, to my knowledge, but he's celibate."

"He's Catholic?"

I shrug, blowing out a puff of air. "Sure. Let's go with that." I mean, I've heard him mention things he's done with a few popes.

That has to make him at least an honorary Catholic. Though a few of the stories may have canceled it out.

"Damn. He's really cute. What a waste."

"I think Peter would disagree."

She yanks on some hair wrapped around her brush far harder than she has any need to. "I have no idea what you're talking about."

What she'd said earlier finally hits me. "Wait. You saw Abby in her dress. Does she look amazing? Oh, I can't wait to see it. I mean, I know she can wear anything, and I'd still think that she's the most beautiful woman in the world, but just the thought of her dressed up all fancy, in my arms as we dance, kissing me after we say our vows. Holy shit, Sandra. I think I might be gay."

The brushing stops as she erupts into laughter and takes a good long while to collect herself. "I did not see that coming."

"I'm sorry you had to find out this way. I hope it doesn't make things weird between us."

"I think I'll live. As long as you don't try anything in the next"—she checks her phone—"twenty-eight minutes before you're a married woman."

"I think I can keep my hands to myself."

"Good. And yes, I saw her dress. Ashley needed my help with something. Now there's a credit to her species. I didn't know they came as sweet and genuine as her." Of course they like each other. It's like looking in a mirror. "I mean, I'm not into fiends or women, but even I felt something seeing her in that dress."

"Ashley or Abby?"

She blushes. Both? Sputtering, she replies, "I already said I'm not into fiends, but I meant Abby. That dress really suits her. I wish you could've seen the old her in it."

"I don't need the old her. I love *this* her just fine. I'm still sad about all the time we lost, but she's not a different person no matter how different she may look. She's the same woman I've always loved. And you already said you were into fiends, like, not even two minutes ago."

Grumbling, she returns her focus to my hair. "Well, I'm not into girl fiends."

"Aww, but it'd be cute. You and Ashley could straight at each other. That's how it works, right? When two straight girls develop a crush on each other? I mean, it's totally natural."

I see her rolling her eyes in the mirror. "She and I both have boyfriends, and if I was ever going to experiment, it sure as hell wouldn't be with her."

"Speciesist."

Another eye roll. "So if you don't still wish she was the old her, why do you keep buying her things the color of her old eyes?"

I attempt to face her to chew her out, but my hair stays where it is and yanks me back into place. "Because I know *she* still wishes it. I suggested that she paint our pictures as we both are now, but she wasn't willing, the same way she hates having a mirror."

"I can hardly blame her. I sure wouldn't."

"I love how she looks. She's perfect. Until she can see the same, I thought it'd be nice for her to have a reminder of who she was. I know sometimes she's scared that she's just a monster, fiend..." I am not having Sandra be the one to correct me. "That she just has the memories of the girl whose body it was, and she's only possessing it. Sometimes, I think she's scared that even that's not true, and that this is all she's ever been. I hear how much she frets in her dreams, how she shakes. I know they're not all hunting dreams. I won't let her forget that she's still a person."

"Is she, though?"

I glare at her reflection, not wanting a repeat of last time. "Of course she is."

"A person who never ages, is unkillable, looks like a giant zombie, and has a constant craving for human flesh?"

"Yes." She turns away from the mirror, letting go of my hair. "She is. Should I be looking for a new maid of honor last minute? If you still can't support us, I don't want you here."

She turns back, her eyes wide. Even in the reflection, I can make out tears. "No, Liz. I'm sorry. I'm still having some trouble getting used to the whole thing. All I've ever wanted for you two was, well, this." She gestures at my dress, the chapel next door, and all around. "I want your happily ever after. You both deserve it."

"Then why do you keep doing this?"

She sighs, squeezing a few strands of my hair. "It's scary. I don't know how you take it. I lived my whole life knowing full well that all of this was make-believe, and now my best friend is marrying a wendigo. Even if that wendigo is the love of her life, for a normal person, it's a pretty terrifying prospect. Every movie I've ever seen has taught me that the monster trying to take away the girl has to be stopped, not that they need help picking out a wedding dress. Which I did, and it turned out perfect. I'm managing. I'm sorry. And before you say it, I know it's fiend. I messed up."

I allow a faint smile. She *is* learning. "Do you promise you haven't reported this place or our wedding to some *Men in Black* sort of agency that's going to break in and hunt everyone down?" I don't think it's realistic, but she's been a bit of a bigot, and I'm still having a lot of trouble shaking the fear. Though no one here will tell me if such an organization exists. It would be really nice to know.

"Are there really men in black?"

I shrug. "No one will tell me."

"Well, I sure as hell wouldn't know how to contact them."

"*And* wouldn't do it?" I gesture for her to keep going.

"And I would never do anything that could ruin my only chance at being maid of honor. Come on. I would at least wait."

She has a point. "All right. Fine. I believe you. Just don't do it in the future, either."

"I won't."

"Okay. Back to torturing me, then."

She tugs at my hair, attempting to wrangle it. "Why do you do this to your hair?"

"What?"

"I don't understand how it can be both this short and knotted, but you don't even condition it. What do you expect me to do with this?" Her hands jab at my lifeless hair, emphasizing the fruitlessness of her endeavors.

"I didn't ask you to do anything. This was all your idea."

"Well, still. Look at what you've done to your poor hair, girl. Do you know how much work it takes for me to get this? Weaves aren't cheap or easy, and your hair was naturally perfect, but you had to chop it all off and destroy it with shitty hair dye."

I shrug. "I don't worry that much about it. That's why I keep it short in the first place."

With a dramatic sigh, she grabs some hair spray and a comb. "Well, then, I'm at least going to style it."

"You are not making me look like a frat boy."

"But it's your wedding day. I have to do *something* with it."

"You have hair. Do something with your own hair. I've humored you for long enough."

Her reflection glares at me. "You are impossible."

"I don't want to look like a douche at my own wedding. I also don't want to be late."

"You have plenty of time." She checks her phone again. "You have twenty-three minutes, and you're already dressed. I wanted to make you look extra pretty."

"If I agree to let you do my makeup, will you give it a rest?"

She pauses, staring at the mirror, then with another dramatic sigh, she sets the tools down and grabs a small bag from her purse. "Fine. I am going to make you look beautiful whether you like it or not."

"As long as Abby likes it, I'm fine." She spins me around, pinching my chin between her thumb and forefinger as she examines my face. My new nocturnal schedule has left me a good bit paler than I used to be, so I don't have anything we could use. I'm doubting any of her makeup will match me, but whatever. It's a special day; she can have her fun. I'll have my own fun tonight. "Will you get it over with?"

"Don't rush an artist." She hisses, a fleck of spit hitting my cheek. "I will accept nothing less than perfection on this day. I am so glad I found a good match for your skin tone." So she actually bought some. Why am I surprised?

"Well, 'this day' starts in twenty minutes, and I've seen you take over an hour to do your makeup. I still don't understand how that's remotely possible. Will you please just make a decision and get to work? I don't have the patience for this."

"Fine." She draws a few tools from the bag and begins her arduous process. I sit still, cooperate, and do my absolute best to tolerate her.

Okay. Maybe it was worth it. My reflection looks like a whole new woman. Gone are the bags and flaws. I'd expected that—even I can manage that—but I have a new shine, almost as if I've been brought back to life. I'm not sure Abby will be able to wait until the end to kiss me. I wouldn't mind messing up the service for that. I am already tempted to pull her into my arms the second we reach the altar.

❖

It's time. I take a deep breath, staring at my reflection. Wow, I am not used to seeing myself with makeup. I can barely believe that's me. I give Sandra a tight hug. I don't know why I'm scared. I guess since I've spent the last six years avoiding commitment, no matter how badly I want it now, there's still a part of me that's terrified.

I think of Abby, of her smile, the coolness of her touch, her soft fur, and her eyes that could almost burn a hole in me. I love her. I'm ready for this. There are just a lot of people here, and it's such a big thing. Another breath, a gulp, and a reassuring squeeze on my shoulder from Sandra, and I find my feet moving almost on their own. Toward the chapel, toward Abby. I'm ready.

We agreed not to do any "Here Comes the Bride" nonsense. James walked us through everything a few weeks before the rehearsal. We're not two houses joining together—this isn't some arranged marriage—we're two people who love each other and already share every aspect of our lives and just want to make it official. We'll stand there, together, in front of everyone, before the ceremony even begins.

James did want us to have a flower girl and ring bearer to lash so that their scars would be a permanent record of our wedding, but we decided to just go with the paperwork. He's old fashioned, I get it; it's just a little creepy.

Oh. Holy fucking shit. I enter the chapel, approaching the altar, and find Abby in her gown, waiting for me, and I forget to breathe. I've never seen anything so beautiful. It's a more archaic, Victorian design than mine with frills and lace, long sleeves all the way down her massive arms, a hoop skirt that puts mine to shame and pools at her feet, a corset, and a veil. I know I don't want to encourage her hiding her body so much, but she looks so beautiful. I did not know she was going to have a veil. So much for my kissing her in the middle of the wedding.

The guests are still filing in. I have time. I take a step toward her, reaching for her veil. She could stop me, but she doesn't. The veil lifts, revealing the face I'm going to be looking at for the rest of my life. "I love you," I whisper, placing my hand on the back of her neck and pulling her to me for a quick kiss.

She smirks as she pulls away, raising to her full height as if to make sure we don't do that again. "I love you too."

James rolls his eyes. "Can you two seriously not wait the few minutes until I tell you to kiss the brides?"

"Nope," we both say.

He lets out a low groan. "I manage to hold off just fine. I believe in you. Keep it in your pants for a little longer."

I suppose rubbing it in the face of a celibate incubus is a

little mean. We both keep our mouths shut and off each other, waiting for the rest of the audience to find their seats.

Ashley snickers. Her dress matches Sandra's. I guess they coordinated. As a massive being with wings finds his spot, he waves to her, and she blushes, waving back. That must be the guy she mentioned. I feel a little bad for Sandra not getting to bring her boyfriend, but I'm already hesitant enough to let her be here after everything she's done. He doesn't get any leeway.

There are almost thirty people watching. Most are seated, though a few either aren't bipedal enough or are too large for the chairs. I swear we didn't invite this many people. There were a lot of plus-ones.

The last few find seats, and without any sort of signal, the room goes quiet. Every eye turns to James.

"Well, apparently, these two crazy kids decided to trust me with this, God knows why." Warm laughter erupts through the large room. "They made me promise no human sacrifices, no orgies, and no pots of blood, so I guess I'll go with something simple." He looks between the two of us, a soft smile on his lips. It's too genuine. It doesn't suit him. "I have never, in my thousands of years, seen any two people love each other more than Elizabeth Rosseau and Abigail Lester. I include myself there. I know what we all think when we look at them, Stop making the rest of us look bad." Doesn't this stuff usually wait for the reception? I guess when it's the officiator making the jokes, they have the stage, and James certainly seems to want to take it. Although, wow, that was a really tame joke for him. Is he following a script? "I believe they both have vows they want to read, so I'll let them get to that."

Abby clears her throat. She was always a nervous public speaker, and it's only gotten worse since she became a wendigo. You'd think speaking in front of her diet group all the time would have helped, but she almost ran away when she had to speak during rehearsal. "I can't recall a point in my life before I knew you, Elizabeth, but even if I did, my life wouldn't have begun until then. You've been my best friend since we were three. We did everything together. I don't know when my feelings moved from friendship to love or if they were there all along, but because of you, I never questioned my sexuality, and until I ran away, I never had to worry that I would be alone. No matter what, I knew we'd be together our whole lives, whatever type of relationship that ended up being." I smile, urging her to keep going. She gulps but manages to continue. "You've always been the one to get me through every hurdle in my life. Without you, it was like I was only half living." All of the undead members of the audience laugh, and I swear I hear Sandra chuckle. "Liz, you're my everything. I've been waiting for this moment my whole life, yearning for the chance to call you my wife." I tear up, and her hand flies up under her veil to wipe away a tear. "So, I guess I should shut up so we can get to that."

I resist the urge to stick my tongue out. Way to undermine your big dramatic speech. I sniffle. Fuck, that really got to me. "I wish she would've told me any of that back when we were younger," I say to the array of fiends before us, gaining another laugh. "I know exactly when I fell in love with you, Abby. It was the minute I first saw you. I wasn't quite aware enough that it was an option for me to act on, then, but it's why I wasn't able to bring myself to go a day without having you by my side. You've been the most important part of my life since I was a little girl. Abigail, I hope you know by now that I would've helped you get through anything, and you never have to hide from me. You're my world. I love you with every fiber of my being, and I always have and always will. The only life that I can even imagine is one spent with you. I've been terrified of any sort of commitment for so long, but with you, I just want to declare our love to the whole world. Now, let's do just that." I turn to James. At least the end of my speech was a little less tonally inconsistent.

James pats us each on our shoulders, which requires a bit of a stretch for Abby. "I don't have it in me to delay the big kiss any longer. By the power vested in me by the province of Ontario and

Hell, I pronounce you wife and wife because you two weirdos are monogamous for some reason. I pronounce you Abigail and Elizabeth Rosseau-Lester. Both of you, kiss the bride."

Abigail swoops me into her arms, holding me, gently guiding my lips to hers, and kissing me for the whole world to see. I melt despite the cold of her touch. This is all I've wanted.

Abby is finally my wife.

Chapter Twenty-Two

Abigail

On the dance floor, I hold my wife in my arms as the music starts, our hips swaying in perfect sync. I want to say it a million times: my wife. This is all I've ever wanted. Of course, there is a certain issue with having a siren as your wedding musician.

Liz starts to flit away, missing a step of our dance as she turns toward the band.

"Honey." My voice is singsong all on its own. I wonder if I could imitate Caris's voice along with its effects, but I want it to be my voice she responds to.

She does. She turns back. "Sorry." Her eyes meet mine. "I'm here. I love you."

Caris is still singing. I can't believe that worked. She really is head-over-heels for me. I twirl her and hold her mere inches from the ground. We've been practicing a lot…in the woods. We didn't break into the school again.

"I thought I was the one leading."

"You got distracted."

With a smirk, she takes over and actually manages to twirl me. We had to put so much work into figuring out how to manage that despite our size difference. "I'm not distracted anymore." She pulls herself flush against me as the music picks up pace, leading me through the song, trying out every applicable move we've practiced.

When the song is done, a few people applaud, and I feel arms wrap around me. "That was amazing." I'd recognize that squeal anywhere.

"Thank you, Ashley."

"You two are such a cute couple. So now that you've had your dance, is the floor open for business?"

"You want to go grab your guy?"

"Of course." I can hear the grin in her voice.

I pull away and smile. "Get to it."

When I turn back, I look for Liz, but she took the cue to talk to her own maid of honor. And have another slice of cake. It sucks that I can't even have my own wedding cake without throwing up. It made cutting the slice for her kind of weird, but the moment was too cute to pass up. At least it's beautiful. We went with a three-layer chocolate cake, made by our favorite satyr bakers. I take the moment to find James. "Thank you. As hokey as that was, it was a wonderful ceremony."

"Just because I think human weddings are weird doesn't mean I don't know how to handle them." He holds a forkful of cake. Incubi are so lucky. "I was happy to help. You two are great for each other. It's almost like you're a whole new person."

"More like I'm my old self."

"Either way, you seem to be happier."

"I really am." I lean against the table, watching my wife talk to her former kidnapper. It's been a crazy year. "I can't believe it all really happened."

"I can."

"What, you called all this?"

"Yeah, Ashley owes me a hundred bucks. I bet her last year that you'd be married within a year."

I shrug. I don't care enough to deal with his bullshit right now. "I'm gonna go grab my wife."

"Have fun."

I join her and Sandra at the cake. "Everything all right?"

Liz clings to my arm and leans against me. "Everything is wonderful."

Sandra smiles. "Can I take a picture?"

"I—"

Liz looks up at me pleadingly. I guess I can put up with it. "Okay."

We line up in front of the cake with me on my knees so we can both be in the photo. Sandra takes a bunch of pictures with the two of us posed differently each time. For the last one, Liz is sitting in my lap and kissing me. Maybe I'll actually be able to handle seeing these pictures. Even I have to admit, this dress looks pretty good on me. Maybe those giant spiders really were descended from Arachne because they sure know how to sew.

"Want to dance some more?" Liz asks.

There are a few things I'd rather be doing right now, but a little more dancing sounds pretty fun. "Of course. After you."

She smirks and takes my hand, dragging me back to the floor. Nora's dance moves have almost caused an earthquake, and she's being led away by that anthropophage I never caught the name of when we start. Feeling Liz pressed against me, her warmth, her presence, is enough to make me both quite happy that I agreed to more dancing and all the more desperate to take her back home.

Caris's voice is very versatile, and we dance our way through an even larger assortment than the night Liz proposed. After the last song, as the reception is starting to come to a close, I carry her back to her chair, her dress sticking to her body with sweat. She hooks her arm around my waist as I set her down. "How are you still fine? You're wearing a corset. There is no way you should be able to put up with all of this better than me."

"Wendigo." Okay, there's one advantage.

She fans herself. "Grab me a drink?"

The satyr couple is cleaning up, but there's still a bit of champagne left. I grab a glass and bring it back. "Your champagne, madam?" I offer, showing my teeth in a goofy grin. With her, I don't even want to hide.

She swallows it in a single swig. "Well, I'm feeling a bit better. Want to take me home and wear me out all over again?"

"You read my mind."

She throws her arms around my neck, letting me swoop her back up in my arms. "Should I hang some cans from you with a Just Married sign?"

With a heavy sigh, I glare. "You're not drunk enough for that joke."

"Get me more champagne?"

"Later." I take her home. We have our whole honeymoon to enjoy. She's taking the next week off from her appointments, and we have no intention of leaving our cabin for anything in the world.

❖

Liz sits across from me, some roast chicken and corn on her plate. My stomach growls. I can handle it. "You sure you're okay?" she asks.

"I'm all right." It's always meat that's the issue. I can't eat it, either, but it reminds me of the one thing I *can* eat. I see Liz, knife in her hand, looking terrified and running away, and I know there's no way I could ever eat human again. I shake my head, and the knife in her hand is just for her dinner, not for me. Still silver, though, but killing me with that thing would be a hell of a lot more work than it's worth.

"You don't have to watch me eat if you can't handle it, Abby."

I shake my head. "I don't want to miss a second of my new life with my wife."

"Well, as long as you're rhyming, you must be fine. Just, if it ever is too much, I'd rather be able to continue spending time with my wife than have her go off on another human-eating spree."

"That was *one time*."

She snickers and smiles, a bit of rosemary on her lips. "One time for four years. I want you here, every day, with me."

"I'll take care of myself."

"You better." She stabs the chicken, and my stomach does its best to continue reminding me of just how hungry I always am.

"Okay, I'll be in the living room."

"I love you."

"I love you too." I throw myself onto the couch, the momentum moving it a few inches. I can still smell the chicken, but that's nowhere near as bad as having to watch her eat it. Some days, it doesn't get to me; other times, it really does. I turn on the TV. We have satellite now, and solar panels, so we don't have to go through so much fuel. I watch some mindless crime drama while I wait for her to finish up. For some reason, the dead bodies in the show don't make me at all hungry.

Before long, I hear her rinsing her plate, and she hurries over to the couch. I move my feet, letting her plop down and burrow between my legs to lay her head on my chest. "I'm sorry."

I run my fingers through her hair. "It's okay. It's just a bad day for it, apparently."

She nuzzles me, fingers winding their way around to the hand on the remote.

"Are you trying to change the channel or hold my hand?"

"Both."

I hand her the remote, and she transfers it to her other hand so she can still hold mine. "What do you want to watch?"

She brushes soft kisses down my chest.

"Or did you want to turn off the TV and go upstairs?" I tug lightly at her hair.

She shakes her head. Her hair tickles me and prompts a giggle. "I'm still worn out from this morning." She taps a button on the remote, angling so she can see the screen, and searches through the channels for anything good. "Want to watch a movie?" she asks after a while. We don't watch enough TV to know what's good. We've only had satellite for a few weeks, and the coverage is spotty at best up here.

"Sure." I try to rise to put something on, but she clings to me.

"I did not think this through." She buries her face against me again, more kisses trailing up to my clavicle. "How about we just cuddle and watch whatever that show was?"

"You're the one who wanted to change the channel."

"And I have made my regret for that decision clear."

I run my hand down her back, gripping her ass and pulling her up another foot, her lips now at my neck. "Fine. As long as you regret it." I snatch the remote and flip back to the crime drama marathon as another episode starts.

"Do you even like this show?"

I shrug. "It's watchable."

She rolls to the side, trapping my left arm under her body and resting her head on my shoulder. I wrap my right arm around her, my hand resting on her thigh. "Then I guess I can put up with an episode."

We end up watching three episodes despite neither of us being into it. We're simply too worn out and comfortable to be bothered to move. When the show ends, her lips trail up my neck and find my lips.

"I think I'm ready for another round."

"I thought you'd never ask." I carry her to the bedroom, and we resume our honeymoon festivities. We only have a few more days before she'll have to go back to work, and we intend to do our absolute best to make the most of it. After all, we only have the rest of our lives.

About the Author

Genevieve McCluer was born in California and grew up in numerous cities across the country. She studied criminal justice in college but, after a few years of that, moved her focus to writing. Her whole life, she's been obsessed with mythology, and she bases her stories in those myths.

She now lives in Arizona with her partner and cats, working away at far too many novels. In her free time she pesters the cats, plays video games, and attempts to be better at archery.

Books Available From Bold Strokes Books

Femme Tales by Anne Shade. Six women find themselves in their own real-life fairy tales when true love finds them in the most unexpected ways. (978-1-63555-657-5)

Jellicle Girl by Stevie Mikayne. One dark summer night, Beth and Jackie go out to the canoe dock. Two years later, Beth is still carrying the weight of what happened to Jackie. (978-1-63555-691-9)

My Date with a Wendigo by Genevieve McCluer. Elizabeth Rosseau finds her long-lost love and the secret community of fiends she's now a part of. (978-1-63555-679-7)

On the Run by Charlotte Greene. Even when they're cute blondes, it's stupid to pick up hitchhikers, especially when they've just broken out of prison, but doing so is about to change Gwen's life forever. (978-1-63555-682-7)

Perfect Timing by Dena Blake. The choice between love and family has never been so difficult, and Lynn's and Maggie's different visions of the future may end their romance before it's begun. (978-1-63555-466-3)

The Mail Order Bride by R. Kent. When a mail order bride is thrust on Austin, he must choose between the bride he never wanted or the dream he lives for. (978-1-63555-678-0)

Through Love's Eyes by C.A. Popovich. When fate reunites Brittany Yardin and Amy Jansons, can they move beyond the pain of their past to find love? (978-1-63555-629-2)

To the Moon and Back by Melissa Brayden. Film actress Carly Daniel thinks that stage work is boring and unexciting, but when she accepts a lead role in a new play, stage manager Lauren Prescott tests both her heart and her ability to share the limelight. (978-1-63555-618-6)

Tokyo Love by Diana Jean. When Kathleen Schmitt is given the opportunity to be on the cutting edge of AI technology, she never thought a failed robotic love companion would bring her closer to her neighbor, Yuriko Velucci, and finding love in unexpected places. (978-1-63555-681-0)

Brooklyn Summer by Maggie Cummings. When opposites attract, can a summer of passion and adventure lead to a lifetime of love? (978-1-63555-578-3)

City Kitty and Country Mouse by Alyssa Linn Palmer. Pulled in two different directions, can a city kitty and a country mouse fall in love and make it work? (978-1-63555-553-0)

Elimination by Jackie D. When a dangerous homegrown terrorist seeks refuge with the Russian mafia, the team will be put to the ultimate test. (978-1-63555-570-7)

In the Shadow of Darkness by Nicole Stiling. Angeline Vallencourt is a reluctant vampire who must decide what she wants more—obscurity, revenge, or the woman who makes her feel alive. (978-1-63555-624-7)

On Second Thought by C. Spencer. Madisen is falling hard for Rae. Even single life and co-parenting are beginning to click. At least, that is, until her ex-wife begins to have second thoughts. (978-1-63555-415-1)

Out of Practice by Carsen Taite. When attorney Abby Keane discovers the wedding blogger tormenting her client is the woman she had a passionate, anonymous vacation fling with, sparks and subpoenas fly. Legal Affairs: one law firm, three best friends, three chances to fall in love. (978-1-63555-359-8)

Providence by Leigh Hays. With every click of the shutter, photographer Rebekiah Kearns finds it harder and harder to keep Lindsey Blackwell in focus without getting too close. (978-1-63555-620-9)

Taking a Shot at Love by KC Richardson. When academic and athletic worlds collide, will English professor Celeste Bouchard and basketball coach Lisa Tobias ignore their attraction to achieve their professional goals? (978-1-63555-549-3)

Flight to the Horizon by Julie Tizard. Airline captain Kerri Sullivan and flight attendant Janine Case struggle to survive an emergency water landing and overcome dark secrets to give love a chance to fly. (978-1-63555-331-4)